Cold Lake Fishing

by

Derek Lukachko

Derek Lukachko

Cold Lake Fishing

Derek Lukachko

ISBN 9798731826525

Derek Lukachko

Cold Lake Fishing

by

Derek Lukachko

Prologue

It becomes apparent to the driver that he could steer into oncoming traffic. If he chooses to target the approaching Volvo, the weight of which is several multiples of his own truck and trailer, the impact will not be survivable. His hands tremble weakly with anticipation and his grip loosens around the steering wheel. A gentle tug to the left and a quick ending. The timing is perfect. The tractor-trailer combination is beginning its descent into the valley which occupies the space between them. He eases off the brake and presses lightly on the gas. Gravity does most of the work. He watches the needle climb easily over the speed limit.

The driver feels extremely aware of his body. His back aches from long hours of sitting. His lumbar support is turned to the maximum with little relief. Despite the stiffness of his back, his body feels uncomfortably loose. His feet are heavy against the floor and his arms are light, floating awkwardly with an apparent lack of dexterity. His heart is hollow and sunken inside his chest. The unnatural motion of the objects passing by his window contributes to what his nerves are doing to his now twisted and unsettled stomach. He swallows heavily with his eyes closed. A cool rush of sweat breaks through his skin and sends a shiver up his spine and into his teeth.

His breaths are shallow. His mouth is dry. He stares over his goose-bumped arms and white knuckles. He can feel himself losing control of the truck and, with it, the power to decide. The Volvo is close. He considers the diagonal slash across the grill. He had been told recently that it was to symbolize their invention of the three-point seatbelt, but never confirmed it. He doesn't care. The driver of the Volvo would survive. For himself and his passenger, the impact would not be survivable.

He tells his hands to pull the wheel to the left, but they don't move. *The impact will not be survivable.* He squeezes the wheel as the high-pitched whining shifts into a dull groan and the Volvo passes beside him. Following the change in sound is a heavy wave of air being hauled along with the Volvo's cargo. It pushes his own truck to his right. Another cool rush of sweat washes over his body as he briefly struggles to stay in his lane. The power to live and die is in his firm grip and practiced reflexes. He could let go and fate would decide. *I can let God decide.* He eases his grip on the wheel as the truck starts up the other side of the valley.

His passenger is unaware that if not for the driver's nerves, the opportunity to again question the speed of the vehicle could have died with him, pressed into that diagonal slash that has become known as a symbol of vehicular safety. The driver assures him that he is in control. The truck slows as it continues its ascent. The passenger is worried that the driver's mental state may compromise his ability to continue. He offers to take over, but the driver assures him that they have almost reached their destination. The passenger is unnerved.

The truck and its two passengers crest the ridge. Directly to their front is an intersection allowing for a safe turn to their right or left. He removes his sunglasses and tucks them in the space between the visor and headliner. As the speed increases, the driver takes a final survey of these options and confirms that there is no approaching traffic.

The oversized stop sign has flashing lights. This implies to the driver that it has been previously overlooked. There is no guardrail to slow the vehicle if the driver opts to ignore the pulsating red lights that encircle the important traffic sign. The whole truck vibrates violently as they pass over the first set of rumble strips. Had he been admiring the scenery or staring into his lap, he would now be aware of the impending danger. The driver ignores this warning and continues to accelerate.

The passenger feels his heart sink in his chest when the driver does not react to the violent shaking. The truck shakes again, this time more viciously. Staring forward, he reaches out and smacks the driver across the chest and arm. It is a last desperate plea with his own deity that the driver is not paying attention. The passenger takes his eyes off the approaching disaster and turns to see that the driver's own eyes are not on the road but staring back at him. The passenger sees no fear but feels it. He considers exiting the vehicle. Bouncing off the pavement would be a better fate than an abrupt deceleration.

His seatbelt does not release. The passenger thrusts and kicks wildly to free himself. The truck passes over another set of rumble strips. He screams and begs the driver to stop the vehicle. The driver does not react. The passenger does not feel that he owns control of his own life. He calms his mind and surveys his jammed seatbelt. To his right, he can see that the belt is heavily worn. He does not have time to contemplate how the belt could have worn so unnaturally. Instead, he thrusts his hips upwards and yanks the belt with both hands. The truck passes over another set of rumble strips and the additional force breaks the seatbelt. In a hurried panic he releases himself.

The driver turns his cold stare back to the road. His foot is pressed to the floor and the hemispherical engine is screaming through its dual exhaust. He wonders if he will be able to see the airbag deploy through the wheel. His passenger is scrambling to get the door open. The driver removes his hands from the steering wheel and places them calmly in his lap. The truck sails passed the flashing stop sign. He closes his eyes and allows himself to go limp.

Saturday

"One does not become a tyrant to avoid exposure to the cold."

-Aristotle

I

He was in a car and could smell it from across the street. Not the body, which would be in the early stages of decomposition, but the alley where the unfortunate soul had transcended, leaving behind its mortal body. What lay ahead was an ascension into paradise, assuming he qualified. If not, eternal damnation, as described in some interchangeable religious text. He stared across the street and pondered with sickening contempt the implications of such a reality. If Roman genuinely believed it, he had never allowed it to become apparent to those who dared to ask. He had spent a great portion of his life avoiding the thought and using energy to argue the contrary.

He found himself disturbed not by what horror he might find just a few steps beyond the police tape, but by how he was able to disassociate. He found it to be unnatural. In just a few hours, his on-call shift would have been over. Had this poor fellow been discovered later, the call would have gone to another. Despite the time, since he was drawn too early from the warm embrace of his spouse, Roman was not fully awake. His head ached, his stomach was unsettled, and he was weaker than he ought to be. These are the unfortunate side effects that one must endure if they choose to partake in the cultural poisoning of one's body. He had spent this morning's happiness last night and although he had made a hasty attempt to clean his teeth and mouth, the nauseating stale taste of gin made its way forward with every breath and burp. He jumped at the sound of a tap on his window, just inches from his ear. Unlike Roman, his partner, who approached from behind his field of view, had surely not indulged himself just a few hours prior.

"Are you just going to sit in your car like an invalid?" he asked. Roman rolled down the window to unmuffle the sound of Moussa's voice, who passed him a coffee. "Let's go. You gotta see this shit." He slapped twice on the roof of the car. Moussa was just a couple inches taller than Roman but flaunted it with perfect posture.

"What's in this? Two milks?" Roman peeled open the plastic lid and sniffed it before he sipped. The smell started his mind working, as if he were a trained dog who responded to simple cues. It was satisfying and improved his mood, yet he held his expression. When Roman looked up for eye contact, Moussa had his face buried in his phone.

"Did I hit my fucking head?" Moussa answered with dry and fabricated anger. "You've taken it the same way since I met you. Now, come on. Got work to do." His eyes stayed glued to the screen as he spoke.

"Man. He isn't going to get more dead. Give me a minute. I just fucking got here." It was not a genuine plea, but a sarcastic one, with the intent to agitate him even further. Moussa's shift would have been over at the same time as Roman's.

"I know you just got here. I got coffee on the way, and I beat you. Is that because you're stupid? Or just lazy?"

"You keep running your mouth like that and I'm going to smack it shut," Roman warned, as he opened the door intentionally hard and shoved it into his partner, who dropped his coffee.

"Man, fuck you."

"Here." Roman handed him his own. He had not meant to cause a spill. "Drink mine and quit being a bitch." The taller detective was clean-shaven. He had a neat fade that was almost to the skin around his ears and long on top, slicked and combed. It never seemed to grow out. They started across the street. The sun had not yet risen. It would be at least an hour before first light. The alley was illuminated with industrial floodlights. Having an awareness of the first and last light of the day was one of the non-transferable skills that Roman had learned as an infanteer. He could also assemble a machine gun. "OK. Fill me in. What do we know?"

"Body was found a little over an hour ago. No wallet. Hasn't been identified."

"That's it?"

"What else do you want?"

"How do we know for sure it's a murder?"

"We know. Look, if you want to go on your fishing trip, I can probably handle this." Moussa's face was still buried in his phone as he spoke. Roman wondered if he might walk into traffic one day. As they approached, the cause of the odor became apparent. It was an alley like any other, a narrow brick canyon with dumpsters and debris lining the sides. The harsh Edmonton winters, accompanied by aggressive freeze-thaw cycles, warped the asphalt, and disrupted the grading. Deep potholes had formed and the stagnant water, rich with city runoff and mildew, had nowhere to flow.

Fucking disgusting place to die.

"Probably not. Captain's not giving that kind of freedom these days."

"Kim going to be mad?"

"Yeah."

The crime scene photographer was carefully reviewing his shots when Roman found him sitting on a concrete staircase a few steps past the body. Obviously diligent with his work, he paid no attention to Roman, who had to lower his head to force eye contact. "Are you finished taking your pictures?"

"Yes, but I'll redo it after they move the body and the sun comes up. So don't fucking touch anything," he answered with a nasally crack in his voice that implied he had not yet spoken that day. When he looked up from his camera, Roman assessed his age, guessing early twenties. His oversized glasses had fallen down the bridge of his nose and he straightened them with his middle finger. Roman disregarded the gesture and turned back toward Moussa.

Talk to me like that again and I will smack those stupid glasses off your head.

Roman put on a pair of latex gloves and stepped over the small stream of drying blood that ran from the body toward the centre of the alley. The young man was sprawled out on his back between the rear entrance to Evolution Club and the communal dumpster. His clothes had been stripped off and thrown unceremoniously aside. The victim's mid-length sandy blond hair appeared to be artificially coloured and did not match the darker brown of his eyebrows. Roman squatted to get a closer look and could detect a heavy layer of cologne. The aroma blended with those of the stagnant water and open dumpster. It hung thick in the air like the steam rising from a

14

bowl of soup. It was hard to tell, but he may have been a good-looking young man if his face wasn't so damaged. Roman deduced from the bruising that the right side of his face had taken the worst of the beating. The orbital and cheek bones appeared to have lost their structural integrity. Roman imagined that if he were to press down on them there would be little to no resistance. The mouth was partially open and, from what he could see, the central and lateral incisors on the right side were missing. The left central incisor appeared to be broken. Roman suspected a broken or missing canine and premolar as well but couldn't see without touching the body. The disfigured bottom lip, caked with dark blood, and broken jaw made it impossible to see any of the bottom teeth. Trying to imagine the victim's sense of self-preservation, Roman looked to his arms and hands for defence wounds. As he figured, several contusions and lacerations covered the victim's forearms. His hands, however, appeared to be much more damaged than one would suspect. Despite the swelling, it appeared to Roman that most of his knuckles were broken and covered in deep cuts. His right hand was bent unnaturally inward, so that his fingertips could almost reach his forearms.

At least he went down swinging.

He was tall and muscular. Around six feet and over two hundred pounds. Through the blood drying on his chest, Roman could hardly make out the word carved to his skin. He stood back to get a better angle. From straight over top of the body, Roman could make out the word "FAGGOT" slashed into the victim's chest.

"So . . . you are thinking murder or . . . ?" Roman had almost forgot Moussa was standing there.

"No shit, eh?" He nodded at the rear entrance. "This is a bar?"

"Gay bar."

II

He would always linger. The screams would wake him up, but the bed would keep him there. The nameless man formally known as Paul Derocher had spent enough of his life locked up to appreciate a good mattress. The Canadian prison system costs the taxpayers five billion dollars every year. Almost none of it went to reasonably comfortable beds. Now that he was free, he never skimped. He wished he didn't have to hear the screams. It made him afraid to go to sleep. Almost every night he would relive the few hours that changed his life. In the morning, his blood would curdle, and he would wake up to the worst noise that had ever fallen on human ears. Twelve years and three months had passed, and the memory had not begun to fade.

"Let's go, Paul!"

His newest friend was yelling for him to hurry up. The French-Canadian accent made Paul feel comfortable. His parents were from Montreal, but the family moved around a lot. It was the unfortunate life a child lived when their parents were both serving members of the armed forces. He was born in Ottawa, and, after a few postings, they ended up in Trenton, Ontario. Paul did not like to blame his problems on other people. In his mind, he was a strong individual. But having not settled down for more than a few years at a time, he lacked the strong core group of friends that an eighth-grader would normally have.

"Paul! Everyone is waiting, man. Let's go!" Danny was getting impatient.

"I'm looking, fag. Don't make me come out and beat you!" Paul was deep inside his overfilled garage. He and Danny had a plan for the evening, but they needed supplies. His parents never fully unpacked. The result was that his garage was always stuffed to the roof with boxes. Paul had to climb on top of the mountain of useless garbage to find what he was looking for.

"Got it!" Paul screamed in excitement. He turned and started crawling off the precarious stack of carboard. He rolled out of the garage and dropped the two cans of spray paint as he fell. Danny flinched and jumped out of the way as they clanked off the driveway.

"Careful, idiot. That shit is flammable. Let's go—they're waiting."

Paul hid the cans in his backpack, and they headed toward the rendezvous point. The sun was getting close to the horizon. It would be dark soon and start getting cold. In his backpack, Paul packed a Nalgene water bottle, bug spray for when the mosquitoes came out, and a sweater for when it got cold. He figured his father would have been proud of him for being so prepared. Paul himself aspired to join the Canadian Forces like his parents. His father spoke often about the Canadian Special Operations Regiment—CSOR. In three years, he could join the local reserve unit of whatever town or city in which they were stationed. Two years later, and after he finished high school. He would join the Regular Force as a combat engineer and move on to CSOR or JTF2. It was made clear by his father that becoming a special forces operator was no easy task, but Paul was strong and confident.

They arrived at Danny's house. Kevin and Pavel were already there. Kevin was Danny's younger half-brother and Pavel had just moved to Canada from Russia. His English wasn't great, but he understood more than he let on.

"Let's go over the plan," Danny announced, making sure the others knew he was in charge and had come up with said plan. "When the sun goes down, we will approach and hide in the trees to the south. After they set up their tents, they will probably go for some nerdy little nature hike. That's when we strike!"

"Why we want to wreck their tents?" Pavel asked. Clearly, he did not understand.

"Did you see that gay little outfit he was wearing at the mall? Those guys are total losers," Danny explained. "They're going on a stupid little overnight camping thing, and we're going to ruin it."

"And we are going to paint our faces so if they see us, we can run away and not get caught," Paul added. "Super sneaky." He made a slow walking gesture toward Kevin, who looked nervous.

They ducked inside Danny's garage to make their final preparations. The sun was setting. The four of them divided up their equipment. Pavel brought two flashlights. Danny took one and clipped it onto his belt. Paul put the other in his backpack. Each took one lighter. Danny's mom was a smoker and there were lots of lighters in their house. Danny, asserting again that he was the leader, showed them all how they worked. Paul sparked a flame on the first try. Danny did the same.

"Mine's not going," Kevin whined. Paul figured his hands were probably too weak. After some quick instruction from his older half-brother, Kevin was able to create a flame. The three of them looked at Pavel, who had not yet tested his lighter.

"Do you know how to light it?" Danny asked, speaking slower than was necessary. Pavel seemed to be contemplating the sentence, or maybe his whole life, as he stood silently with the lighter in his hand. After a few seconds, he stuck his hand out toward the group and lit the flame, swinging his entire arm up and down. Danny and Paul each took a can of spray paint. Kevin had a can of hair spray that was stolen from his mom's bathroom and Pavel had nothing.

"Where's your spray paint Pavel?" Danny was clearly annoyed. "It's not that hard. Simple instructions. Get something that sprays."

After a quick survey of the garage, Paul spotted a can of WD40 on a shelf. "There," he said, pointing. "That'll burn better than any of that other crap."

None were quite tall enough to reach the can, so Danny and Paul hoisted Kevin up to knock it down.

It took longer than they had anticipated to hike to the air cadets' campsite. Paul checked his watch and saw that it was past ten. For the first time, he considered that his parents might be out looking for him. "Let's make this quick. I can't stay out this late," he whispered to the group that was hiding in the trees less than fifty feet from the nearest tent.

"Are they sleeping?" Kevin asked his older brother. There was no motion in the campsite, and no lights on.

"I told you," he answered his younger brother. "They go on

20

nighttime nature walks."

"How do you know so much about the cadets?" Paul laughed as he shoved Danny playfully. "Did you used to wear one of those little uniforms? Is it hanging in your closet?"

"Shut up, asshole! I don't think they are here. What time is it?"

"After ten. Let's make some noise. See if they come after us," Paul suggested, as the first thought of hurting someone crossed his mind. From right behind them, Kevin threw a golf-ball-sized rock toward the tents. The rock didn't make it even halfway. Still no movement. Paul scooped up some smaller pebbles that were scattered around their line of departure. "Follow me," he instructed, as he took off his backpack and stuffed the rocks and lighter in his pocket. It was dark, and the sky was overcast. Still, the moonlight pushed its way through the low-hanging clouds and guided Paul's advance.

Paul crawled on his stomach the way he saw soldiers do it on TV. It was exhausting. Especially with the can of spray paint in his hand. He gave up on the army-style tactic after no more than twenty feet. The grass was tall enough that he could probably crawl on all fours and not get spotted. It occurred to him at this time that they had forgotten to paint their faces. It was dark. No one would see them. Paul made it within throwing distance of the tents. He reached into his pocket and dug out his pebbles. With a large swooping motion, he launched them into the campsite. Paul imagined himself launching a grenade into an enemy trench. The rocks scattered around the nearest tent. Two bounced off the stretched nylon and onto the ground. He immediately dropped to his stomach to listen for motion. Not a sound. After a few heavy breaths with his face in the dirt, after his heart rate dropped, he raised his head above the grass to investigate. Nothing. The campsite was deserted. He turned around and made eye contact with Danny. The two exchanged a shrug and, without speaking a word, agreed that the campsite was empty. Paul reached back into his pocket and started fumbling around for his lighter.

"Let's go!" Danny whispered loudly. He broke into a low sprint toward the nearest tent. He dove to his stomach and covered the last few feet crawling flat on the ground. Not to be outdone, Paul chased immediately behind him, cut off to the left, and dove to his stomach at the corner of a tent. The next-closest tent was to the right of Danny, but Paul left that for Kevin, who would be the slowest runner when they turned to escape.

Paul lit his lighter and lifted the can of paint. He paused and let the flame die. He turned to his right to make his last confirmation that he was not alone in his mission. He could see that Kevin was struggling to get his lighter working and considered running over to help him. Danny had only just got the lighter from his pocket and sparked a flame. The two made eye contact as Danny sprayed the paint through the fire and onto the tent. It immediately took flame, and Danny was running. Paul turned on the lighter and did the same. Heat washed back against his bare arms and was followed by the chemical odor released by burning synthetic materials. The flame stuck to the tent and expanded with demonic haste. He turned to run and noticed Danny had grabbed his younger half-brother by the arm and was hauling him toward the woods.

This may have been the first adrenaline rush of his life. Time slowed inside Paul's head. He had taken only three or four steps from his tent when he heard the first of the screams that would haunt him for over a decade. He wheeled around to look at the first tent that had taken flame and felt briefly reassured when he saw no motion inside, as the flames melted the cheap waterproof nylon to the ground. His muscles could not move as fast as his thoughts, and his vision crawled to his left.

In a matter of seconds, the camp had sprung to life. Another horrifying scream tore through the cool night air as he saw an adult at the centre of the camp fumbling to get an extinguisher working. A teen boy, no older than seventeen from what Paul could tell, was clawing madly at the tent that he had set ablaze. The teenager was not fighting to get out. He was clawing to get in. As the flames quickly grew taller, the tiny shelter fell onto the two trapped inside. Paul was frozen. His heart sank into his stomach. He watched burning arms flailing as the bright coloured tent turned black and stuck to the boy's skin. Another scream poured out of the boy's mouth as he fell to the ground.

Time returned to its normal speed when the flames collapsed under the spray of the fire extinguisher. The man operating it emptied the entire tank before he looked up to see Paul, alone in the field, staring back at him with a lighter and spray paint in his hands. Paul dropped both.

Without thinking, he turned and ran. He did not have time to think about the other members of his party. He sprinted past the line of departure and the backpack that carried his sweater. His heartrate climbed, and he heard more screams and chaos echoing through the night. Paul did not stop until his lungs were burning, and his legs were numb. He keeled over and landed in the freshly-cut grass of a local soccer field. Staring up at the sky, it occurred to him that he did not remember which direction he ran. He was struggling to put the pieces back in order, and realised he could hardly remember anything that had happened. Only a few details remained burned in his mind: the flaming tent collapsing into an airtight coating around the boy trapped inside, the man with the extinguisher staring directly at him for an eternity, and the screams.

Paul never remembered how long he spent on his back trying to catch his breath before his life was slammed back into real time. His backpack landed heavily on his chest.

"Man, I think you killed someone." Danny was standing over him. "Where the fuck is Pavel?" Paul tried to stand up but Danny shoved him back into the grass. Moonlight caught the blade of a swiss army knife in Danny's hand. "Listen to me, Paul." It was hard to tell if Danny was afraid or angry. Tears glowed in his eyes and started to run as he spoke. "Don't ever tell anyone what happened here. Not for me. For you. We were not here! Understand? If you tell anyone that I was here . . . ." The blade was an inch from Paul's nose. "If you tell anyone that we were here, I will fucking kill you."

The two never spoke again.

Paul stared at the emptiness before him. The earth spun unnaturally against his back, and stars crawled across the sky. His heart beat heavily against his chest as he struggled to draw breaths of the still night air, rich with the smell of spring. His mind raced and wandered, blurring the reality of his recent memories of death. From behind closed eyes, he watched them burn, and with each passing blink, the sky and earth rotated. The grass carved mercilessly into his smooth and delicate skin as an unseen force pressed him upward, holding him from the abyss. The only noise Paul could hear was the faint rumble of traffic in the distance, and the screams in his head.

III

Without saying a word, Roman reached across the table and scooped the bacon off Moussa's plate with his fork and knife. Moussa did the same with Roman's toast. It was a ritual they had performed many times over the years they had worked as partners. The sun was coming up, and the photographer would be taking daylight pictures of the alley. There was no rush to finish breakfast.

"Guy was infuriated." Moussa had a mouth full of toast, but politely covered it with his hand. "Like, personally offended."

Roman appreciated the gesture. He had made it abundantly clear how irritating he found it when people spoke openly with food in their mouth or, worse, chewed with their mouth open. "Didn't he make the call? He's not going to know anything."

"He called and went home. That was his whole story. It still makes sense to ask him a few questions." Moussa habitually unlocked and relocked his phone with his free hand, while squishing his brown toast into an egg yolk. "Maybe someone else saw something."

Your phone would let you know if you got a message.

"And this other person said nothing? They just casually wandered by, like, *there's a body back there. Not my problem.* And then, later, the manager calls 9-1-1. No one saw it except him. I'm sure of it."

"Just go talk to the guy and I'll run over to the morgue and see if anyone identified the body. Then, maybe go home and take a shower."

Do I stink?

"Fine." Roman drained the rest of his coffee and looked over his shoulder for the waitress. "So, they went anyway."

"Who?"

"Kim and friends. Not fair for me to ruin the weekend for everyone. Anthony can back the boat into the water." The waitress came by and filled his mug without saying a word. "Thanks." Roman made sure to smile and make eye contact. He was always polite to the people who handled his food.

"Are you worried?" Moussa was checking his phone again. "I hear they manufacture smart phones to be as addictive as possible. Worried about what?"

"Kim. Camping. Beer. All manner of general merriment," Moussa explained, waving a piece of toast around.

"What are you trying to say?" Roman knew exactly to what Moussa was alluding, but he wanted to make him say it.

Moussa tilted his head back and let his mouth hang open in an over-the-top *sorry I offended you* motion. "I'm not saying anything." His voice rose to a comedic level, and he slowed his rate of speech. "I'm just asking if you're worried. I have a wife. I trust her. And I love her. But I would not send her out drinking. In the woods. With a bunch of hooligans. And go to bed. By myself. Three hours away. And sleep soundly."

"I'm not worried. Just the three of them are going. And Anthony is there. Guy's got my back." Roman checked his watch. Lots of time. "About this body, though. Someone will post something on social media. There will be a video and fifty witnesses. Whisky-fueled hate crime that got out of hand. Probably three hungover farm boys with deleted Facebook accounts shitting their pants and staring through the curtains."

"So, what? They should get off easy because they're good ol' boys just having fun?"

"No. They're going to prison. For sure. All of them. Probably get a DNA match off the guy's knuckles in a day or so. He fought hard for his life. You see his hands?"

No response. Moussa was glued to his phone. Roman stared.

*   *   *

The guy was definitely not happy. Roman could see that as soon as he entered Evolution Club. Walking into a night club during the day, he felt out of place. Like swimming with your clothes on or driving an unfamiliar car. Mechanically, it was the same, but it didn't feel right.

The place was quiet and the lights were on. Only a few hours before, it would have been packed beyond capacity with hundreds of sweaty half-dressed teenagers. Being there reminded Roman how fast he was aging. Not too many years ago, this would have been his kind of place. *Sort of.* The lights exposed the filth. The floor was heavily stained and grabbed his shoes as he walked. The floorboards had a layer of permanent grime built up. *Its dark when there's customers.* The air was thick and musty. It smelled to Roman like hormones and shame. He could taste the vomit crawling up the back of his throat and onto his tongue. Finding a stool without a ripped cushion was a harder task than it should have been. He made a mental agreement that the least worn stool was probably the cleanest. It didn't make sense and he knew it. He leaned on the bar and quickly pulled away when he felt that it was still wet from a spilled drink. Instead, he shoved his hands in his pockets and waited for the man behind the bar to acknowledge he had arrived.

It was obvious that he was being ignored. The man was smaller than expected, and younger. He was clean-shaven and had his hair cut like a wet paintbrush. Both ears were pierced. Eyebrows were waxed. Soft, smooth skin. Good physique for a smaller guy. Shiny black T-shirt and tight, dark pants. He was working aimlessly at wiping counters and loading bussing trays. Whoever spoke first would lose. Frustrated, Roman smacked his hand on the counter.

Sighing, the man decided to finally give Roman a minute of his time "Fine! What?!"

"What do you mean, *what*? You know why I'm here. You own this place?" It was more believable up close. The man aged as he approached and the lines on his face became clearer. The scruff on his neck looked thicker and the hair on his head, the opposite. Still, he definitely took care of himself.

"Told the other guy that I don't have any information for him."

"You may know more than you think. Gotta say, though, from across the bar, I would have believed you were twenty-five."

"I would get a few drinks in you and let you believe whatever you want. I don't know how much help I can be." His vowels were soft and his consonants sharp.

Don't be prejudiced. You don't know.

"Any fights break out last night?"

"At this place? Seriously?" The attitude in his voice was amused, and clearly not genuine.

"You have security here?"

"Anyone who shows up with a security shirt and wants to work for ten bucks and hour under the table. It's not a rough place."

"Then why the security?"

"Insurance."

"Who's in charge of them?"

The bartender made a point of surveying the room sarcastically and looked back to the detective. "You're lookin' at him."

"You see any big blonde guys? Muscular. Over two hundred pounds. Good-looking before he got his face smashed in."

The bartender's attitude was thick and blending into comedic sarcasm. "You want to know," he paused to chuckle softly, "if there were any good-looking, muscular guys here last night? At Evolution Club?"

This guy is pretty funny.

Roman chuckled back and redirected: "How often do you go out in the alley?"

"After we close. We don't serve food, so there isn't a lot of garbage. Usually, we pile it up near the back door and take it out at the end of the night."

"Who found the body?"

"Same guy that runs security."

"Got any cameras? Maybe scan the IDs when people come in?"

"I don't even have real security. Do me a favour?" He was trying now to sound at least a little serious. "Try not to make this into a big 'dead boy at the gay bar' thing. I already barely make a dime here."

Roman's phone buzzed once in his pocket. He ignored it. "You might actually be busy for a while. People are weird. Adrenaline junkies love crap like this. As though the same thing is going to happen again." The single buzz was followed by a familiar pattern. "I have to take this. Don't go anywhere." Roman stepped outside and answered his phone. "Moussa."

"Hey Roman, I'm sending you some pictures. I guess we could call it a lead. Let me know what you think."

"Is it good or bad?"

"Don't even know what it means yet."

Roman checked his phone. The first text came through when he was still in the bar. The number was not saved in his phone and the message had only three letters: *BP N*. Roman immediately deleted the message and waited for Moussa to send pictures of whatever clue he had uncovered.

I hope this is good.

Derek Lukachko

IV

He could have worked that day but chose not to. Max had a promise to keep.

Dolphin Maximus Cardinal was his full legal name. It was stupid, and he hated his parents for it. He looked in the mirror at the mess he had become. Max hadn't shaved in days. His hair was long and greasy. He had milky, bloodshot eyes that were sunken into his skull. Dark bags hung down his cheekbones. Years of sun damage left his skin leathery and coarse. In Max's early twenties, he had been a heavy hitter. Stronger than most men his size, with contagious confidence. But now, under one hundred and fifty pounds and looking ten years older than he was, he hated his appearance. He would not let her see him like this.

Years of service had taught Max how to clean up in a hurry, but he was in no rush today. The most important thing was to clear up his skin. After a quick shave and shower, he tied his hair behind his head and generously applied moisturizer.

It would take at least a pot of coffee to get life back into his eyes, so he got it brewing. He opened his fridge to look for something salty. The sodium would cause him to bloat and make his face look fuller. Bare shelves. Max couldn't remember the last time he opened his fridge to see it stuffed with fresh food. Every few weeks he would have a delusion of getting clean. He would head to the grocery store with the best intentions and stock up on fruit, bread, grade-A Alberta steaks, potatoes, bacon, and eggs. On his way home, he would always stop at the Liquor Depot. Can't have steak and potatoes without beer. He wouldn't cook the steaks or the potatoes. The food would rot, and he would throw it out. He settled for stale crackers that he did not remember buying. Breakfast of champions in the City of Champions.

The coffee table was a mess and needed to be cleared to make space for his laptop. Most of it was garbage. He grabbed the stamp bag of heroin and shoved it in his back pocket. The rest he shoveled off the table and into a black garbage bag. Max paused, staring at the blank surface, then dug through the bag to retrieve a business card. The name and number on the front of the card did not matter. The back was important. There was a date, time, and address. Max didn't need to look it up to know that it was for St. Joseph's Basilica.

Just another Catholic church with some faggot rapist priest.

The date and time were for a Narcotics Anonymous meeting. It was tomorrow, and he had promised he would attend. Despite having several less favourable traits, Max believed that a man was only as good as his word. Although he didn't care about hurting the feelings of the redheaded God Boy from work, he had said he would go, and intended to keep that promise. Max placed the business card on the shelf under his coffee table, beside the loaded Browning 9mm that was illegally stored there.

He opened the computer and saw he still had time before the Skype meeting. Max did not get along with his brother but maintained contact with the last family member that would still talk to him. He turned on his camera to see how he looked.

A neat and tidy pile of shit.

33

He adjusted the angle of the screen to show his campaign star that was proudly displayed on the mantel shelf over his shoulder. His online banking confirmed that he had received his end of the bargain. Max had once again traded two weeks of his life holding up a STOP and SLOW sign to protect the skilled roadworkers and, in return, he was paid $1,658.76. It was enough for a plane ticket if he ever wanted to run.

I wonder if there's anywhere they wouldn't find me.

Max had drifted off. He was daydreaming about a beach in the South Pacific when he was startled by the artificial ringtone prompting him to start the video chat. He stood up and quickly walked two laps around his living room before answering. Max wanted to convey falsely that he was not waiting for the call and made sure to be buttoning his shirt as he answered.

"Hey Lulu!" Max didn't have to use a fake smile. His niece was in her first year of post-secondary, attending the University of Ottawa.

"How's it going, Uncle Dolphin?" Max wanted to believe that the flatness in her voice was an act to appear more mature. She was the one and only person that he allowed to call him by his first name.

"Busy, as usual. How's school?"

"We only just started, but it's so much fun!" The excitement was intentionally fake.

"Meeting lots of people? Any boys?" He wanted to sound comical, but cared to hear the answer.

"Yes, Dolphin, considering half the people here are boys."

"Don't you sass me. I just want to make sure my favourite niece is staying safe." It was thrilling to speak with someone who did not wish him harm. In the years since his release, he had grown accustomed to advantage being taken of him at every opportunity.

"I don't want to be rude or anything, but I have a lot of studying to do this weekend. So we can't talk for too long." Lulu was clearly distracted by something off camera.

Probably some new friends.

"No worries, I have a lot going on today." It was a lie, and he hated it. He wouldn't let her know about the shitstorm of a life that existed outside of her view through the laptop camera. "Who are you looking at over there?"

"Just some new friends." She was looking at her phone while she spoke. "Hey, I hate to do this, but I had some expenses come up. Mostly books. Dad says he doesn't have the cash right now."

He would not have been so easy to manipulate if he knew that she had gone drinking across the border, where she was legal. Lulu had way too many vodka crans for an eighteen-year-old who weighed barely more than a hundred pounds and had woken up with an even tighter budget than she had the day prior.

"How much?" Max asked, hoping it would be small.

Lulu cringed as well as she could fake and quietly asked: "Eight hundred?" She folded her hands as if in prayer and stared quietly at the camera, while Max looked at his bank account.

He had over drafted his account by nearly five hundred dollars before he got paid the day before. He was looking at $1,178.98 that didn't belong to him when he answered, "Sure." He sent the transfer.

"Thanks, Uncle Dolphin!" She only had to half-pretend to be excited. "But I'm really sorry—I have to get going. My study group is waiting for me."

Max could tell she was lying, but he felt good for helping her out. "No problem. Don't work too hard. And tell your dad I said hi."

"I will." The call ended.

Max sat in his filthy apartment, listening to the buzz of the city outside and the fan blowing the smell of dirty laundry around inside his bedroom. He felt empty. Buyer's remorse—except he had spent his money on a morsel of friendly conversation. She needed the money more than he did. She was a student. *Students need money.* It was the right decision. His mouth was dry, and his body ached from the hangover. Sunlight peeked through the curtains and spotlighted the suspended dust. Max pressed the 9mm to his head and stared at his dark reflection in the computer screen, contemplating the hollow feeling.

*   *   *

They watched him exit the building. His eyes were closed by the sun. He turned toward the fence that separated the parking lot from the construction supply store. If they didn't intercept him, he would jump the fence and briskly walk to the Liquor Depot. Max didn't work again until Monday, and they couldn't risk losing him for two days.

The two brutish men got out of the car and powerwalked toward Max, doubling his pace. They quickly gained ground and, once within earshot, the closer one yelled out, "Hey Max! Where you going?"

Max broke into a sprint. He was faster than they expected and opened the gap quickly. The chase was short. If there were no obstacles, they may have never caught him. He slipped on his first attempt climbing the wooden fence. It was still wet from the rain that had fallen the night before. The blunder cost him his lead, and they didn't give him a second chance.

V

"You have to think critically here. If it were an obvious clue, why would it be there?"

Moussa and Roman were walking up the stairs to Kyle Brown's apartment. *Awful name. Kyle.* The body was easily identified only hours after arriving at the morgue. The Forensic Identification Services Section of the EPS would be picking through and photographing the entire apartment. Roman had wanted to question the roommate before they got there.

"Let's just explore all avenues. It could be a room number. Part of a phone number. Who knows?" Moussa was reaching.

"I know it could be. But why?"

"Sometimes these people want to get caught. They leave pieces of evidence and make a game out of it." Again, Moussa was face down in his phone.

"Are you recording this conversation?" Roman noticed the voice memo adding time on Moussa's iPhone.

"It's a new strategy for working out problems. Instead of writing it, I record it. It helps me to not forget ideas."

"Eighteen twenty-two. It could be military time. Either for something that happened yesterday at 6:22 or something happening in the future." Roman tried to buy into the idea.

"See? That could turn out to be the revelation that solves this case. And now I don't even have to write it down." Moussa was waving his phone, showing off that it was recording.

It wasn't a great building. The halls were tight. The lights were dim. The carpet was well worn and stained. No underground parking was available. Perfect for students. The University of Alberta was in the heart of Edmonton. Any building within reasonable walking or bussing distance was prime real estate. Forty thousand students attend the school. If the tenant complained about the state of the hallway, there would surely be another to take their spot.

The door to Kyle's apartment was open. As they previously figured, EPS had dug through what remained of his life, trying to find a connection. None remained. This was likely another dead end. The architecture of the apartment was an extension of the hallway. The entrance was hardly wide enough for the two detectives to remove their shoes. Roman was careful not to touch the walls, worried that the filth would stain his clothes. Once he had his shoes off, he squeezed into the living room and noticed the plushness of the rug. Clothes, books, shoes, and a gym bag were scattered around the floor. The single bedroom door was closed, and the roommate was sitting on the couch watching TV.

"Not a lot of street noise in here." Roman wanted to start with easy conversation to make her feel more comfortable. "One of the nice features of old buildings, right?"

"This place is a dump. I try to make it a little nicer, but you know. Lipstick on a pig."

He could sense a little disinterest in the conversation. *I knew we should have gotten here first.* He sat down beside her on the couch, intentionally lowering himself to her eye level and placing himself to face the same direction.

"They already ran you through the basic questions?"

"Twice. And very aggressively. Am I a suspect?" She scowled at him with her arms folded. He could sense the contempt.

"I'm sorry about what happened to Kyle. And no, you aren't a suspect." Again, he was trying to soften her up.

"I barely knew him. A friend of a friend said he needed a place. He didn't have a lot of money. I don't have an extra bedroom, so he agreed to sleep on the couch for three hundred bucks a month. He needed a computer, so I gave him my old laptop. He never bothered to change the password. He moved in at the start of the month and I never even got one month's rent. That's basically the whole story."

"Students are usually poor. It gets better later in life. Kyle ever talk about people he didn't get along with?"

"No. Like I said. I barely knew him. He was out a lot. And I don't need a life coach right now. Don't feed me shit about how things will get better. Just do what you need and leave. Please."

Roman noticed that she had barely taken her eyes off the TV since they arrived.

Jesus, girl. Show some emotion.

"What did he do when he was home?" Moussa cut in casually.

"He spent most of his time on the computer. It's behind you on the kitchen counter. I unlocked it for the other guys, so feel free to have a look."

Moussa went over to check it out.

"I'm going to leave you a business card." Roman pulled one from his jacket pocket. "If you think of anything else, let me know.

OK?"

"I will. How long before someone comes to get his stuff?"

"The other guys didn't take it?" The roommate waved her hand around to indicate that the living room mess was Kyle's. Roman was a little surprised they would leave the dead kid's stuff for some poor student to deal with.

Moussa piped up from the kitchen. "For a broke student this guy played a lot of online poker. And for a lot of money."

"Maybe that's how he paid the bills. Can you see if he won anything?" Roman put his hands on his knees for leverage to stand up. He started for the door.

"His account balance is at zero, but he had some big games. Looks like he won over a few thousand dollars a couple times. Lost just as much, from what I can tell."

"Do you want to take that back to the office?" Roman was putting his shoes on in the hallway.

"No. We should get FISS back here to clean up. Look how they left this place."

Roman and Moussa were halfway down the hall to the stairs when Roman stopped. "Did it seem weird that she didn't really care about her dead roommate?"

"I mean—if they only just met. . . . Maybe she's tough."

"I'll let it sink in a little and come back tomorrow. Might just be shock. If we press her now, she'll never trust us." The crew of FISS staff was coming back up the stairs and heading for the apartment. "Hey, clean this place up," Roman snapped as they went by. "Grab the computer. You can't leave it like that."

"We just got here, man." The cop hardly acknowledged Roman as he walked by.

"I have somewhere to be. Do you want to go back and sort this out?"

"Sure man, I'm on it," Moussa lied.

Roman left the building and checked his watch. About a thirty-minute drive. No huge rush. He pulled out two sticks of Nicorette and stuffed them in his mouth. Kim had taken his truck, and he had her Camry for the day. The AC was broken, and he drove with the window down. He did not notice the person following him.

VI

He had aspired to be more. A signaler stood at either end of whatever construction or maintenance project was blocking a lane of traffic. His job was to communicate with a radio to the signaler at the other end and decide when to flip their signs around to indicate which way traffic could flow. The work was tedious, and today he had agreed to work the morning shift, leaving the afternoon to himself. A flagger was usually a fresh employee early in their career, putting in their hours on the low end of the pay scale, or a degenerate that could not be trusted with any more complicated tasks. The nameless employee, who formerly went by Paul, was the latter. Had he turned his life around earlier, he could still have made them proud. Now that his mother had passed, he lived only to serve himself and God.

Two years. It was two years that Paul had to serve to make right what he had done. At least that was the case in the eyes of the juvenile justice system. Paul and his family had pleaded guilty to involuntary manslaughter. They had no choice after the eyewitness testimony of his accomplices labelled him as the kingpin. Paul was to serve two years at the Roy McMurphy Youth Centre in Brampton, Ontario. The lawyer hired by his parents made a case that Paul's education should not be compromised, so he was allowed to attend private school, and, for the duration of his sentence, he would spend his weekends at home.

Late in his career, Paul's father had switched occupations in the military. His constant deployments and postings were putting stress on his personal life. He had opted for the slower-paced role of a weapons technician. Still, on the tail end of the Afghanistan campaign, his country called on him to serve an eight-month tour of duty in the Kandahar province. The notice he was given was short. The deployment was non-combat, and the fighting had all but ended. His third journey to the country should have been the least perilous. Paul did not remember the specific details, but his understanding was that his father would be assisting in the training of weapons technicians for the Afghan National Army. His last weekend at home before his father left was in August. It was one month after Paul had started serving his sentence. Mechanically, they had a perfect family weekend. Though the words spoken were positive and the expressions on their faces were cheerful, the tension was strong.

Paul was being dropped off on a Sunday afternoon at his second home. It was the third time he had had to say goodbye to his parents in this location. As always, it was a long-winded goodbye from his mother. In the previous drops, his father had not said a word and waited in the car. Today, for what would be their last conversation, Paul's father came with them to the front door of the correction facility. His powerful hand rested softly on Paul's shoulder, making him feel pathetically small. Paul stared up at the stoic face of a combat veteran who was searching for words. Paul spoke first.

"Dad. I'm sorry." Paul could feel the corners of his mouth being pulled downwards. He pursed his lips to hide it. Time was passing too slow, and he could feel the wateriness building in his eyes. There was no way to hide the complete desolation he felt.

His father squatted down so he could speak at eye level. He nodded softly as he spoke. "They have good people here. Work with the therapist. I know you can turn this around. This will not be how your story ends." He patted him twice on the shoulder and rose to leave. With his massive arm around the soon-to-be widow's shoulders, he walked back to the car.

Paul's sorrow turned to rage as he was marched by detention staff to his dormitory. He threw his bag on the floor and stretched out on his bed, cradling the back of his head in his hands he stared at the ceiling. "I can't believe they fucking left me here. My parents don't give a shit."

"Shut up, man. You burned a kid to death. You are one of the people that actually deserves to be here." Paul would not remember his roommate's name, but he did remember Ryan. The second boy he killed.

Paul lived two separate lives. On Saturdays and Sundays, his mother would smother him with lame family activities. He was intuitive enough to know that she was not as excited as she acted about the Science Centre, or the PG movies to which she would drag him. It was insulting to him that she would not just say that she didn't trust him to be left alone. He was a toddler that had to re-learn what was right and wrong. Don't hit people and don't say mean things. Don't lie, cheat, or steal. He was not allowed to use the internet or to play video games. He had a collection of books that were hand-chosen to only have the most wholesome stories. Shortly after his father left, he would yearn for the weekdays at the detention facility.

To his horror, he learned that his mother had lobbied to allow for one extra night at home. What Paul did not realise was that it removed the financial strain of paying for his transportation on those days, between school and jail. She would pick him up from private school on Friday at 3 P.M., immediately after the final bell dismissed the students. Part of the agreement was that she would walk him straight from class to the car and deliver him to the same class on Monday morning. Being escorted by detention staff on normal days made Paul feel like a hardened criminal and, on those days, Paul was revered by his peers. On the days that he was escorted by his mother, the effect was the opposite. St. Michael's Catholic Secondary School was a private all-boys school that served grades seven through twelve and, on Mondays and Fridays, his mother was the only woman that nearly a thousand teenage boys would see outside of their own homes.

Paul's routine was straightforward. He had lame weekends with his mother and classes with his peers. He would see a therapist twice a week to talk about his feelings. Aside from his regular homework, he had to keep a journal and review it with Dr. Asshole, who was arrogant and condescending. Paul was not permitted to play on sports teams or join any after-school program. Despite the catcalls thrown at his mother twice a week and the relentless and tormenting bullying, Paul warded off any desire to be violent. His lawyer, therapist, and both of his parents had made it clear that his privileges, however few, could be revoked if he were to become aggressive.

After word got out to his classmates that Paul could or would not fight back, every day during their recess, Ryan would beat Paul senseless.

After the bruises on his face became noticeable, Ryan, who was a year older but no bigger than Paul, would avoid hitting him in the face or head. On some days, Paul was able to run away and maintain enough distance that he could escape his daily punishment. Unfortunately, the violence became a source of entertainment for some of the other students. The savage poundings that previously entertained only one disturbed individual evolved into public embarrassment.

Paul strongly considered looking to his mother for help or advice. His fear, which was justified, was that her involvement would hurt the situation more than it would help. He knew his reputation would paint him into a corner, and that the story would be about how a violent child murderer was tormenting the innocent Catholic boys. He could ask to be removed from the school, but after failing to mesh with the righteous students at St. Michael's, he figured the list of schools willing to admit him would be shorter than before.

At night, even with the techniques he learned from Dr. Asshole, Paul would struggle to sleep. Bruises, hidden by his clothes, and deep internal pain from his beatings made it impossible to find a comfortable position. He feared his nightmares, which grew in intensity every day. His head spun from the two major thoughts he could not escape. The first was the disappointment he would feel when his father found out he was not able to attend a private school and had to be educated at the Roy McMurphy Youth Centre. The second, as always, was that day in June when he ruined his life. The lack of sleep was causing Paul to feel confused and disoriented.

His last day at St. Michael's was November 11. As the class stood quietly on the eleventh minute of the eleventh hour, Paul watched Ryan, who had been held back a grade, whispering to another classmate. Paul felt the rage building inside as the two boys laughed and looked at each other's phones.

Despite his better judgement, Paul stopped Ryan in the hall between classes. "Hey, Ryan, I know you and I have had some differences, but I would really appreciate it if you stayed quiet during the moment of silence. Please. This day is bigger than me and it's bigger than you."

"Everything is bigger than you. Child-killer." Paul was under slept, but he knew he had made a mistake.

"You know what, I'm sorry. I shouldn't have said anything." Paul was trying to remove himself from the situation without causing any more damage. He turned and started walking.

"Where the fuck are you going?" Ryan was yelling, and the usual crowd was gathering. Paul increased his speed. "I said, where the fuck are you going?!"

Paul increased his stride, with his head on a swivel. Desperately, he peered through doors and windows to find a teacher. The students were without adult supervision. Paul broke into a run. "I think I forgot something back in the other classroom," Paul yelled, trying to draw attention. He didn't know who, and never would, but one of his classmates stuck his leg out, below Paul's field of vision. Their ankles locked and Paul fell forward, landing on his chest and hands. Before he could scramble to get up, Ryan landed heavily on his back.

"Got somewhere to be?" Paul didn't respond, and Ryan hooked him hard in the ribs on his right side. Paul's hair was just long enough on top for Ryan to comb his fingers through and squeeze to gain control of Paul's head, pulling it back so they were face to face. Ryan snorted and drew saliva from the back of his throat. He ejected it forcefully onto Paul's face and followed it with a right-handed open-palm smack to Paul's right ear.

Paul's head was pounding, and his ears were ringing. He raised his forearms to protect his face and cupped his hands over his ears. He rolled onto his left side and raised his knees to his chest. "I'm sorry. I don't want to fight you."

Ryan stood up and toe-punted Paul in the lower back. "Fight me, pussy!" He turned his head left and right, as if looking for his something to do with his quarry. Ryan grabbed him by his belt and collar and started dragging him. "Can you fly, little birdie?"

Paul saw that they were moving toward the staircase. He thrashed to his feet and wrapped his arms around the knees of his tormentor dragging him to the ground. As Paul was struggling to break free and climb to his feet, another student, maybe the same one that tripped him—he would never know—kicked him hard from behind and between his legs. Paul collapsed to his hands and knees. The pain from his groin fired up toward his stomach. He gagged and threw up in his mouth. There wasn't enough time to recover before Ryan's arm was around his neck and he was being pulled to the stairs.

"I said. . . . Can. You. Fly? And I want to find out." As they approach within a few feet of the stairs, Paul adjusted his weight and used their momentum to drive Ryan into the wall, momentarily pinning him there. Both of their backs were facing the stairs. Paul tried to drop his weight to avoid a backward roll that would put them over the edge. With his free left hand, Ryan shoved his palm in Paul's face and crushed his nose. He intensified the discomfort by shifting his hand back and forth, with pressure. "You like that, birdie? Time to fly!" Ryan lifted forcefully to move Paul's weight backward.

"Fuck you! Let me go!" If Paul had seen their homeroom teacher running down the hall to break up the fight, he may have waited longer. Paul turned his head so that his chin pressed into Ryan's ribs. The headlock immediately began to loosen. He wound up his right arm and, using all the force he had, drove a fist into Ryan's crotch. The noise from the crowd implied they were offended by the low blow. His head was almost free. He wound up and delivered an even harder punch to the most sensitive spot on the human body. The crowd was not pleased. The arm around his neck loosened, and Paul stood straight up and made a perfect connection. The back of his head impacted his opponent's nose. He was free. He used his left shoulder and right arm to push off and stumbled to his knees.

Time slowed. The eyes in the crowd grew together. Each pair of eyelids stretched open, horrified with anticipation. Their focus was not on Paul. His homeroom teacher came barreling through the students and stepped right around him. Paul turned. First his eyes, followed by his head and finally his whole body. The teacher wasn't fast enough. Ryan was cascading down the stairs, rotating in the air. His hands were moving to break his fall but did not arrive in time. His left hand touched first. The momentum of his body folded the teen boy's arm in half. His right arm was too far behind in the turn. The bridge of Ryan's nose connected with the corner of a step, and the impact rolled his head downward. The next step met the top of Ryan's skull and stopped the motion of his head. His upper spine could not bear the weight of the teenage body and the momentum it had generated after falling halfway down a flight of stairs. His neck buckled under the pressure and his body rolled over top.

Time returned to normal speed as the limp body stopped on the first landing. The teacher was only a second behind and ran to check on the boy. Ryan was lying motionless, flaccid, with his mouth and eyes open, staring through the ceiling into an endless, skyward abyss. There were two dozen witnesses. On a normal day, Paul lacked the vocabulary to describe how much he despised him. But right now, he really needed Ryan to get up.

VII

Thirty minutes from downtown, in the northeast corner of the city, Roman entered the pub style chain restaurant. On the lounge side, there was a poorly-maintained pool table, a few booths, and a bar that served generic draught. It would have been empty if not for the fellow second-generation Ukrainian-Canadian, Oleksandr Boyko, who sat alone in one of the booths. Sacha was a year younger than Roman, shorter, stockier, and, after letting his beard grow thick, having adopted a constant upward pressure from his lower lip, and never quite opening his eyes all the way, he could pass for ten years older.

Roman sat down across from him and grabbed the folded *Edmonton Journal* that was on the table. "Done with this?"

"Yes," Sacha replied, in a thick eastern European accent. "How was the fishing trip?"

"OK, *Oleksandr*. You're laying it on pretty thick." Having known the man since they attended training at the Saint-Jean Garrison, Roman was one of the few people outside of his family that could identify Sacha's accent as being fake. Roman admired the newer appreciation for their mutual heritage, and, in the company of others, he would let the accent slide. "They went without me."

"Oh." His accent faded, and he stared deeply at the empty table between them. Then he shook his head, as if to dust off his confusion.

What are you thinking about?

"I just thought you were coming back tonight," Sacha continued, "I must have my dates mixed up. Long week."

The waitress came by with two tankards of Rickard's Red. The glass was opaque and ice cold. To Roman, there was hardly a more satisfying sound than when she placed the beer down on the bare table. The weight of the glass was evident in the depth of the thud. Roman wiped the frost from the handle of his beer with a napkin, motioning a quick *cheers* toward his friend. "Na druzi," he announced, and swallowed deep.

"Are you having anything to eat?" The waitress was placing branded cardboard coasters on the table.

"No. I think we're OK," Roman answered, before taking another, smaller drink from his glass.

"Cactus cuts," Sacha said flatly, not even raising his eyes to meet hers.

"Please," Roman added, getting a smile in return before she walked off.

"How are things?" Sacha asked robotically.

Their friendship had diminished over time and Roman knew that Sacha did not actually care to hear an answer. "Things are good."

"Thirsty?" Sacha was staring at the Roman's tankard, which was emptying fast.

"I eat fast and I drink fast. Plus, I've had a bit of a day." Roman exhaled strongly, stretched his arms above his head, and cranked his neck back and forth. "Some kid got beat to death downtown. Case is going cold by the minute. No witnesses, owner of the bar had nothing, roommate didn't even know the guy. Most of his family lives in Calgary. I'm sure we'll pull a mountain of DNA off the body, but he was dancing all night in a bar. Without a suspect, we basically run it through the database and hope for a match."

Again, Sacha stared a thousand miles into the distance, as if he could solve the case in his head and, again, he shook out the dust. "What do you do with a case like that?"

"The usual process. Sometimes shit comes up. We have a clue, but I doubt it will take us anywhere. Moussa figures it was left intentionally, to pull us into a game."

"So, what's this big clue?" Their cactus cuts had arrived. Roman figured from the speedy service that they were sitting under a heat lamp. Sacha reached in with his dirty fingers and touched twice as many as he took. He shoved the whole stack of chips in his hand into the dip. Roman grimaced when he noticed the tip of Sacha's index finger also contacted the dip. Sacha licked it clean.

"They carved a number into the bottom of his foot. Don't know yet what the number means, but it actually tells us more than you would think."

"What does it tell you?"

"First, that this was an injury inflicted after his death. Nobody is walking around on that. And it was too clean and precise to be done while he was fighting back. Second, it tells us that they wanted to leave a message. It's bait, for sure."

"What do you mean *bait*?"

"He expressed his motive as being homophobic. The carving in his foot adds nothing. Whether it was for us to find, or the media, or even the family, it doesn't matter. It's not a clue. It's misdirection. He wants us to chase it."

"He was gay?" Sacha was hammering through the appetizer. He pushed it toward Roman, offering his scraps.

"I'm not eating that. And, yeah, probably gay. Killed behind a gay bar. Had 'faggot' carved into his chest. It also tells us that our killer was arrogant. He took the time to leave a message. It must have taken him at lease a minute or two to get it done. Could have easily been spotted from the street. It was really important to whoever killed him that we see this number, and that we know that it was done after the murder."

"Why, though?"

"Well, Sacha, that's what we're working on." Sacha made eye contact with the waitress beside the bar. He gave a nod and motioned for another round. Roman didn't even notice he was half a tankard behind Sacha now. "And *I'm* thirsty?"

"You always drink like a bitch. Try not to get too close to it."

"The case?" Roman was a little offended but tried not to show it. "What do you mean?"

"You know what I mean."

Roman poured the remainder of his Rickard's Red smoothly into his stomach and burped inside his mouth. "OK, so what do you need?"

"Guy's name is Igor Kovac. Pulled over for speeding. Asshole had an arrest warrant for an unpaid fishing ticket. By the way, did you know that if you don't pay that crap, they put a warrant out for your arrest?! Seriously."

"What did he do? Poaching or something?" Roman caved to his hunger and picked a burnt chip from the side of the basket.

"Not even. He was fishing legally at Crimson Lake. Pulling out yellow perch. They're a fucking pest. Invasive species. Anyway, he didn't have his license on him, so he got a fifty dollar fine. Never paid it and it turned into a warrant. Fucking bullshit, really. Obviously, they knew about the warrant, stopped the guy for speeding, and brought him in this morning."

"Scrubbed his apartment?" Roman asked, already sure of the answer.

"It's tight. Like he was never there."

"What are they going to come up with? How bad is he?"

"He keeps it clean. I don't think there is anything lying around to put him away, but this guy is in deep. Just want to get ahead of it. What are they after?"

"Fuck, man, I didn't want to go back in today. Who made the arrest?"

Sacha did not know who had made the arrest. He had no further information, or opted to keep it to himself.

When the second round came, the two robotically clinked their glasses together. "Na zdorov'ya," said Sacha, before tapping his glass on the table and drinking. Roman did the same. The two old friends forced a pleasant and unfulfilling conversation while they finished their drinks.

Roman left the restaurant slightly buzzed.

Empty stomach. Gross-ass Sacha.

He got in his car and rolled down the windows. The AC was

getting fixed on Monday. Roman discretely unfolded the newspaper just enough to check. He didn't need to count it, and stuffed the paper under the passenger seat before pulling out of the parking lot. He was still unaware that he was being followed.

VIII

His new name was Rick. He was sitting in the gravel parking lot beside Busters Pub on 118th Avenue. His destination was just two blocks away. After working every day for a month in the oilfield, this day had been earned several times over. He had become part of the Witness Protection Program after testifying in court to have his own, unrelated charges dropped. In hindsight, hiring a prostitute in plain daylight may have been a mistake. Unfortunately, Rick had certain tastes that could not be satisfied by his wife and, when he saw what he wanted, he had no strength to resist.

Two blocks west from his location, on the north side of the street, was Paradise Massage. Today would be his last visit. It was Rick's regular establishment, because they could satisfy those unusual desires and dealt primarily in cash. Cash was the only way to hide the transaction from his wife. It had been two years since his arrest. He had done the counselling, both personal and couples', but she still refused to trust him.

He left the car and started for the massage parlour, jittery with anticipation. A spring jacket, ballcap, and oversized sunglasses, he thought, would do the job of concealing his identity. Despite those great efforts, he was easily recognised. The withdrawals he had made were minor. At every opportunity, he had converted his time into cash, often lying about his whereabouts and working under the table. The envelope was heavy and constantly reassured him, with every step, as it pressed lightly against his chest. He forced himself to move slowly. Perspiration began to form under his arms and across his back. The sun pounded against the dark jacket.

He was not aware of his pursuer. He had his eyes lowered to the sidewalk. He popped his collar and lifted his shoulders. The neighbourhood was not one with a good reputation and if, by some incredible fluke, his path was to cross with an acquaintance; he would be without an explanation of his business there. Inside his pockets, he gripped his phone in one hand and keys in the other. A salty bead of sweat crawled from under his hat and made its way to his brow. It stung when he blinked, and when he tried to wipe it away quickly, with a shaky hand.

The sign on the front was subtle. The name of the establishment, the phone number, and a neon 'open' sign. Upon arrival, in an unintentionally conspicuous fashion, he looked over his shoulders before deciding that he would not be seen entering. No one appeared to be following him, and he slipped inside. He tripped, without falling, on the single step, and became comically entangled in the two-door system.

"*Sneaky.*" Across the street, his pursuer spoke to no one and laughed. It was unfortunate that Rick had been so amusing. The task would be easier if he had no personality.

Upon entering, the weight of the world lifted from Rick's shoulders. He removed his jacket and hung his sunglasses from the collar of his soaked T-shirt. "How's it going? Is, um, Jamie in?" His voice came out with no strength as he caught his breath, which he only just noticed he had been holding.

"Already expecting you, Rick. Upstairs. Last door on the right." She spoke with an emotionless smile and thick accent. It was welcoming, friendly, and weirdly judgemental.

"I know."

Rick climbed the stairs and opened the first door, which led to a tight hallway. The building was soundproofed well. He was alone with his footsteps. Although no sound filtered through the doors, the smell was unmistakable. It was humid. Sweat, leather, flavoured lubricant, and generously applied perfume that would often be described as 'stripper spray' hung in the in the air and stuck to his skin. On the laminate floor, which was designed to look like hardwood, his feet crunched on the unswept dirt. The colour scheme, which he assumed was to make the establishment feel more feminine, was a careless combination of bright pinks and purples. Rick arrived at his usual portal and knocked quietly. The custom in this location was to create the least noise in the hallway, to avoid disturbing the other patrons.

"Enter," he heard Jamie's soft and slow voice beckon from behind the wooden door. He pressed himself against it and basked in the sound. The short delay of gratification would intensify the experience. Behind the door was pure ecstasy. He quivered as he exhaled, his throaty breath shaking grotesquely as he reached for the doorknob. He closed his eyes and stepped into the room.

"Hi, Rick. Been a while."

IX

Roman was sweating through his shirt when he rolled up to the station. With the windows down, the rhythmic pounding in his ears had been maddening, and this afternoon he found himself to be especially irritable. *I should be fishing.* The truck was already hooked up to his boat when he left that morning and decided it would be easier to borrow the car. It turned out to be the right decision, because the three remaining campers were able to go on the trip without him. Roman left the passenger side window cracked when he got out of the car. He considered for a moment the newspaper under the seat, but let it go. It was the last pitstop in a long day he should not have worked. He would make sure it was short.

Roman sat at his desk and turned on his computer. He shuffled around at his desk, trying to look busy, until he saw his target walk into the break room. He followed casually, careful to not seem too nonchalant. Being legitimately thirsty after driving there in an oven, he filled a paper cup with water and downed it. He filled it again and intercepted Higgins. "What's up, man?" Roman patted him on the back while Higgins was brewing a coffee.

"Thought you were off today! Going fishing or something," Higgins replied in an uninterested tone. He had expected more, but not rightfully so. They had no solid foundation of friendship.

"Technically, I was on call until six. Call came in at four. Two hours and I would have been home free."

"Oh . . . For that, uh. . . hate crime, right?" Higgins was stirring his coffee, still not entirely interested in the conversation.

"Yeah. I thought about leaving it for Moussa, but the Captain would launch if I blew off a murder to go camping. The others went without me."

"Shitty."

"Not for them. I'm sure they will be fine without my company." It occurred to Roman for the first time that he hadn't heard from any of them since this morning. "I heard you brought in a guy for a fishing violation?"

"Jesus. Word travels fast. No one cares about the fishing violation. But he sold to an undercover last week. He still doesn't know. We're not even interested in this guy. The fishing warrant was just to get him talking. We let him make a call and set his mind at ease."

"So? What's the plan?"

"It's a beauty. My own little masterpiece. Like I said, I don't care much for this guy, but we know who he's linked to. Now that we have him all docile, I'm going to drop the hammer."

"Savage. Who are you after?"

"Big fish. Front page, *Edmonton Sun*. Going to work him for a name drop. Have two targets to bring down, and we know their locations. We know this guy is tied up with them."

"How do you get him to sing?"

"Police work. Igor is Canadian. But *new* Canadian, you know. Just got that social insurance number last year. Has a family, too. Wife and kids. Going to introduce him to his buyer from last week and start throwing around some big words. 'Deported' being the scariest one. He'll burn out, and we'll get our name."

"You need a warrant."

"I need a warrant. Judge wants verbal confirmation. Just a matter of time. We have sixteen hours to crack him. Even if he says it in passing, we are good." Higgins drew out the last few worlds with a subtle confidence. He went back to stirring his coffee and poking around in the fridge.

"You still haven't told me who it is."

"And I'm not going to." Roman tried to hide his disappointment, but Higgins shared Roman's natural ability to read people. "Nothing against you, though. Just keeping quiet for now is all."

Roman laughed believably, and gave Higgins another pat on the shoulder. "Go shine your badge."

Pleased with himself and amused by the scathing jab he had taken at his by-the-book colleague, he carried his smirk back to his desk. For several minutes, long enough to appear busy, he shuffled aimlessly around, and then opened Facebook on his iPhone. He updated his status: "Long day. I'm exhausted." He sent a text to Kim to see how the trip was going, and one, mockingly, to Anthony: "No fish pics? Must be a slow day." As he proceeded downstairs and out toward his car, he was met by his long-time partner, Moussa. He smiled loosely, feeling the effects of three tankards on an empty stomach. "You sort out the cops at our guy's apartment?"

"Just a miscommunication," Moussa lied again. "You left your window open."

"I know. The air conditioning is broken. Can't you tell?" He raised his arms to show the sweat under them. As predicted, Roman's phone vibrated silently in his pocket.

"You're disgusting. Antiperspirant. You can buy it at any drug store. You're not worried about someone breaking in? Stealing something?"

"At the police station? Fuck off." Moussa didn't respond. He was drawn in, once again, to the intentionally addictive personal device. "Hey, listen. I'm burnt out. Calling it for the day. You want to get a beer?"

"Not today, man. It was my day off, too, and the wife is waiting at home."

"Right. OK, take it easy." Roman got into his car, disappointed that he would be drinking alone on a Saturday. He had missed the phone call. He quickly paired his phone to the Bluetooth and waited for it to ring again. No reply from Kim or Anthony. *Probably have their phones off. Or Kim does, and Anthony hasn't caught anything.* The thought made him laugh.

The car audio was way too high, and the phone ringing made him jump. He turned it down and answered the call without speaking.

The voice on the other end started: "Roman."

"How far?" Roman asked flatly.

"All the way," the voice answered with the same lack of inflection.

"All right, listen." Roman was convinced, correctly, that he was speaking with Sacha. His tone was dead serious. "You have a problem."

X

The sun was getting low on the horizon and light poured through the south-facing windows of Busters Pub. A waitress sauntered over and got to work on the blinds. Rick sat alone at the bar. To his rear, there was the unmelodious snap and crack of a few local Eskimos fans pushing around the balls on the pool table. With so many pints in them, any strategy was absent from their game. A local band of middle-aged men with a female vocalist were setting up for their gig on the far end of the establishment where Rick would have his last hurricane cocktail. He decided not to stick around for their performance, predicting that their music would be an unrehearsed and offensively loud cluster of noise. To avoid offending musicians during a live performance, he decided to leave before they started.

The bartender brought around his fourth drink of the late afternoon. Rick, in a state of bliss, handed her a ten and dumped all his change in the tip jar. He paid no attention to the slightly offended expression of an over-tipped bartender. His gentle sips left a sweet and sticky residue on his lips, causing him to be constantly licking and wiping his mouth. Busters was not a pretty place, and far from a classy lounge, but right then, that didn't matter. After the hour he spent with Jamie, his world was soft and easy.

He planned to be home in an hour with his beautiful family. He would shower off and see if he had enough endurance for round two.

It would have been a much different and less thrilling experience than he had with Jamie, but one that was necessary for the time being.

Rick grabbed an unused coaster from the stack beside the salt and pepper and placed it on top of his cocktail. He drank at Busters so often that he did not need to ask for directions to the washroom. Rick floated across the room, whirling, in his euphoric state, to the men's room. Coming in the other direction was a tall man in a hurry. It did not offend Rick that they bumped shoulders and he did not stop to apologize. The blissful state in which he found himself was not vulnerable to the unpleasantries of fellow patrons.

After completing his business, Rick returned to his seat and removed the coaster from on top of his drink. The screech of an electric guitar being plugged in broke the silence. Rick spun around in his stool to view the pool players stumbling drunkenly around the table. Good enough entertainment for right now, he figured. Rick drank deep from his cocktail and placed it on the bar behind him.

He reached down and pulled the vibrating phone from his front pocket. It wasn't phone call but a sequence of text messages from his loving pig of a wife. He contemplated the extra stops he would now have to make on the drive home and turned around to order another drink.

Can't hurt the mood I'm in.

"Another of your finest hurricane cocktails!" he announced, and slapped another ten on the counter. The gesture was funny in his mind.

"You've had a few, Rick. Are you driving?" the aging bartender asked. She looked to be in her late fifties, and had her hair dyed bright red. Rick figured she was desperately, ineffectually trying to hold onto her youth.

"Of course not!" Rick lied. "I'll take an Uber. Or maybe Jamie can drive me."

"I don't know who Jamie is, but last time you told me you were taking an Uber, I watched you get in your car and drive away. Just want you to stay safe." She unenthusiastically poured him a water.

"You aren't much fun," he stated, feeling a little defeated. He pouted his lips and pretended to sulk as he drank his water.

He finished slowly, over the next few minutes, and she poured him another one. He drank that too.

"Now can I have another cocktail?" Rick could feel the alcohol in his voice as he struggled to string his words together.

How many have I had?

She brought out the drink and Rick reached into his pocket to pull out some cash, but came up empty. Confused, he reached into his other pocket all pulled out a small wad of bills. He became concerned as he was struggling to choose which bill to put on the counter.

Didn't I already pay?

"Rick, you already paid for this one. Do you want your change?"

Suddenly, she was right in front of him.

Where did she come from?

He waved his hand to say no, afraid of what might come out if he tried to speak again. Rick tried stuffing the cash back in his pocket, but found the task more difficult than it should have been.

How many have I had? It wasn't this many.

Rick brought the fresh cocktail to his mouth and had another sip. "Hey." He couldn't remember his bartender's name. He had known her too long not to know her name. "Maybe. . . maybe you should call me a cab." She wasn't in front of him anymore but miles away, at the other end of the bar.

"I thought you were taking an Uber," she called back.

"Right." Rick felt abandoned. Who were his friends here? He heard laughter from the men playing snooker behind him.

Or was it a pool table? Are they laughing at me?

A few loud, percussive noises echoed through his head. He struggled to maintain focus as he turned around to see the source of the disturbance. The band members were also laughing.

Are they laughing at me, too?

"Rick, you look a little sleepy. Maybe you should give me your keys."

He spun around again to look for Angie. Her name was Angie. She wasn't there.

Out of the corner of his eye, he noticed a man at the end of the bar, close to the front door. "You're the man that bumped into me. Maybe you should give me your keys." The stranger paid him no attention and Rick quietly turned back to the bar. He stared into the cocktail glass.

Is she pouring me doubles?

The uninhibited and belligerent euphoria was usually later in the evening. "Hey, man, are you OK?" Again, someone was talking from behind him. Rick flinched as if the voice had come from nowhere. He spun around but did not reply, wondering how long he had been staring into his drink.

Am I acting funny?

There was no one behind him. "Everyone stand still!" he ordered, as the slurring of his speech worsened. "Stop spinning me around." He wheeled around in his stool to face the bar. This time, he lost his balance and fell. The impact on the ground jarred him back into reality. He looked around as he climbed back to his seat. No one seemed to notice his fall.

I need to leave. Ricky pulled his cash out again and place two bills on the counter. *That should cover what I owe.*

He made his way past the pool players, toward the men's room. As he entered the hallway, he started losing his balance. Trying to save it, he stretched his right arm in front of his body and his left to lean against the wall. At the intersection in front of him, he had to make a right turn. He pressed off the wall with his left hand and tried to land across the hall with his right. Misjudging the distance, he waved his hand at the picture of a celebrity who had probably never entered Busters Pub and fell forward. His off-balance weight pulled him down and he impacted face first into the wall. The strength in his legs abandoned him, and his whole body collapsed to the ground. He paused to catch his breath.

Using the top of his head for balance, he made a tripod with his hands. Once he was confident he was in control, he climbed the wall to get back to his feet.

I'm on the right wall, I think.

To the left of the intersection, there was a glowing exit sign.

Rick had forgotten about the exit. Knowing that he would lose his balance again in a few steps, he decided it had to happen fast. Rick made two wobbly steps, bracing himself with his hands on either side of the hallway. *Almost.* He released his anchor points and lunged with all his force at the push bar where he made contact before falling again. The cool, fresh air rushed over him. It was the smell of victory. Rick crawled with all his strength through the partially-open door and rolled onto his back, listening to the street noise. He looked up at the stars in the sky and listened for the door to latch behind him. There was no earth or asphalt beneath him. It was as if he was floating weightlessly. All sensation of touch was lost, as were his motor functions.

Stars? How long was I in there for?

The door didn't latch behind him and the stranger from inside the bar stepped over him. No response came from his body when he attempted to roll onto his stomach. *What do you want?* The words were silent, and he wheezed out no more than a gentle squeak.

XI

Max's long hair touched the swirling water that washed his crackers down the drain. With each heave, the intensity increased as cramps pressed from his navel, through his stomach and into his chest. His hands shook violently as he struggled to stop the flow of water, and his legs crumbled under the weight of his body. His shaky arms could no longer hold the faucet, and he fell to the floor in his bathroom. Adrenaline and a sense of self-preservation had gotten him home. He had decided not to die in the garden of some rundown building complex, feeling stupid. He knew they would return.

A few hours before, he was savagely beaten and left helpless in the sun. They had dragged him to the corner of the yard, where not so carefully manicured hedges would hide him from the world passing around. He was sure they had intended to kill him. It had taken all his fortitude to drag himself over the fence. Had he failed, the key to his apartment would be lost in the jungle of weeds and grass that were unkept on the other side. Max had, with his last clear thought before being torn to the ground by his assailants, jettisoned the key from his possession, and over the fence. The room number was stamped on it. Had they found the key, Max was sure they would enter his home take anything they deemed valuable, whether sentimental or monetary. The journey over the fence and back had taken most of his strength.

On his right side, in the fetal position, he stared distantly at the base of his toilet.

When was the last time I cleaned behind there? Have I ever?

It was an arm's length away. He could touch it with the tips of his fingers, but knew he would lack the strength to climb to it when he needed. He wanted a hot shower or bath. He could feel himself getting colder. Another fit of chills was drawing near. He would do it with his clothes on, afraid to see the damage that had been done to his already-frail body.

I can do this. A small victory was all he needed. *Embrace the suck.*

It hurt to shift. His ribs, his stomach, and his groin exploded with pain as Max rolled onto his back. With an eye swollen nearly shut, the burnt-out bulb in the centre of his bathroom ceiling was both inches from his face and a hundred feet away. Reaching skyward with his left hand, he weakly grabbed at the towel hanging from its rack. It was still damp. His hand was swollen, and he fought to close it.

Fuckers probably broke my hand.

He was satisfied that his grip was sure, and he used the leverage to turn his body so that his back was against the wall. Reaching above his head to grab the towel with his right hand, he pushed with his legs against the base of the toilet until he could raise himself into a sitting position.

Small victory.

The change of elevation caused pressure to build inside his skull, and he noticed his head was thundering. His heart was pounding against his chest and the bathroom was spinning. Max lowered his arms across his chest and hugged his shoulders in a lonely embrace. He was freezing. He heaved dryly from the pain, but his stomach was empty. It was followed by a painful burp that reminded him of the stale crackers that were his breakfast. He felt he wasn't going to make it to the tub. Weakly, he grabbed one end of the damp towel and pulled it from his drying rack to lay it across his chest. It had been a day, almost two since the last time he used. Tonight, it would get worse, and Max would not sleep.

He was cold, and weak. His head throbbed and ached, the pain increasing with every beat of his heart. He started leaning to his right, preparing to sleep on the linoleum, and felt a lump in his pocket. Salvation. Had he made it to the tub, it would have been ruined. They had searched him, but quickly. Through his loose-fitting jeans, they had missed it. It was only a stamp bag and low-quality, worth less than a breakfast at Denny's, but it invigorated him.

I have to get to my garbage.

It was a fresh mission that promised the greatest prize. Crawling on his hands and knees, he had to cover twenty feet, maybe twenty-five, to the kitchen. In the living room he paused and took a break, face down on the dusty carpet, balancing on his forearms and nose.

This place is disgusting.

After some heavy breaths, he gathered his strength and raised his head. Beside the entrance to his kitchen, hanging from the wall was a Dene dreamcatcher. He hated it. It perpetuated stereotypes. Yet he refused to get rid of it. She had made it in school and presented it proudly to him as a birthday present. If Lulu ever came to visit, how would she feel if he had thrown it out? Max, from his pitiful pose, stared up at the homemade piece of garbage and wondered how his ancestors would perceive him. Would they be proud? "Fuck you!" he barked at the inanimate, offensive, and poorly-constructed piece of garbage, and continued on his odyssey.

At the doorway to his kitchen, before the last leg of his journey to paradise, Max decided he was being pathetic and that he should rise to his feet. After a few more deep breaths in his four-legged stance, he forced his head to the heavens and planted a foot out front. The throbbing in his head increased and he lost his balance, stumbling into the wall. Using it for balance, he pressed his body weight and planted his other foot.

Small victory.

Max placed a hand on either side of the doorway and stared at the tied bag of garbage beside his sink. When he stretched his leg in front, a new, razor-sharp pain, originating internally, from within his pelvis, passed through his abdominal muscles. The tearing sensation collapsed him, and he missed the counter when he reached for support.

You are pathetic.

Max was gagging again from the pain. He was thankful all his crackers had already been washed down the bathroom sink. He sat, shivering and exhausted, until the pain in his stomach faded. Feebly, and from the seated position for which he had had to work, he extended his arm and snatched the bag of garbage. The scream he unleashed through his closed teeth was an expression of joy, as much as it reflected his pain. He tore through the bag, spreading it on the floor, and found the discarded needle. After a few more swipes, he found the rubber band that he would tie around his arm.

Almost home.

He needed his legs one more time. He knew it would hurt, but he would fight through it. Quickly, and biting down hard on the spoon that he had taken from his drawer beside his head, Max stood up and leaned across the counter. He turned the burner on high and slid down the front of his stove to the floor.

He knew the quality was bad but, at this point, the purity was not an issue. His hands were shaking as much from exhaustion as they were from withdrawal. Sniffling because of his runny nose, he tapped the powder into the teaspoon and placed it on the element, leaving the handle over the edge for easier access. He tied the rubber band around his arm and pulled it tight with his teeth. Wincing in pain, he realised for the first time that some of his teeth may have been cracked. Soon, he would feel no pain. Max slapped his arm near his elbow to expose the veins.

Go time.

Using a discarded napkin, Max carefully took the hot spoon down from above his head and placed it gently on the floor between his legs. With careful precision that had been developed over years of repetition, he filled the syringe through the hypodermic needle and flicked it to float the air bubbles to the top. Max tightened the rubber band again and smacked his arm harder this time. At eye level, he carefully pressed the plunger and watched the dark substance bulge at the hollow tip.

Max closed his eyes to enjoy the nirvana in his mind. He would not work tomorrow. He would not feel pain. He could forget about his debts, and the men pursuing him. He would not see the redheaded God Boy tomorrow.

What was that kid's name? He had made the kid a promise, and now wondered if he could keep it. *Fucking God Boy. Telling me what to do.*

He opened his eyes pressed the needle against the scarred skin overtop his favourite injection point and rolled his thumb onto the plunger. His hands were still shaking. Across the floor of his filthy kitchen were the rotting remains of steaks he would never grill and potatoes he would never boil.

Fucking ginger Bible-thumper.

He was breathing heavily. Staring around the mess he had made of his life. Thirty-five years old and he had two things to show for his time: a campaign star for his service in Afghanistan and a Browning 9mm that had been purchased illegally for less than a week's pay. Max removed the needle from his arm and squeezed the syringe in his palm. His hands were too swollen to break it. "Fuck you!" he screamed as he closed his eyes, launching the syringe across the kitchen and into his living room. He did not want to see where it landed. "Fuck you!" he repeated as he raised the stamp bag over his head and mashed it into the hot burner. Max collapsed to his side. Now sweating, and again in the fetal position, he braced himself. The night was going to be bad.

XII

Roman woke up with a sore neck and a headache.

Why is it so easy to fall asleep on the couch?

He figured it was late without looking at his watch. Poker was playing on the sports channel. "Not even a sport," he said to himself as he sat up, blinking heavily, and wondered where he left his phone. He wandered lazily into the kitchen and dug a bottle of Tylenol from the cupboard above his stove.

What's better for headaches? Aspirin? Or should I find Aleve?

He settled on the Tylenol, and swallowed two, before he grabbed a glass to fill with water. His Brita was full, and he had two large glasses and returned it to the fridge without refilling it.

Problem for tomorrow.

He grabbed a can of AGD and dragged himself back to the living room couch. The top of the can popped off with a satisfying *crack* and *hiss* as the pressure equalized.

His phone was buried between the cushions. It was past midnight and the last message he had received was from Kim hours ago: "Goodnight. I love you." He responded with the same.

He had not received a reply yet from Anthony, so he hit him again. "Did you fucking die?" Roman typed out. His smart phone corrected the message before it sent.

Yeah, that's what I meant.

"Almost. Had to bail on the trip." Roman was a little surprised by how quickly Anthony responded.

"Yeah? You sick or some shit?"

"Exactly. Couldn't get off the can this morning. Sent the girls without me."

"They left the camper?"

"Just took the boat. Got a hotel room in town. Girls' weekend sort of thing."

"Come have a beer." Roman had finished his first can and was heading to the fridge for another.

"Some other time. Not feeling 100% yet."

Roman was watching a professional poker player pretending he was unsure of his hand when he was startled by his phone. Anthony was calling.

"What's up? Why don't you text like a normal person?" Roman was always a little annoyed by his friend's insistence on making a phone call when a text would suffice.

"Not much. I saw that murder on the news. You're working that one, right?"

"Obviously. That's why I bailed on fishing. How short is your memory?"

"Just wanted to check in. You know they're saying lots of weird stuff about the body. Thought it might be hitting close to home or something."

"It's fine. Where are you calling from?"

"What?"

"You're like, echoing."

"Throne room," Anthony laughed as he answered.

"You're fucking disgusting."

"You want a selfie? Don't answer. I'm sending one." He did.

"Seriously, though. I thought it may have been a hate crime that got out of hand. Some hillbillies from out of town that had a few too many light beers. But they left a clue. Like they want me to chase them."

"First of all," there was a lot of attitude in Anthony's voice, "how do you know it was more than one guy? Second, don't keep me guessing. What is the clue?"

"First of all . . ." Roman was, for the first time, second guessing his original breakdown of the crime scene. Despite his crude language and laidback personality, Anthony was a clever guy. On more than one occasion, he had helped Roman steer an investigation in the right direction just by asking questions about it. Some sort of Socratic method of argument. "First of all," he repeated, sarcastically mimicking Anthony's voice, "I don't know for sure that it was more than one guy. But this kid was big and athletic. His hands were busted up pretty bad. I'm thinking he returned some damage before he went down. Second of all. They carved a number into his foot. On the bottom. Like they want us to chase them. But it's too obvious. Are they trying to get caught? Or is it just some bullshit?"

"What's the number?"

"Oh yeah? Like you're going to figure out the whole thing. You have every number in the phone book memorized? One-eight-two-two. Go ahead. Solve it, smart guy."

"I don't know. An address or something," Anthony suggested. It reminded him of Moussa.

Really reaching if you think he left his address.

"That's it, I'm going to bed." Roman figured he was sedated enough to get back to sleep. "Beers tomorrow, though. And steaks. I got a new barbecue."

"Deal." Anthony hung up.

Roman's phone buzzed, and he regretted looking at the shameless picture that Anthony sent of himself in the bathroom.

Fucking weirdo. Roman had a genuine smile while he was brushing his teeth. *Why send me that?*

He took a quick shower and crawled into bed. The case was spinning in his head, every detail relentlessly prying. No detail occupied his mind more than the beaten, bloody, and grotesquely familiar face of that young man.

I should have one more beer.

His phone buzzed again as he was throwing the covers off. He looked and saw Anthony had sent him a message. *Better not be another picture of him in the bathroom.* He reluctantly opened the message and, again, regretted it, but for a different reason. It was followed, seconds later, by another text from Anthony.

"Smarter than I look, eh?"

"I hate you so fucking much. Couldn't have waited until the morning?" Roman quickly shot back.

"No way. Get it while it's hot."

Roman carefully read over the first message a few times before conceding to the fact that Anthony had actually helped him. He looked at the time. *Twenty-three minutes. It took him twenty-three minutes. Asshole.* He went back downstairs, grabbed another AGD, and Googled the message, to confirm his friend was right.

"Leviticus 18:22."

XIII

It echoed metallically when the back of his head hit the solid surface hard. His neck was stiff, and his stomach was in knots.

I was with Jamie. And then the bar.

His whole body bounced again off the cold surface and, again, his neck whipped back, driving his skull into the floor beneath him. Rick grunted loudly and tried to reach back to check for damage. His fingers were laced and his hands would not separate. It was cold, and he could feel that he was moving. He rolled to his left to avoid the next skull-shattering blow. The taste of stale vomit was on his tongue, and he heaved dryly, the quarter-roll disturbing his already-tight stomach. It became apparent to Rick during this motion that his feet and knees were pressed tightly together and were not free to move, either.

"Hello?" Rick's voice echoed in the small space. The returning sound was higher-pitched than his own voice.

Sounds like metal.

Again, he was bumped off the floor and, this time, he hit the left side of his head when he landed. His eyes were closed, and he was not able to force them open. He craned his neck and rolled his head in all directions, attempting to remove whatever binding forced his eyes shut. It was sticky and pulled his hair when he moved. *Tape?* With his hands together, he raised them to his face to uncover his vision, but found his hands were bound in a similar fashion. His whole body ached, and he rolled onto his knees. Panic was setting in.

What the fuck is going on?

He worked quickly and aggressively to find an angle that would allow that ball of tape around his hands to pick at the similar wrappings on his face. The momentum of his metal prison stopped suddenly. With no reference point to balance, Rick found himself floating weightlessly. His own momentum was stopped when the top of his forehead met another solid surface. The impact echoed again metallically in the small space, and a powerful shockwave passed from his head and neck into his shoulders and ribs.

That was dumb. Am I in a vehicle?

"Hello? Can anyone hear me?" Rick called out, louder than before. *Stay calm.* He pulled hard to separate his hands. He heard the driver stirring in the cab. "Let me out!" He breathed heavily and was flushed with fear, when he heard the door to the cab open and close. He was sitting quietly as the footsteps moved around the front of the vehicle and down the passenger side. He could hear traffic passing on the driver's side. "HELP!" Rick screamed, as the back door unlatched. Cool air rushed over him and with it came the smell and taste of exhaust fumes. He could feel the suspension sink, and the back door closed again. His captor was in the van with him.

The unknown person slammed him down and pinned him with most of the pressure against Rick's chest. The weight restricted his breathing, but he forced himself to speak. "Who are you? What do you want?" From the strength of the assailant, and from the artificial fragrance he wore, Rick decided it was a man. He had a leg on either side of Rick and was pinning his arms to his body. There was a familiar tearing sound of duct tape being pulled off the roll. Rick barely managed to get out one more plea for mercy before his mouth was covered. His hair was gripped, and he could feel and hear the tape being passed several times around his head.

Good thing my nose isn't stuffed.

The back door opened, the suspension raised, and the door slammed shut. This time, the steps went around the driver's side, between him and the traffic. Rick was wondering how much time had passed.

How long before my wife calls the police?

To avoid more slamming of his already swollen and bruised head, he inched into a corner and braced himself in a sitting position. His breaths were deep and deliberate. Although he could get more than enough oxygen through his nostrils, the tape covering his mouth made him feel claustrophobic.

How long do I have?

Rick started working his legs back and forth in a pedaling motion, to loosen his feet. At the same time, he was rubbing his face on the metal wall of the van, attempting to free his vision. He was frustrated he had only just realised he could have stayed quiet and used his teeth to work at the tape on his hands. *Fuck.*

The van rolled around a corner and Rick heard several metal and plastic objects bounce across the cargo space to his right.

Could I use any of them to help me?

The ride was not long enough to work himself free and the van stopped again. Rick vomited in his mouth and swallowed it. It was more from fear than from his hangover. *I was at the bar.* The van pulled to the right as it backed up. *Last stop.* His breathing was getting heavy. The steps were loud and crunchy as they moved around the front of the van.

Gravel? Where am I?

The passenger door of the van opened. Rick tried to listen through the metal as the driver rummaged around. The door closed and the steps continued to the rear of the vehicle.

Rick was sweating. He was fighting desperately not to wet himself. His body was trembling, and he was struggling to breath. He listened carefully to the clanging of metal outside the rear of the van. Eventually, he heard a heavy snapping sound as metal broke, stopping the audible struggle. Then there was fast rattling sound, like a chain being pulled through a fence.

Is he breaking in somewhere?

The back door of the van opened. Rick tried to scream but managed to deliver nothing more than a high-frequency hum through his nose. A quick sound of Velcro being pulled open was followed by the stretching of leather over skin. Immediately after, a second sound of Velcro was followed by leather again being pulled over skin.

Gloves?! Rick started kicking and squirming violently. An adrenaline-fueled rush was rising over him. *No! Not today!*

Rick banged hard on the metal of the van trying to produce as much noise as he could manage before he was grabbed around the ankles and dragged out into the cold air. His head banged hard on the way down, and he landed on his back. Dust filled his nose and gagged his flow of oxygen. The ground was rough and sharp. He was now sure that it was gravel. Before he could squirm for freedom, he was dragged across the rough surface by his feet. His T-shirt rode up and his back scratched against the ground.

Rick was left seated on the ground with his back against a cold, rough surface, as the footsteps calmly walked back to the van. There was a high-pitched, hollow scraping sound of something being removed from the back of the van. The steps paced evenly back until they were in front of him. His earlier attempt to hold his bladder failed, and he felt the warm liquid pour down between his legs.

Which way would he swing? Rick raised his bound hands to cover the left side of his face, and the changed his mind and covered the right side. He was trembling and started whimpering. He wanted to beg for mercy. Eventually, he lowered his chin to his chest, and covered both sides of his face with his elbows. For an eternity, he sat, waiting, with his taped hands above his head.

It was beautifully cool outside, relieving the sweltering, unnatural heat of the September weekend. The ground beneath him was sharp and jagged. The wall to his rear was hard and cold. Stale, regurgitated hurricane cocktail was sharing his mouth with the toxic taste of adhesive that had seeped through his lips. The ammonia from his urine mixed with exhaust and burned his sinuses with every inhalation. Through his fleshy earmuffs, to his right, was light evening traffic and rustling leaves being disturbed by gentle wind. To his left was the dull hum of the engine that was still running.

I guess he plans to make it quick.

To his front, the still atmosphere was disturbed by a long, thin object hurdling through it. The sound of the breaking air gave less than a second's notice before he was struck on the back of his right arm and across the bridge of his nose. He winced and curled forward. The second blow caught more of his forearm than anything else, but connected directly on the bone. Rick curled his broken arm into his chest.

My head is exposed.

The following blow to the right side of his head removed any conscious awareness of the situation. He rolled forward and to his left, landing face down in the gravel. Every muscle in his body tensed. His legs extended fully, and arms stretched downward, locking straight out. His final thought was of Jamie.

XIV

He was lying on his back, staring up at a starless night sky. Overgrown grass and dandelions crowded his vision. He raised his head and looked toward his feet, observing that his lack of clothing should have led to irritation from the flora that engulfed him. The air was still, thick with pollen, and cool against his skin. He sat up and brought his knees to his chest, searching for context. Paul was overly aware of the magnitude of the space that surrounded him, and his pitiful self, that could bear none of its force. There was no recollection of the events that had preceded. It was eerily quiet. He struggled to balance himself in the overwhelming stillness that surrounded him. His hands shook and his head was too heavy for his neck. Despite the thickness of the air, he struggled to draw satisfying breaths. Pressure was building inside his skull with each increasingly heavy beat of his heart. He scanned across the landscape and was alarmed by the lack of distinguishing features. As if stepping through a mental portal, he had the sudden realisation that he was in a soccer field that was not his destination. He departed it with unrelenting ambition, pumping his legs forcefully, but feeling his movement to be restricted.

He was lost, wading, waist deep, through a sensationless grass ocean. Hills surrounded him in every direction, rolling like monstrous waves. Motion and stillness produced no sounds. The world was taunting him. It was vast and he was small. Guided desperately by moonlight, Paul thundered through the valley that separated him from the glowing orb in the sky. As he crested the first ridge, he saw that he had made no progress, and repeated the action. Each knoll was its own island, surrounded by a rippling clover universe. Paul spun to check his progress and could no longer see the field that had birthed him into this world. He spun again, to reset his course. Standing before him, silhouetted by moonlight, was a massive human. In his own dark shadow, the man's features were not visible.

"DAD!" Paul's voice cracked as he called out. The man turned and started down into the next valley. Paul raced after him but could not close the distance. "Wait!" Paul's screaming was muffled, as if there was not enough air in his lungs to project his voice. The grass was thick and hindering his movements. As the distance between Paul and his father grew, his panic increased. His motions were becoming less deliberate, and his confidence was wavering. Paul was thrashing, fighting against the ground that seemed to hold him in place. He raged, squealing unintelligibly at the figure. Paul leapt out, hopelessly clawing at the air, but his father's unresponsive ghost moved easily from his reach.

He found himself face down in the dirt. The grass and roots had scratched his face, and Paul welcomed the sensation. His body was heavy. His arms were almost too weak to move. He raised his head and made eye contact with his dead father. "Dad! Where is the camp?"

The unusually featured figure that was surely his father turned to his fallen son. The powerful build of the former special forces operator was shriveled and pathetic. His skin was pale and cracked. Stoic, piercing eyes sank into his skull, and veiny, dark skin surrounded them. His normally neat hair was long and thin, hanging in front of his face. When he opened his mouth to speak, his teeth were yellow and broken.

"They killed me, Paul." In was an airy whisper, and the sound became Paul's totality.

"Dad!" His voice was cracking. He could not hide the twisted face of a crying boy, and let tears run down his cheeks. "Where are they?" He tried to rise, but his feet were tangled in ropy weeds that grew in the grass.

When the grotesque figure moved his mouth to speak, only an airy, dying breath wheezed through his cracked and broken lips.

"Fuck you!" Paul was scrambling but lacked the strength he needed to rise. "Tell me how to find them!"

His father lowered his head, bending unnaturally at the waist, and rotated his head sideways, until his eyes were inches from Paul's. His expressionless face curled into one of anger. Through clenched teeth, he spoke with serpentine hate: "You are weak. You will be judged. This is not God's plan." As the last words crept from the monster's mouth, its jaw loosened and fell to the ground, exposing a grey and rotting tongue that licked the air where its lower teeth should have been.

His withered body straightened and he let out a disappointed exhale before turning into the moonlight and continuing his impossible pace. Paul reached down to his feet and saw his laces were wound into the ground. Terror did not allow him the dexterity to untangle himself. He breathed slowly, trying to steady his hands. *Slow is smooth. Smooth is fast*. He was free. Paul rolled over onto his hands and feet and stood to find his disfigured father.

He was no longer alone, and stood where his life had changed. The nylon tents were unburned, and the camp was quiet. There were no screams. He had made it. He whirled around to locate his teammates in the copse of trees that would be behind him, but saw no one. A young boy exploded from his tent and rushed toward the centre of the camp, where the first aid kit and safety equipment were kept. Paul watched in puzzled amusement at the boy desperately digging around for something. For a moment, he considered speaking up, until he saw that the boy had dug out the fire extinguisher. He watched helplessly. His feet felt cemented into the ground. When he opened his mouth to speak, he could not make a sound. It was the second boy he had killed.

"Burn, little birdie!" Ryan was laughing as flames exploded from the nozzle. Fire engulfed the camp. The heat blasted through Paul's exposed skin and frozen body. The delicious spring air that had previously filled his lungs was now a mouthful of ash. Skin peeled back off Ryan's laughing face as he continued hosing the camp with flames. The smell of Paul's own burning flesh and hair blended into that of toxic burning nylon. Children fought desperately, wailing and crying, to escape from their melting shelters. The laughter from Ryan's skeletal face faded, as if the source of the sound were drawing farther away. The heat and smell dulled, and Paul sank. The immense pressure of the children's screams darkened his world, forcing him downward and inward.

He was on his back, appreciating the comfort of not being in a prison cell. The unnamed man was afraid to open his eyes. He lay perfectly still in his bed, waiting for the world to be quiet again. After a few slow breaths, he opened his eyes to the darkness of his room. He was soaking wet. *I hope that's sweat.* He wrestled free from his covers and sat his pale body on the floor beside his bed. He had no air conditioning, and his bedroom was too hot. Still, he shivered in his damp underwear. Seconds before, he had been burning. He had watched, and smelled, the skin melting off his body. Using his shaky hands, he combed sweaty hair out of his face. He whispered to himself: "I need to pray. I need to confess."

I wonder what he will think about what I have done. And what I am going to do.

Sunday

"I will carry out great vengeance on them and punish them in my wrath. Then they will know that I am the Lord, when I take vengeance on them."

- Ezekiel 25:17

"Don't think about zebras."

-Unknown

I

Roman felt it would end soon. Those inside were fulfilling their end of the weekly bargain, made with this Catholic version of "God" whom they served. The trade was ninety minutes of boredom so they might leave with a mild sense of virtue. Either way, the disinterested detective stood on the steps of St. Joseph's Basilica, finishing the last few drags of his cigarette. Between each relieving breath, he stared with contempt at the thin paper tube whose chemical contents had managed to possess his unwilling soul. He had been able to avoid the first two services by arriving early. His previous stop had been at Mary of Help, down the street, and he had sat through an agonizing hour of preaching, to find that the priest, once again, had no information. The original plan, devised by Roman, had been to do the questioning from home. Over the phone, they could have covered more ground. In person, Moussa had suggested, they could be more effective. Roman stuffed his butt in the concrete planter beside the door when he heard the parishioners stampeding outwards.

Sacrilegious?

He leaned back against the balustrade that extended between opposing stone staircases to allow them to pass around him. The doors flung open, and they spilled out, loudly reviewing the service amongst themselves. He typed out a quick text to Moussa while he waited for the crowd to thin. "Any luck?" He did not get a reply.

When fighting upstream offered less resistance, Roman

politely stepped between the stragglers and entered the church. The vast hall softly echoed the murmurs of the few that remained. Two rows of wooden pews were flanked by a sophisticated system of columns and pointed arches. Roman wondered if it was for the congregation or their God that such magnificent structures were used for worship. Above the arcade, the stone walls rose several stories to a vaulted ceiling. Light diffused through the stained-glass windows and mixed with the dim chandeliers that hung deeply above the passageway between the pews.

There must be a more efficient way to light this building.

Roman made himself smile. Hoping to make his visit as quick as those that had preceded it, he asked one of the volunteers, who was straightening between the pews, "Where can I find the pastor? Priest?"

"He takes confession immediately after service." The elderly man smiled forcefully and indicated with an open palm in the direction of the booths.

"Great," Roman whispered to himself, before raising his voice to become audible. "How long does it take?" He spoke through a hidden hostility he knew the innocent man did not deserve. Had the world been created to hasten his own interests, he would not feel bound to the slow progress of this morning's proceedings. He directed that frustration on this man, whose path had happened to cross his own.

"Well," the man spoke slowly, drawing both breath and thought with great effort, "that depends on how long the line is. If you want to get in, you should probably make haste."

Roman exhaled hard and nodded, with his eyes on the floor. "OK. Thank you."

There wasn't much of a line. Just one young redheaded man, patiently waiting. Roman took a seat next to him and checked his phone. Still no reply. He sucked his teeth and tapped his feet. The dusty and dry air contrasted painfully with his memories of the lake where he should have been that morning. With his eyes closed and arms crossed, he imagined his feet dangling in the cool water to balance the heat from the unrelenting sun. A lighthearted conversation between Kim and his friends would be taking place behind him. Fueled by discrete consumption of canned drinks, it would require none of his own participation. His own attention could be paid to the delicate sensation of his bait, bouncing, over a hundred feet below.

Instead, he sat beside some God-fearing stranger, who surely had his mind focused on how he might please his deity this week. "Hey," Roman whispered, "I haven't done this before. Can you run me through it?"

"Are you recently converted? Or have you, until this day, lived a life so righteous that you needed no confession?" The words were condescending, yet he whispered with an enlightened tone that implied he was wise well beyond his years. His expression was soft, flat, and showed no impatient hostility, opposite to that which Roman had projected to his previous advisor. He raised his eyebrows slightly and stared steadily at Roman. It was welcoming, in some celestial way, and Roman felt drawn into an open conversation.

"No. I'm not religious. I don't mean to offend. But it's just not up my alley. I need to speak with . . ." he couldn't remember the priest's name, and trailed off, turning his head to break the uncomfortable dialogue.

"—Father Edmund," the young man finished for him, and leaned in close, so that their shoulders were pressed together. "You know, he probably wouldn't mind speaking with you after. A lot of people take these confessions very seriously. Myself included. Please don't make a mockery of my religion."

"Like I said," Roman shuffled and shrugged the young man off his shoulder, "I don't want to offend anyone. My business is time-sensitive. Will Father Edmund not speak with me?"

"I cannot tell you what Father Edmund will or will not do." *That tone again.* "But I can tell you this. If you take your confession seriously, you will feel better after. Might even get some more sleep." The young man's eyes dropped just below Roman's, and he made an almost impossibly subtle gesture at the bags under Romans eyes. "Can I ask you something?"

"No." Roman was annoyed. His posture slumped. He leaned back in his chair and stuffed his hands in his pockets, searching for his gum.

"Why don't you believe in God?"

"I don't have time to get into this right now."

The young man surveyed the room with his eyes before landing his smug gaze back on Roman. "Is it not the time or place?" A humorous smile stretched across his lips. "You're going to have to wait as long as I am."

"Fine," Roman started, no longer straining himself to whisper, but still not disturbing the peace of the nearly empty church, "First of all I never said that I don't believe in God, which I don't. I like to think objectively. Is there any proof that God exists? And, possibly more importantly, is there any proof that he wants me to confess my sins? If I could see and touch and feel this all-powerful immortal, I would consider its existence as a factual possibility."

"Is the proof not all around us? The earth, sun, moon, and stars? Atheists seem to be hung up on the loose theory of the 'big bang.' But without a physical force to start the universe in motion, your own theory requires a higher power, does it not? Without one, would Sir Isaac Newton not roll over in his *Christian* grave? Furthermore," Roman could tell at this point that the man was well practised in his side of the argument, "how can our perfect design be the result of random chance? Each person has between twenty and twenty-five thousand different genes. These are the blueprint that our cells follow to build us, to repair us, and to reproduce us. In our short existence—and I would guess that we disagree on the duration of that existence—how could all the pieces of such a wildly complicated puzzle just fall into place?"

Still speaking softly, and now with some attitude, Roman answered: "I do not give two licks of shit if Newton was a Christian. If we filled the holes in science with 'God did it,' we would never have advanced this far.

"That's—"

"—I am not finished. If we are going to namedrop, let me tell you a story. Unlike a lot of what you hear in this building, this is a true story. You obviously know who Abraham Lincoln is." The man nodded, and Roman continued: "At one point in his life, Lincoln was boarding with a pastor, or a reverend, or some religious leader. But at night this leader would be awake, watching the sky. It has never been uncommon to witness a shooting star. But on this particular night, there were hundreds, or thousands. And this all-knowing religious leader, being so educated by the Bible, saw this as the stars falling to the earth. Part of Revelations, if I am not mistaken. He thought the world was ending. So, he wakes everyone up. Tells them to repent. It is the end of days." Roman waved his hands sarcastically. "Mr. Lincoln, who was also raised as a Christian, gets up and went outside to witness the apocalypse. He sees the stars falling and heads back to bed. He went on, at some point, to explain that, although he did not have an answer for what was happening, he was sure that God was not ending the world. The point of the story, if you're still with me, is that he did not have the answer, but he knew that there was one. He knew that there was an answer better than 'God did it.'"

"That's a true story?"

"As best as I can retell it. I don't know the exact details," Roman exhaled, "but my understanding is that it was a meteor storm. Not the stars falling to the earth."

"God. I would've guessed that, between the two of us, I was the preachy one."

Roman didn't respond. Instead, he pursed his lips, exhaled forcefully through his nostrils, and stared at the confession booth, as if to somehow hurry its occupants.

"I would guess," the young man started again, "based on the fact that you are carrying a sidearm, that you are a cop."

Probably felt it when he leaned into me.

"You would guess right." Roman was edging forward, looking at the booth for a clue as to what was taking so long.

"So, you protect the law, and stand for what is right?"

Roman was being led, but allowed it to happen. "I like to believe so."

"Are your laws not written based on the teachings of the Bible? Without religion, without God, what is right and what is wrong?"

"That's another lame argument for religion. Right and wrong." Roman was hooked. Being pulled into the age-old debate that would not be resolved here in this queue. "The laws of your religion are based on empathy, an emotion that predates religion by two hundred thousand years, or more. If you hurt another person, it makes you feel bad. That exists with or without the body of Christ. Or a confession. Or a grand spectacle of a building for worship. If your dog bites you, and you feel pain, your dog will feel bad, and it knows nothing of God."

"Perhaps during our creation, God gave us empathy, so that we might follow and obey his laws without direction."

"Empathy is an involuntary reaction. When you witness an emotion, you mimic it. Some more and some less. By recreating the expression in your own face, you are forced to feel that way. God's laws, or those written in the bible, do so much more harm than good."

"You want to back that one up?" The young man's voice had dropped from his previously sophisticated tone to a more natural one. Roman figured he may have struck a nerve.

"How many people have been killed in the name of their God? How many wars have been fought over minor differences in beliefs?" Roman's voice was rising. "How could one follow a religion that would make a normal, sane, individual turn violent? Why should an innocent man be dragged into the street and beaten to death because of the words written in the Bible?"

The young man did not reply. The door to the confession booth opened and a nondescript middle-aged woman exited. Roman indicated with a nod of his head, "You're up."

"No. I think you should go first," the man answered, "You need it more than I do."

If Roman weren't pressed for time, he would not have taken the offer.

II

Father Edmund slid open the wooden cover and looked through the lattice at the exhausted face of a man who appeared to be in his mid thirties. It was not a man that he recognised, and certainly not one whose confession he had taken.

"You're Father Edmund?" the man asked unequivocally.

"Usually, you start with, 'forgive me father for I have sinned.' But, yes, I am Father Edmund. Go ahead, tell me your sins." Since he had not taken the man's confession before, he tried to exude a friendly and welcoming tone.

"Detective Roman Owen. EPS. Homicide division." The man identified himself in a monotone and commanding voice, not increasing his volume. He held his badge to the lattice so the priest could confirm his credentials. "Can I ask you a few questions?"

Father Edmund shifted his voice from friendly and welcoming to business-formal, without implying any hostility, and answered carefully. "You are welcome to ask me any questions that you have, and I am happy to assist. I will let you know that direct, personal questions regarding the confessions that I take are confidential. Unless, of course, someone was to confess to a violent crime or the intent to commit one."

"Yep, heard that a couple times today." Sounding slightly exasperated, and after taking a few minutes to read robotically what sounded the standard rights regarding questioning, the detective started: "Has anyone confessed to committing a violent crime, or the intent to do so?"

"Not in my entire career," he answered with swaggering confidence. The priest forced his eyebrows together and stared deep into his memories to confirm the answer he had so easily given. Before anything came to mind that would cause him to ask for a pardon, the next question was delivered. This one came with the same lack of conviction as the first.

"Are you aware of any religious groups that could be dangerous?"

"No. Fortunately, I am not."

"I want you to rethink that one in a little more depth. Not that I don't believe you, but it's easy on the surface to assume everyone has the best intentions. Are there any religious gatherings that seem to not like new members? Or maybe some groups that work together on projects that don't seem to have a clear objective?"

The question came with a slightly accusing tone, implying the speed and confidence with which he had been answering was less than genuine, or that no thought was being given to the responses. The truth in it stung, as he had not taken more than a second, either time, to reply. Father Edmund realised now that the detective had also been speaking slowly, and figured this must have been to reduce the feeling of being pressured. Introspection, he had always thought, was an important skill, especially for a man of the church. Speaking to an officer of the law, even when innocent or oblivious to any wrongdoing, felt, for some reason, uncomfortable. He furrowed his brow deeper than before, cleared his throat and head equally, and spoke with greater confidence.

"Not off the top of my head. I am sorry. But I will keep my eyes and ears open for you."

"Have you noticed any strange behaviour? Maybe a member of your church who seems stressed more than normal, or anyone asking irregular or dangerous questions? I understand this is vague."

"Once again, not off the top of my head. I will try to watch for you. When it comes to strange behaviour and irregular questions, however, I must decline to respond. It is not wise to compromise the trust of my position. If the members of my congregation received word that I was directing the law into their lives, especially without good reason. . . . I want you to remember that the confessions I receive are str—"

"Confidential. I know," the detective cut him off. "I'm not trying to press or be rude. I want you to understand that I am not here looking for someone who committed trespassing or shoplifting. Since this is strictly confidential, as you have made so abundantly clear, I feel like I can tell you that we are investigating a murder. It was violent, and appears to have been premeditated. From what we can tell, it was motivated by religion. Please use your discretion. I don't need to hear about who vandalized someone else's place of worship."

"Thank you. I think I understand."

"Are there any outwardly homophobic members of your church?"

"Well, that is an interesting one. Homosexuality is forbidden in the Bible. Obviously, in modern times, the church must adapt to be more accepting. Yes, there are members of the church who outwardly condemn homosexuality. The list likely wouldn't help with your case."

"Why do you say that?"

The priest drew out the start of his answer, moaning, as if discomforted: "For starters, I'm not sure that I would be willing to compile such a list. More importantly, because most of the names would belong to an older generation. The sort of people who would struggle to beat down a twenty-year-old body builder."

"I never said anything about that." The detective's voice was slightly humorous, as if he had caught someone in an obvious lie.

"It's all over social media. The homosexual boy found in the alley. Also, us priests and religious folk, we talk to each other. I got a text message shortly before you got here. I wish you the best of luck with your case. Honestly. But I don't think I can offer you any assistance."

"I'm going to leave my card on the seat outside," the detective explained, seeming to understand that this interview would need to end shortly. "If anything comes to mind, do not hesitate. I want you to call me. Thank you for your time."

The detective exited the booth. Father Edmund stepped out and grabbed the card before returning to hear the last confession, which came from a familiar face, this time.

There was a long pause before the young man spoke. "Father, I need guidance," he nervously started. "I have committed many sins in my life, and for those I have been prosecuted. But the time I served was sentenced in accordance with the laws of our courts, the laws of man. In their eyes, I have atoned for those sins. I have also committed myself to the church. To be absolved of these sins in the eyes of the Lord, I can do nothing less than spend my life doing His work."

The veteran priest noticed the young man's voice was slow and deliberate, as if he was being careful to use the right words. There was more he had to tell. "You sound quite rehearsed. And it seems that you have made all the right decisions since taking the path of the Lord. What is it that's troubling you?"

"What would one do?" The man paused several times when he spoke, and chose his words with careful precision. "What would one do if they were faced with a situation where the laws of man, and the laws of God, did not assert the same action?"

"If you were to explain to me the specific situation, I could offer you specific guidance." Father Edmund was thinking of the detective. "It does sound like you may intend to commit a crime."

"I have committed many crimes. Violent crimes. I guess the real question is, would one risk imprisonment? Is the sacrifice of freedom of one's mortal body an atonement worthy of preserving one's soul? Would the lack of action be a sin in God's eyes? This opposite would mean freedom. Freedom during one's short earthly existence, but eternal damnation." The man's head was down and appeared to think deeply as he spoke.

"The laws of man, as you call them, are the laws that govern this county. Those laws are based on the commandments of the Bible, and the morals that it teaches. In which passage is there a lesson being taught that would supersede modern laws?"

"In many passages of the Bible, Father. I will pray on this. And through that prayer, I hope I will find the answers that I seek. Thank you for your time, Father. And for your guidance." The boy stepped quickly and confidently out of the booth.

Father Edmund's old legs did not allow him the strength to rise as quickly as the young man. When he exited the middle door of the confession booth, there was no sound in St. Joseph's Basilica except for the last few echoing footsteps as the man pressed hurriedly toward the door. He dug into his pocket to feel for the detective's business card. He twisted it slowly between his fingers and pursed his lips.

I, too, will pray on this.

III

He was freezing. He had destroyed the last of his heroin on the stove the previous night. Max lay on the rotting linoleum floor of his rental kitchen, soaked in sweat and vomit. The evening had lasted several lifetimes. Max's cell phone was soaking in a filled kitchen sink. He had previously attempted to call for another stamp bag of nirvana, and destroyed his avenue before completing the order.

The pounding inside his skull and aching behind his eyes was some combination of withdrawal, dehydration, and the savage beating he had received the day before. The pain in his abdomen had reduced, but his legs were still hardly sturdy enough to climb to his feet. Leaning on the counter, he opened the cabinet and found the bottle of extra strength Tylenol.

Four should do it.

He dumped them into his palm and, shaking, threw them into the back of his throat. He filled his hands from the standing water that had destroyed his phone, and used that to forcefully swallow the pain relievers. After he was sure it had settled, he filled his stomach in the same fashion.

"OK, Max. Never again."

The symptoms had faded, but Max knew they would return. The sour smell of his regurgitated stomach contents mixed with the uncirculated air of the slum he was renting.

First thing. I need to clean that.

After eating what remained of his stale crackers, Max gathered a mop, a bucket, and various cleaning supplies, and sorted out the mess in his kitchen. The pills and crackers came back up, but he made it to the bathroom to avoid another mess. The simple task drained him and, exhausted, he slept on the couch, with a second attempt at the Tylenol. This time, he used fresh water.

Food.

When Max woke, he had another, more natural sensation in his withered and bruised abdominal muscles. This one he could easily cure.

He knew how he looked, beaten and limping. He could sense the extra space the strangers gave him when he walked down the sidewalk. It wasn't far. No one had chased him this time. He exited though the parking garage and painfully dragged himself over the fence. The smell of the trash can outside the nearest fast food location was not as bad as his own apartment, and Max dug through until he could find a receipt from the previous day. After a brief argument with the teenager who was employed there, and an even quicker exchange with the manager, Max hustled a full bag of junk food.

They know I'm lying, but they want me gone.

The greasy cheeseburgers and cola sat well. After a heavy burp and a fresh coffee, Max was starting to feel alive. The water in his shower was ice cold to compensate for his burning skin. The hot and cold flashes were common symptoms, and Max altered the temperature several times before he felt normal enough to dry off. Like so many previously failed attempts, today was a new beginning, and the morning had been productive. Max rested again before opening the laptop and staring into the black mirror at his weak and sunken face. His bank account was overdrawn again. He chose not to check which automatic bill payment was the culprit. Another hot flash was coming on, and Max opened his sliding door all the way and aimed his fan to fill the apartment with outside air.

They were expensive. Any that cost more than what he had in his bank account were nice. There were rehab facilities he could afford—those that were funded by taxpayers and weren't as nice. Still, the pages of the online pamphlet were filled with laughing, smiling, lying faces. It would not be so easy that he would laugh and tell jokes and sing in a circle.

"This is all bullshit." The Tylenol was wearing off, or he was exhausted from internet research. He closed the laptop and sat still, with his elbows balanced on his knees and face cradled in his palms. His stomach was twisting again. He inhaled and exhaled slowly. He could not afford to lose his breakfast. Max heaved once, softly, and again, heavily.

It was five slow and smooth steps to the kitchen, where he filled a glass with water and dumped three dissolving tabs into it. Cold sweat was escaping through his skin, and his face was boiling. The crisp taste of the Alka-Seltzer started the relief, and he poured the whole glass into his stomach and chased it with another. He rested his weight, using his head and arms as an anchor point, against the counter.

Max was startled when the buzzer beside the door disturbed the quiet hum of his electric fan. He shuffled over and hit the button to talk. "Hello?" His voice was raspy and dry.

"It's me. I'm in a hurry. Let's do this." He recognised the stern voice.

"I don't need. Go away."

"Yes, you do. You called last night and hung up on me." The voice was getting agitated.

"Look, man. Sorry to make you come down. I'm getting clean." He was looking for a way to get rid of his dealer. He hardly had the strength to argue. "I'm broke, too. Overdrawn. And I lost my job." It was only half a lie, but the connection ended.

Thank fucking Christ.

Max dragged himself back to the couch to continue his research. He had to wait for the drugs to settle his stomach, and drifted into a painful, quivering sleep.

He woke up when an object bounced off the coffee table in front of him. He was groggy and slow to move around as he looked for the culprit. A crumpled ball of paper was on his living room floor. It was heavy and taped together. The light of the late morning was blinding. He squeezed his eyes shut the way a child might if he had eaten a popsicle too fast. With one eye barely open, he unwrapped the gift that was airmailed through his open balcony door. There was a rock from the garden, a stamp bag of low-quality heroin, and a note.

"On the house."

Max left the rock and paper on the coffee table and took the heroin to the bathroom. He lifted the lid to the toilet and held out the bag. Using the counter for support, he rocked from his toes to heels and back. His apartment was quiet again. There was the dull and steady hum of the fan, and an obnoxious buzzing sound above his head. The bulb flashed off and on once before a brief pause, and then died completely. He closed the lid and stuffed the bag into his back pocket.

Just in case.

IV

The body of Rick Van Pelt was discovered in the gravel parking area that separated Paradise Massage and Victoria Fancy Sausage. The body had baked in the sun for hours before its discovery and had already been identified when the detective arrived. The area was small and hidden from the street by a row of tightly-spaced Swedish aspens. A shadow cast from the eastern building covered the entire space and made the body impossible to spot from the street or sidewalk until the late morning.

Upon arrival, Roman noticed the fence was chained and locked before the murderer broke in. Roman considered that he had taken the time to cut through the lock before placing the body there.

So deliberate.

His eyes were forced closed by the sun, and he peeked through a squint at the scene before him. The sweltering heat had caused him to sweat through his dress shirt, which was now untucked and partially unbuttoned.

"Your air conditioning still broken?" Moussa asked.

"Since yesterday? Yeah." Roman was irritated more by the implications of a second victim than by the question itself. After stuffing a Nicorette in his mouth, he chewed and drew a long breath in through the nose, before releasing it quickly through his mouth. "The fence was cut. We find this body here, between a greasy sausage shop and a brothel."

"Massage parlour."

"Whatever. The tracks end before the gate. He cuts it and pulls the guy out—gagged, I would assume."

"Or dead."

"No. I don't think so. He drags the victim," Roman indicated with his palm at the disturbed gravel, "from the gate to the brick wall. He kills him—and, when the forensics guys come through, I'm sure they will back me up this—violently." Because of its condition, the body had already been photographed and moved; but the dried blood in the gravel confirmed Roman's theory. "The question I am dealing with is, *why*? Why did he—or she, who fucking knows—bother to gag the guy and move him? And kill him after?"

"He could have been dead when he brought him here."

"I really don't think so. There would be no reason for all this blood. Do we have pictures? I want to look at them while I'm here."

"We do." Moussa walked back to his issued Hyundai Elantra and returned with an issued tablet. The file was already open, and Roman swiped through as Moussa spoke. "His name was Rick Van Pelt. He didn't go home last night, and his wife called this morning to report him missing. Body was found around the same time. She gave a positive ID."

"You talk to her?"

"Not yet."

Roman perused the pictures, lining each up so he could see them as part of the scene landscape. Rick had been lying naked in the gravel between the brick wall and a dumpster. His clothes were tossed carelessly aside. The markings on the ground implied that he was dragged, but only to the wall.

He was in a sitting position and collapsed during the beating.

The similarities between the two victims were as expected. The right side of his face was severely beaten. By inspecting some of the closer angle shots, Roman identified what looked like a broken cheek bone and several shattered teeth. His nose was bent unnaturally sideways. There were defence wounds on his hands and forearms, but his knuckles were not smashed, unlike the first victim.

The blood that pooled behind his head and neck was mostly absorbed by the gravel and dried by the sun. It was not "FAGGOT" that was carved into his chest. The killer had been creative and gone with "HEDONIST." Roman swiped until he found a picture of the dead man's feet and confirmed what he already knew. The killer had left a clue carved into the bottom of his foot.

"J7."

"So, it's a serial killer." Roman paused to think as he squeezed the flavourless gum between his teeth and handed Moussa back the tablet. "And we know the guy was moved. I saw a couple pictures of tire tracks in here. Maybe we get lucky, and they can identify a tire type, but I doubt it."

"Come on man, you have something cooking in there. Some kind Detective Owen shit." He tapped Roman forcefully yet playfully on the forehead.

"I don't think our killer goes wandering around brothels and gay bars and just *happens* to stumble across two guys in two days who he decides to kill. There's no fucking way. It's too easy. Tell me I'm wrong."

"You think they were targeted? Because they have less-than-traditional sexual desires?"

"I don't know what I think. But it really irks me that he moved the guy alive, and killed him here. He killed him on that wall," Roman pointed, "and not that one. He wants to put a really big stamp on it, that he didn't like that the victim went in that massage parlor. How big of a difference is it, if he just kills him and throws the naked body in the alley back there?"

Moussa didn't answer. He pondered, staring at the dried black-red stain between them. "Fuck, I can't wait for the media to be all over us," Moussa said sarcastically. "You have any luck this morning? At the churches?"

"No, and Captain's going to be pissed. We have two bodies, and no clue what's going on. And 'hedonist'? What is that all about?"

"Huh?" Moussa had his eyes in his cell phone again.

"Like. The first time was so crude and offensive. 'Faggot.' But 'hedonist' is just so . . . specific." Roman was shaking his head and staring deeply at the ground.

"You think maybe they cater to *all* desires in there?" Moussa pointed with his thumb at the massage parlour.

"You would know."

"The first body was beside a gay bar. This one. . . ." He shrugged. "I'm betting we get some answers in Paradise Massage."

"You are going into a massage parlour, f-flash your badge, and ask if they offer male-on-male . . . uh . . . services? Wow. We really have nothing." Laughing, Roman could barely get the words out.

"So, what do you figure we do, asshole?"

Roman's phone buzzed and he checked it quickly and stuffed it back in his pocket, shaking his head. "What do I figure? I figure its Sunday and I'm soaking in sweat. How about you go question whoever is working at the 'massage parlour,' and I'll go home and have a beer and a cold shower?"

"How about I punch you in the balls, and then if you can manage to stand up, I'll go next door and tell them you want to apply for a position."

"Counteroffer. I'll take a look around here and see if anything jumps out at me. You go talk to the brothel next door. I'll owe you a favour. Next time you want to bail and leave me with work, no questions asked."

"You are one lazy piece of shit. Deal. But I'm still going to punch you in the dick." He tensed up and cocked a fist downward. Roman flinched.

"You know what? You're right."

"You want your dick punched?"

"Let's get the media on this. See if we can get cleared to release names. Pictures, too. I want to see if we can find out where else he was. Maybe someone calls us?" He was halfway to his car when he finished speaking.

V

"I'm just saying, it's not a bad idea," Samantha spoke from under the Bimini Top. The air was almost still, causing small waves that gently rocked them in the direct sunlight. They had extended the cover, with some difficulty, to protect her fair, freckled skin. Like her cousin, Sam had dark hair that, when left alone, would curl slightly at the ends. She had to style it to avoid looking like a teenage hockey player.

Kim, whose ancestors were from the southern region of Spain, suffered from no such affliction, and laid out on the padded bench over the engine, basking in the heat. Her hair was straightened, lightened, and cropped almost to the skin on one side. Her exposed skin glistened with sweat and stuck to the vinyl cushions. It had darkened since yesterday. Had Kim been alone or with her boyfriend, the top of her whimsical two-piece Budweiser bikini would be below her on the back seat allowing her to tan evenly. Her face, which had started to burn, was covered with a straw hat. Squinting her unadjusted eyes, she raised them to speak.

"He gets insurance through work; I'm included on it."

"They don't cancel each other out, and it costs almost nothing. We got a good policy for Anthony. Even if he were to get burned or something at work, it pays out fairly well."

"Adulting, right? Talking about insurance and stuff." She rolled into the boat, ending in a sitting position at the stern.

"Adulting? You aren't even wearing sunscreen."

"Are you jealous, because you can't endure more than five minutes of sunlight without getting a second-degree burn?" Kim peeked both ways to confirm the distance to the nearest boat. They had moved to deeper water, for privacy and because they did not really intend to catch any fish.

She opened the smaller cooler, which maintained the temperature of canned Caesars and pop. She chose the former, opening it low, so that any curious wildlife officers, known more commonly as fish cops, or RCMP with optics, would not see. The larger cooler was mostly empty, containing bait and ice to cool any large trout that met the unrealistic regulations.

"I'll look into it when I get home. I guess Roman could get killed at work or something."

"And then, how would you pay for the boat?" Sam asked, being funny.

"The boat is paid for."

"What?! How much are they paying detectives these days?! And with our hard-earned tax dollars. Unbelievable."

Sensing that although her friend's tone implied that she wasn't truly concerned with the distribution of government wealth, she was curious. For what was essentially a single income household, Roman and Kim did very well for themselves. Kim's commission-based employment allowed her the freedom to work as much or as little as she chose. Lately, she had been choosing the latter more than the former.

"Roman has a second source of income."

"Really?"

"He calls himself a 'rounder.' Sort of like a low-level professional poker player. He doesn't play huge games or anything like that. He sits at the no limit tables with the other sharks and waits for some wasted teenager to wander over from the slots or roulette. They'll hit a big win and decide to double up on 'one-two no limit.' They get drawn in and cleaned out."

Before Samantha could sort out a follow up question, the bell rang. They had one line in the water. To avoid paying any attention, Kim had braced the rod, quite precariously, in the wakeboard tower, and hooked on a bell that would serve as indicator of success.

"Fish on!" Kim shouted, excited that, despite no effort, they had managed to get a bite. She grabbed the rod and worked it free, tossing the bell aside.

"Is there actually a fish on there?"

"Maybe." She held it gently in her hands, waiting for a second tug. If she tried to set it too early, she might scare it away. In a forceful and uneven manner, the end of the rod fluttered. Prepared this time, Kim jerked it upward and moved one hand to the reel, where she turned it rapidly to maintain tension. The rod dipped downward, submerging to the second eyelet. The fluttering increased, harder than before. Having been taught by her more experienced boyfriend, Kim realised the drag was too high, and released it slightly. The reel whined as fishing line was pulled off the spool. She reeled slowly, letting the fish run when it wanted while being careful not to let the line go slack.

Each time the fish slowed and stopped pulling, Kim pulled it upward gently, reeling in more line as she lowered the tip of the rod to the water. The technique was to keep the weight and resistance in the arched shape of the rod, and not on the mechanism. Lake trout fought hard, grew big, and made great adversaries. After each break, which seemed to increase in duration while Kim drew it closer to the surface, the fish would become invigorated, and dive back down.

The fight, which had been fought thousands if not millions of times before, was a matter of life and death for one, and sport for the other. Her heart raced, her shoulders ached, and her grip softened. Her technique began to falter. Exhausted, she sat on the bench, bracing the rod between her thighs. She was able to maintain the tension, but lacked the strength to draw the fish any higher.

"Do you want to take over?" Kim asked of her friend, who stood awkwardly with the net, holding it close to her chest like a scared child with her toy.

"Not really."

Kim sighed and leaned her weight back pulling the fish, which was still at an unknown depth, with her. Again, she reeled as she rolled her weight forward. The slow and exhausted process was repeated for a few cycles, until the line was no longer pulling straight down, but sideways, and alternating directions.

"It's close. Can you see it?"

"No." Sam had moved to the swim deck, prepared to net the fish when it came to the surface.

Kim played the exhausted trout for another minute, until it became visible. Her heart almost stopped at the sight of it. Below the surface, with its fins stretched out in desperation, it was monstrous.

"Kim! It's huge!"

"Woah!" She was just as excited. She had never caught or even seen a trout that size, aside from pictures. "It's like three feet long. Get the net ready."

Kim worked the fish to the back of the boat and Sam, who was a beginner, scooped at it. She missed the first attempt.

"Scoop from its head."

On the second try, Sam did as she was bid, netting in such a way that it would swim toward the net, not away from it. She lifted too early, having only half of the beast inside the net, and it flopped, splashing wildly back into the water. During the second attempt, the secret lake trout rig, known only to Roman and a few friends, came loose. The line went slack, and the fish dove beneath the surface. Its slow, oscillating motion was tauntingly causal, powerful, and graceful. Light refracted from waves on the surface and rippled across its back as it disappeared from view.

VI

There was already a beer waiting for him. The glass was opaque with frost and a few slushy chunks floated its rich, dark contents. They always used the same restaurant but a different location, choosing randomly, to avoid predictability. This one was as generic and unmemorable as the last. Sacha was eagerly waiting for him, and his own glass was more than half-empty.

"You were right." Sacha was speaking before Roman even sat down. "We have a problem."

"Now when you say 'we,' I hope you mean you and your associates." Roman sat and had a healthy swallow of the beer. He drank like a dog eats, consuming any and everything that was available, worried that it could be taken away at any time, and restraining himself only enough to remain functional, when required.

"No," Sacha corrected, "I mean all of us. My 'associates,' myself, and you."

"Good one. Why don't you go ahead and tell me what's going on."

Sacha pulled a folded piece of paper out of his pocket. "There are two names on here. Both got pinched. Currently in custody. Already got the lawyer in there."

"So? What do you want? They're fucked. Unless your lawyer is, like, worth his weight in gold or some shit." He chuckled, nodded at the waitress who didn't look busy, and asked for cactus cuts when

123

she made eye contact.

"He is. He is." Sacha quieted his voice, as if someone might be listening, "They have a lot. I mean. We didn't get quite the heads-up we needed. You know. Your boys grabbed them last night. Cleaned out the whole house. They are looking at doing some serious time here."

Roman shrugged. "So? What do you want me to do? Sounds like they're in deep shit. Cut your losses, man." Roman didn't bother to lower his voice. He lifted his glass and made eye contact again with the waitress. "And one more of these when my food is ready. Thanks." He made sure to smile on the last word.

Sacha leaned in closer, peaking over his shoulders before speaking. "They are. But listen—"

"—Are you about to tell my why the fuck you're acting like a character in a movie?" Roman was upright and expressionless.

"The one guy is going with a public defender." Sacha nodded his head to Roman, like that should mean something.

"And?" Roman's voice was rising with his temper. "You brought me here to act all cryptic and shit? What do you want?"

"Listen. You know how it goes. Our lawyer gets him less time. Maybe a plea bargain. Maybe he gets off. Who knows? Public defender is bad news, though. Once he separates from our guy, this cheap asshole gets in his ear. I don't know the whole process like you do. But they start offering witness protection for names. Guy gets the idea that he starts singing and he'll walk free."

"Sacha, I'm about to shove my fist so far up your fucking asshole. You better get to the point. Your boys got busted. They are going to do some time. If they want to run their mouths to get a shorter sentence, then so be it. They're criminals. What do you want me to do?"

"OK, man. We just kind of want to make sure we all know what's at stake here."

"What's at stake is your stupid fucking skull retaining its shape. I swear to god, if the next words out of your mouth aren't explaining why I am here right now—"

"—You need to do something." Sacha finally said.

"No," Roman answered, "I don't *need* to do anything."

"Evidence. They have a lot. It would be a lot *easier* to keep our guys' mouths shut. If, you know, they didn't have as much."

Roman nodded at the waitress. "Cancel the beer." He turned quietly back to his old friend. "Did you hit your head? I don't know what kind of movies you and your loser friends watch. There's not just like, a closet full of evidence that I can walk in and take. Are you fucking stupid? And even if I could, I wouldn't. You know, giving you a heads up when shit is going down, that's one thing. Now you want me to commit a crime. Get fucked." Roman stood up to leave.

"It doesn't work like that." Sacha's voice was sterner than Roman was used to hearing.

"What?" He sat back down. "I'm not playing games here. Consider this *arrangement* over. Understand?"

"Games? Is that it? We are playing *games*?"

"I'm out." Roman stood up again.

"Out?" Sacha moved to block him. "You think you're out? How

many times were you *not* out? All that money? You are *in*. You are in *deep*. You don't just walk away from these people."

"Get the fuck out of my way." Roman spoke through closed teeth. His eyes were wide and still.

For a moment, Sacha stood in front of him, staring back into the cold and unrelenting eyes that seemed to stare through his own feigned toughness. When Roman raised a hand to make space, Sacha reacted by clearing his path.

"Hey, Roman," Sacha called out. Roman stopped at the door to hear what he had to say. "There is no *'out'*."

Roman pushed through the door so hard that Sacha thought it might come off the hinges.

VII

The church was a bi-level, which allowed natural light in the basement. Max wasn't sure if he was more or less comfortable here than in his own home. It was clean. The carpet had no stains, and the air wasn't stale and mildewy. He stared at the light pouring in. In the middle of the afternoon, it hardly made it halfway across the floor. It was clean, and not broken by the stagnant particles that would be hanging in the air in his slummy rented apartment. The room would have been dim if not for the light fixtures inlaid in the soundproofing tiles above his head. His chair was the folding kind, and good quality. It was comfortable enough to sit in for a few hours, but not so much that an addict might fall asleep and disrupt their meeting of self-serving, arrogant assholes. How much had they actually used? How severe had their withdrawal been? One after another, they would swagger to the front of the room to tell an embellished story of heroism and personal growth. Every second speaker would thank *God* for *His* guidance, and the strength *He* granted.

Max couldn't believe how cliché it was—cookies and coffee on a folding table beside the entrance. They were mostly untouched and only served to make people feel more comfortable. The gesture would be wasted on Max, who, despite dangerous volumes of Tylenol, was still dealing with the aftermath of a savage beating.

This is a good place. Come. Eat. Speak. Fuck you.

He was hungry, and would have eaten more than his share, if

127

not for the fear of regurgitating it on their pretty, clean carpet. He was sweating. The room wasn't too hot. It may have been the withdrawal, or the fear of speaking in front of a room full of people who thought they were his better. He would not do it. He wouldn't tell them about how hard his life had been, and how alone and afraid he was. He ducked when they asked. As he predicted, the first order of business was new members. A few had volunteered themselves and told their stories. The promise he made was that he would attend. Not that he would speak.

He continued surveying the room as another of the recovered prattled on about his journey. There were more chairs than people. Almost double. Max thought that it wasn't because they were expecting more attendees. It was to leave space for the anti-social people who would be scared off if they had to make new friends. Almost the entire back row was empty. Max had the seat closest to the door, with a buffer of three empty seats to his left.

It was a young woman, probably in her early thirties, who sat closest to him, on his left. He was having a hard time guessing her age. In a crowd like this, it was hard to tell. Her hair was dark and lazily tied behind her head. It contrasted with her pale skin. If she had not been wearing a heavy layer of makeup, he figured her eyes might carry dark circles like his own. She was small. Shorter than average, and on the thinner side of healthy. Max was worried he had been staring too long, and lowered his head and eyes to the floor, leaning his elbows on his knees. The motion caused his stomach to turn. He eased back in his chair and dug into his pocket for another chalky, pink tablet. He chewed with his eyes closed, forcing long, steady breaths in for a count of three, and out for the same.

When his stomached was settled, he leaned forward again. He hadn't seen the colour of her eyes, and was wondering. With the pale skin and dark hair, they could be anything. He decided he would peak over, as subtly as he could, to satisfy his curiosity. He turned his head slightly and stared at the floor, raising his eyes slowly. Her clothes were plain. The word *basic* came to mind. He smiled to himself. She was wearing flats, which implied to him that she was traveling on foot or via transit. She had the same black yoga pants that every millennial woman wore, and a UofA hoodie that hung loosely. Her arms were crossed and she had her hands tucked into her armpits.

Why are women always cold?

He looked to see her eyes and saw she was staring back at him. He quickly returned his gaze to the floor, hoping she wouldn't notice the dark bruising that encircled his right eye and spilled over to a smaller pool below his left. Her eyes were green. He did not expect that.

An embarrassed flush rippled from his face, which suddenly felt too hot, down his body, ending with a tingle in his fingers and toes. It was chased by a wave of cold sweat.

I should go.

From his peripheral, he saw her stand up and start walking over. She was moving quietly and deliberately, so that she wouldn't disturb the speaker. She sat next to him.

"Do you mind if I sit here?" Her voice was soft and broken. The way it comes out after a long, hard cry.

He was caught off guard and struggled to pass for normal. He worried about his breath, and his heart started racing. In any normal social encounter, Max felt out of place. In this room, surrounded by these people, he was now sure he would have been more comfortable in his revolting apartment. At least there, he would be judged only by himself. His words didn't come, and Max managed nothing more than a slight head nod and crooked smile. He dug around in his jeans and retrieved a pack of gum that was purchased for today's festivities. He popped a piece into his palm and held out the pack as an empty gesture. To his surprise, she took him up on his offer.

"Thank you," she whispered.

"No worries. I don't want to breathe coffee breath in your face." Max nodded at the refreshments. His voice was unsteady. He fought hard not to tremble.

"I didn't think you had any. I watched you come in." They were both looking at the floor. Max was more comfortable without the eye contact, and he sensed the same was true of her. "You don't have to speak if you don't want to. I don't."

"Well, I guess I don't have to do anything I don't want to. Just didn't want the pressure of being pulled to the front. Especially on my first meeting. Probably my only meeting."

"Why do you say that?"

"I promised someone that I would attend. He is going to ask me about it tomorrow. This isn't really my thing."

"Are you trying to get clean?"

"Yes, and not for the first time."

"Same." She replied, "I don't know how many times I flushed

it, and then regretted it the next morning."

"How long—" Max realised he may offend her and paused. "If you don't mind me asking, how long have you been clean?"

"Three weeks," she answered, without the same uncomfortable pause. "A personal record. You?"

Max laughed a little when he started. "About forty hours. Almost two days."

"Tell you what. I'm not a huge fan of the sponsor thing. But it is a hard thing to do alone. Why don't I text you tonight, and make sure you rounded out your second day? You can help keep me honest at the same time."

"I don't have a phone."

"Get one." She pulled a pen a notepad from her purse and wrote down a phone number. She crushed it into a ball and forced it into his hand. Her touch was cold and clammy. Her hand felt weak, even compared to his own.

The room erupted in applause, as if the speaker he was ignoring had accomplished some great feat. It was just some other entitled asshole that had finished his story, and the meeting seemed to be coming to a finish. *It wasn't that bad.* Max made sure he was one of the first people out, so he wouldn't have to introduce himself to everyone while they crowded around the pathetic display of refreshments.

Outside, at the base of the steps, he sat down to think in some shade, and lit a cigarette. The sun was pounding the asphalt and he could see the heat rising. He had the rest of the day off. If he went home, he would have nothing to do.

131

Idle hands.

A young man with red hair that Max recognised was standing on the sidewalk, watching him. He approached and took a seat. Max hadn't come for a lecture, and hardly acknowledged the man's presence.

You want to have a talk, God Boy? You start.

"How was your first meeting?" Like he had with the woman inside the church, they faced the same way, avoiding eye contact.

"Pretty fucking stupid. Everyone in there is so self-serving. They're all heroes. Acting like they cured cancer. Fuckin. . ." Max was motioning with his arms to imply a heavy strut.

"Everyone is a hero in their own story."

Max didn't reply verbally at first. Instead, he pointed at his own face and laughed, turning to make sure God Boy was watching. "Yeah. Big time. I should be wearing a cape."

"I didn't think you would stick around after. Kind of thought you would run home and dwell on how shitty your life is."

"I think that might be the first time I've heard you swear. Maybe there's hope for you, after all." Max laughed and exhaled smoke through his smile and nose. "Truth is, man," Max cleared his throat, "I can't really head home. I owe these guys some money, and they know I just got paid. They'll probably pound the piss out of me if I show up at home with nothing."

"I know what it's like to be down. And to have nowhere to run or hide. It can be a scary place."

"What do you fuckin' want, man? I don't need a lecture from you. You're barely off the tit and telling me about being down and out. You don't know shit." Max stood up to leave, flicking his cigarette butt into the grass.

The young man watched Max from the steps, leaning back and resting an elbow to support his weight. The weak and sickly-looking man, who looked to be twenty years his senior, strutted with confidence to the sidewalk. He paused, looking to his left and right, and then drew another cigarette from the pack and placed it between his lips.

"I don't mean any offence." God Boy had caught Max as he was fumbling for a lighter. "I noticed that you don't know which way to go. Do you need directions?"

"I'll go wherever the fuck I want. I didn't ask you to drag me to this stupid meeting of losers, and I don't need your help."

"Don't you?"

"What do you want, anyway?"

The younger man with red hair was not stirred by Max's emotion. "You are lost. And if you wander, with no clear path, your story will end sooner than you like. All I want is to give you a place to stay. I am sure my place is nicer than wherever you are right now. All I want, in return, is that you come to this place every week. Once for service, and again for your meeting."

"Why?" Max was dumbfounded.

"You have nowhere else to go."

"No, why would you help me?"

"Because you need help."

VIII

"So. The guy goes into this place, from what I gather, all the time. He likes to see someone named Jamie. Problem is, 'Jamie' isn't around, or so they tell me. They're all worried I'm here to bust them, even though I clearly explained that I work in the homicide division, and that I really don't care about their operation—just need to ask some questions. English on their end isn't great. Throw in my accent, and we basically have a communication failure that ends with them understanding that I'm a cop and they don't want to talk to me." Moussa was frustrated and almost yelling through the phone.

"You don't have an accent. Not really." Roman flagged down a waitress. "When do we get to talk to this, uh, Jamie?"

"Probably never. I left a card. Asked if they would pass it along. We both know that isn't going to happen. Another dead end. Where are you?"

"What?"

"I can hear it through the phone, man. Are you drinking?"

"We had a deal. I got the afternoon off; you go and do the questioning at the brothel."

"You had the afternoon off so you could shower, and maybe review what information that we have. I figured we would try to put something, *anything*, together, so that the captain doesn't fire both of us tomorrow."

"What do we have to review? We have two dead bodies,

religious crap carved into their skin, and a list of dead ends. Should have the toxicology back from the first guy by tomorrow, and an official autopsy. We work off that. DNA is coming next. They'll find a match from the two scenes. We run it through the database and, ninety percent chance, we already have a sheet on the guy. Unless you have a better idea."

"Tell you what. You go in tomorrow. You tell that to the captain. Just like that. Use those same words and that tone."

"I'm going to."

"She's going to fire you. What do we do about tonight?"

"Tonight?"

"Two deaths in two days, Roman. Pattern killing and targeting homosexuals. If there is going to be a third, it's coming tonight."

"What do you want to do? We got the story out. It's all over social media. What else? Put out a statement that the gays should stay in tonight? You want to talk about getting fired—"

"—Whatever." Moussa wasn't satisfied, but felt he was gaining no ground. "I'll see you tomorrow."

Roman ended the call and slid back to the blackjack table. He gave his placeholder to the dealer, and she dealt him back in. There was a reason Roman played here. Each table played with only four decks, as opposed to the usual six. The dealer didn't draw his second card until all the players had finished. Roman sat in the anchor position, so that he could play his hand against the dealer. He was dealt a six and a seven. The table erupted with joy when dealer laid down a six for herself. In an almost choreographed fashion, each player in turn waved off their option to draw another card. To the apparent horror of the other four players, Roman softly tapped the table beside his thirteen.

"Are you sure?"

After a short sigh, Roman pursed his lips and gave a quick nod of his head. He then repeated the gesture a second time, clearly, so the camera could see.

"This is a bust card. You should stand on thirteen and see if I draw two face cards." Her tone suggested that she thought him to be a rookie. The other players agreed, each adding their support for the advice that she gave. Roman took a quick glance around the table and added up nearly three thousand dollars, all riding on the next two cards being high enough to push the dealer over twenty-one. The ensuing tip would likely double her wage for the evening.   "Hit me." Roman instructed, firmly, so that his intention would not be questioned for a third time.

The dealer pulled a card from the top of the deck and placed it beside Roman's six and seven, "Twenty-one!" she stated, almost in disbelief. Roman gave a comedic bow to the other players, who seemed as annoyed as they were impressed.

"Alright, two big ones." Roman broke the silence that followed his impressive play. The first card drawn by the dealer was a six of hearts. The other players started pounding the table and begging the gambling gods for a monkey. Roman moaned audibly when the dealer drew a nine of hearts. After a few choice words were thrown his way, and after he received an unsolicited lesson from the other gamblers on odds, Roman coloured up left the table.

He took a seat at the empty bar in the centre of the casino. The typical chaos of gambling surrounded his little island like a hurricane—the centre of which served cocktails. Before he had a chance to order, the bartender, a neatly-groomed blond man who appeared to be in his mid- to late thirties, placed a drink in front of him. Roman eyed it, and the bartender, quizzically.

"What's that?"

"Double gin tonic. We ran out of Hendrick's, so I made it with Tang10. Hope that's OK."

Roman looked over his shoulder and eyeballed the distance to the blackjack table where he had been playing. *Forty feet.* "You knew what I was drinking?"

"Not that busy in here. And you tip well, Detective."

The bartender, dressed in a white dress shirt under a vest that would be the third piece of such a suit, went busily about his duties for a few minutes, while Roman waited for an explanation. He resolved that he would have to prompt one.

"How do you know I'm a detective?"

"Like you were just saying, it's all over social media. Everyone knows what's going on."

"You were listening to my phone conversation?" Roman tipped his head back and drained the glass. He tapped the rim. "Another. Please."

"It's not busy in here. You made the right play. She would not have busted," he explained as he poured the drink with smooth and subtle grace. The bottle seemed weightless in his hands, as if it poured itself, and the bartender merely caressed it.

"I know what happened. I was there." He looked over his shoulder again, to confirm his first estimate. "You seem to have taken quite an interest in me."

"You know, Detective, you ought to keep your eyes open. There could be things that you miss. Especially if you let this all get in your head."

"Not to be rude,"—Roman searched quickly for a nametag and took note that he wasn't wearing one—"Barkeep, but I am sort of an expert in keeping my eyes open. Some might say that I am a professional noticer of details. You, on the other hand, pour a damn decent gin and tonic. Now let me ask you something. What makes you think that you, first of all, know anything about the case I'm working on? And, second, have any reference point for what might be getting in my head? Not to offend. Just asking."

"You do not have to worry about offending me. Not the way you tip. Your case is all over social media. It may, in fact, be blowing up more than you know. It doesn't take a professional detective to notice two things. The first being that you were talking about two murdered homosexuals. I don't think that happened twice this weekend. The second point of note is that you are dressed for work. But instead, you are here drinking. It is Sunday. It is the middle of the day. Let's say that I don't know you from Adam. That is not exactly characteristic of an officer of the law, in the middle of an investigation."

"I'm off the clock."

"For a man who is 'off the clock,' you were having what seemed like a very 'on the clock' kind of phone call."

"I'm fine. Thank you."

"I'm not saying that you're not fine. You seem like a nice guy, and I have been in this game a long time. So, please take my advice. Don't let this case get in your head. Don't make it personal. And watch what is happening around you. It's all in the details."

"Thanks for the tip." Roman finished the second drink slowly, allowing the bartender to go about his business. He spun around in his chair and, through the dull roar of conversation, broken sporadically by bells and whistles that implied a big win, struggled to make out the words being spoken around one specific blackjack table. From his pocket he pulled out a roll of chips and thumbed one off the top and onto the bar, flicking it with his index finger as it landed to make it spin.

Silently, the bartender watched Roman walk away, and paid no attention to the black chip settling beside an empty glass.

IX

The conversation was about the pistol. Max's only possession with any monetary value was that Browning 9mm. In his dingy, poorly-ventilated, and sparsely-furnished second-floor apartment, he stood at odds with the young man who had offered him room and board in exchange for only few hours of his time on Sundays. The young man who seemed to entrust his safety to some immortal, all-knowing, yet unconfirmed being saw no use for the weapon. Max, the older and more experienced of the two, could not fathom leaving without it.

"Man, they probably know I'm here," Max pleaded. Despite the almost comical precautions they had taken to prevent being spotted, he was sure they would find him. "And, if they do, they are going to follow me. I'm not leaving without it."

It had not taken long for Max's trust in his new friend to blossom. Aside from taking him in, he had, without hesitation, agreed to use his own credit to acquire an older-generation iPhone with a data plan. He had also agreed to access the apartment building through a rear entrance, darting through the alley like a parody team of action heroes.

"I will not allow this to become an impasse. You can keep it, with two conditions. You will take a weapon-handling course, so that we can avoid any unfortunate accidents. You will also properly register and store that weapon in accordance with federal laws.

Agreed?"

Some civilian is going to teach me how to handle a firearm.

"Agreed."

Max stuffed the loaded weapon in the back of his pants, covering it with his shirt. His friend cringed. They worked as a team to gather some of the few possessions that Max deemed valuable and stuff them in a garbage bag with his clothes.

Calmly, he looked through the apartment for the last time. To his friend, it would appear as though he were searching for anything that may have been forgotten. He was, however, quietly reminiscing about the withdrawal symptoms, compounded with the aftermath of a savage beating, that he had endured the evening prior. The last stop was the kitchen where he had slept, shivering, but not from the cold. He left his key on the counter and the front door unlocked.

X

Unlike his demeanor, Roman's house was perpetually clean and orderly. He had Kim to thank for it. His overstretched mind relaxed for the first time since he had decided he would send his better half on an overnight trip without him. Given the opportunity, he would have explained that his ability to carry the stress of his employment was afforded by the relief he felt in her company. She had made it home safe. The truck and boat were parked neatly in the driveway, and the freshly-cut grass was drying in the afternoon sun.

Try not to bring it home with you.

He found her working through a mess of paperwork at the worn marble table in their kitchen. The refinisher was under the sink. Roman had promised Kim, and himself, that he would restore it this summer. The likelihood of that was slipping away with the last few days of the season. *This fall, maybe.* He dropped a kiss on the top of her head. She hardly looked up from her work.

"What are you working on?" Roman was walking over to the fridge, which would be fully stocked.

"Insurance. Thinking of increasing our policy. Anthony and Sam are out back. He's cooking steaks."

"On *my* barbecue!?" Roman's frustration that his cousin-in-law would dare to use the new Weber before Roman himself had had a chance was only partially sarcastic. "I'm going to have a talk with him." Roman pressed the cold can against her neck and laughed when she flinched. "Come on. The sun is over the yardarm, and we have company."

The lawn in his backyard was as freshly cut as the one in front. His deck stretched across the width of his house, and at the other end was the confirmation of what he had previously been told: the bastard was grilling.

"Asshole!" Roman yelled and under-armed a full can toward his encroaching friend, careful to make sure that Anthony would only notice the motion as he turned, attempting to increase the difficulty of the catch. "You come into *my* house, cut *my* lawn, cook on *my* new grill, and now you want to drink *my* beer?" Roman turned his attention before he got an answer and placed a second beer on the patio table next to is cousin. "What's up, Sam?"

"I didn't even put the meat on the grill yet. Just warming it up for you." Anthony was tapping the top of his can to reduce the inevitable spill that would come from a recently airborne beer. "Hope that was helpful last night. I was half-awake."

"Yeah, we've been hearing about this thing all day. What the hell, right?" Sam cracked the AGD and ripped open the top. As satisfying sounds go, opening an AGD was near the top of the list.

"Fuck, I don't know. Couple murders. Looks like a religious thing. Case seems to be going nowhere." Roman grabbed a seat beside his cousin and peeled the top off his own can.

"Any DNA or anything?" Anthony cracked his, to relieve the pressure without opening it. "Two crime scenes. You must have something." He placed his beer on the table and pulled out a pack of Export As.

"Nothing yet. It's a weird one, that's for sure."

"So, what do you do?" Anthony didn't wait for Roman to respond before he continued: "When you have a case like this, how do you go about solving it? Do you just wait, and hope for DNA evidence? Or do you actually follow clues, like a movie?"

"It's hard to explain. There is a process, but I guess everyone goes about it their own way. I, um. . . ." He paused for thought. "Here. An exercise in detective work." From his back pocket, Roman retrieved a small notepad, the same size and thickness as a passport, and carefully ripped out three pages. He passed one to each person at the table. He then took his mechanical pencil and placed it in the centre. "OK, so here is the question. Imagine the earth was a perfect sphere, with no mountains or valleys or oceans, but uniformly smooth. You want to lay a rope around the equator, right on the ground, and another suspended exactly one foot above the surface. What would be the difference in the lengths of those ropes? First one to answer correctly wins."

"Wins what?" Kim asked.

"My respect. Who cares? Bragging rights."

Immediately, Sam grabbed the pencil and started noting something down. "Do we get to know the circumference of the earth?" she asked.

"Google it if you want," Roman answered with a shrug, as if it meant nothing. He checked his watch. The three participants all started searching on their phones, scrolling and typing with haste. Sam was scribbling on the paper. Roman had another sip of his beer and leaned back. He amused by how well his demonstration was going. He checked his watch. "Okay, time is up."

"What?" Sam drew out the word with sarcastic disbelief. "That was like ten seconds."

"About thirty," he corrected. "And more than enough time."

"Then what's the answer?"

"6.28 feet. Approximately." He paused again for dramatic effect. "Or just two pi, measured in feet. You have to listen to the question and rephrase the scenario. The circumference of the earth doesn't matter, neither does the length of the rope. What I actually asked you was, if there are two circles with a difference in radius of one foot, what is the difference in circumference? Obviously, that is a simpler problem."

"What does that have to do with solving a murder?" Anthony asked. Roman could see that he had genuinely piqued his interest.

"I handed out paper. That implied that you would need to write something down. I gave you one pencil, which presented a problem. You now have to share that precious resource or find another way of writing. That problem would direct your attention from the task at hand. I phrased the question in a way that suggested there was more, and possibly relevant, information to be discovered. The circumference of the earth. Once again, that directed your attention away from a simple math question. The logical response is to take all of the information provided and attempt to fit it into the solution. Murders are not logical. What needs to happen, is we need to step back. We cannot assume that every clue or piece of evidence is part of the solution. It's like assembling a one-hundred-piece puzzle with two hundred pieces. I look at every clue individually. I look for connections. I look for patterns. Thirty seconds is more than enough time to multiply pi by two, but if you spend twenty seconds trying to solve the circumference of the planet, and another ten trying to find a pen, not so much."

"Maybe if we knew that there was a time restriction, we would have gone about it another way," Kim suggested, reasoning with her own failure.

"I don't know when I have a time restriction. I don't know if there will be another murder tonight, or in a week, or in a month. After today, my killer could be on a plane to God knows where. The trail could go cold. Or maybe I have all the time in the world."

Without speaking, Kim stood up and went inside. Roman considered that his own tone had become slightly condescending.

"Could you be any more of a stereotypical Italian labourer?" Roman was referring to the way Anthony rolled the cigarettes up in his sleeve.

"Why don't you just keep them in your pocket? Also, toss me that."

Anthony flicked the pack across the table to Roman and, while lighting his own cigarette said, "I thought you were quitting."

"I'm working on it. After this case, maybe."

"Of beer?" Sam teased.

"Well, don't get too close to it." Anthony seemed seriously concerned, although he tried to hide it with a humorous smile.

"You know. That's like the third time I've heard that in two days. I get that everyone is concerned for me, but I'm quite sure I can handle it." Roman was trying to brush it off, but he knew it was hitting close to home. He and Sam briefly met each other's gaze and, without words, confirmed with her that she knew what they were talking about.

"Leave the man alone," Sam cut in. "It's Roman. He's got this."

"Yeah. Fuck off, Anthony." Roman wasn't being fully serious, as he usually wasn't with these people, and it came off in his tone.

"Fine. I'll drop it," Anthony conceded. "One more thing, though. I was talking to Sacha—"

"—Fuck that asshole. I don't care what he thinks."

"I was talking to Sacha, and he said you were all wound up. I don't know if he knows what I know. But he seemed genuinely concerned. Said you guys almost got into it a bit."

"What does Sacha not know? Some big secret?" Kim appeared in the doorway with a plate full of raw striploins. "Also, are you going to cook these?"

"Yes, but I just got home. Let me have one beer while the thing heats up and I'll do it. And I'll tell you about it later. It's a bit of a story. Come on. Sit down." Without standing, Roman grabbed the plate from her and placed it on the table.

"I thought you were quitting." Kim was looking at the still-unlit cigarette resting between his fingers.

"I am. After this case. It's stressing me out. And word on the street is that it might hit close to home." Roman took Anthony's lighter off the table and lit his own cigarette. "Also, Anthony, do me a favour and don't listen to anything that prick Sacha says. Guy's a fuckhead."

"Thought you were old army buddies?" Anthony had finally

147

opened his beer and took a long sip.

"We are. But just between us, he's not exactly on the level. You know? Just. Watch your back around him is all I'm saying."

"I'm a big boy, Roman. I can handle a pussy little *Uke*. But if it makes you feel better, I'll try not to spend too much time around him. You, on the other hand . . . don't let this case stress you out. Don't make it personal is all."

Roman didn't like the way Anthony dragged out the word 'personal,' but decided to let it slide. "I'm done talking about my work. What's going on with all of you? I haven't seen you in two days."

"Well, first of all, Roman, dickhead, I'm not a fucking labourer. Journeyman electrician and a business owner. It is boring as shit. But you should hear what Sam has going on."

"What I have going on is a beer that's just about empty."

"I'll grab you one." Anthony was on his feet, stuffing the cigarette butt in the ashtray. "Seriously. Tell them about the church. The, uh, program that you're running."

"You guys are getting married in a church, right?" Kim asked.

"Hey. Hey. Hey. None of that shit. Tell us about the program." Roman instructed playfully and nudged his girlfriend with his elbow.

"OK." Sam's eyes lit up as she started. "Basically, through the church, we help people find work."

"Riveting." Roman was sure that his sarcasm wouldn't hurt his cousin's feelings.

"And other jobs, too." She blasted through it without skipping a beat. "We get these guys and girls. Usually with nowhere to turn.

Sometimes addicts. Sometimes criminals. They start coming to church. We help set them up with meaningful employment. Even find them a place to stay. It really feels like you're helping. Most of them are really good people. I had this one guy. Really nice. He has a horrible record. It's really violent, but you would never guess. He's the sweetest guy, and really well-spoken. We found him a job as a road worker. We got him a place to live. Cheap rent, and in a decent neighbourhood. It's been months, and he is really on track. I'm super proud of him. But from his record, you would think he was some kind of psychopath."

"This guy have a name?" Roman asked, feigning humour.

Sam paused, as though she were searching her internal records. Anthony broke the silence by placing four more AGDs on the table. "A couple more and I have to get going. Early day tomorrow."

"You know," Roman's tone changed to the serious one he uses for questioning, "some of these violent psychopaths have a really welcoming personality. It's the weirdest thing. It's almost like they disassociate. They are the nicest, friendliest people. But in those few moments, it's like a different person. I've met a few. I've even questioned them. And it never ceases to amaze me how normal they seem."

"All right, Freud. Shut up about psychopaths. Sam's doing good work. And start cooking already."

XI

He sat, upright and stiff, unable to enjoy accommodations that were far better than those in his own desolate apartment. Despite constant reassurance, Max would not allow himself to match the disposition of his friend. Time dragged on as he considered the events of the day and how they had unfolded.

Am I dreaming?

No words had been exchanged since their disagreement about the firearm. Max wondered if it had caused offence. He placed the loaded Browning on the coffee table and checked the time. Minutes had passed in this new home, but it had felt like hours. His heart refused to settle, and the care he was putting into the pace of his breathing was doing more harm than good.

He stared across the unnervingly clean and organised room. A grotesquely detailed crucifix filled the space from the mantle to the ceiling. Unlike most that he had seen, upon which the saviour's head hung pathetically to his right, with his eyes lost in thought, this version stared forward. His eyes appeared originally to display the same painful sorrow. But after Max sat and stared back, they became passionately judgemental. He could feel the contempt weighing on him as they followed him around the room.

"Would you prefer a TV?" His new friend's voice broke the silence.

"No, it's . . ." Max had to paused to catch his breath. "It's a really nice . . . uh . . . piece?"

"Are you comfortable?" God Boy took a seat to Max's right, facing the kitchen and leaning forward. The distance between them was an awkward arm's length. Like the scrawny depiction of his saviour, God Boy's eyes stared deeply, unblinkingly, and accusingly at Max.

"Yes. This couch is really nice. Your whole place is. How can you afford this? On what we make?" He chose his words carefully, as one would during an interview for which they had not prepared. He could not shake the feeling that this wasn't free, and it loomed over him. In his mind he created countless scenarios where the young man would ask for the favour to be repaid.

"God took my hand and thrust me from the abyss. This is one of His many gifts. I spend my life doing His work, and I find that I am rewarded."

His work and road work.

His new friend's deliberate motions and calculated sentences drew a deeper panic. Max started to feel the cold sweat returning. He was trying to hide his discomfort, but another wave of withdrawal was upon him. He dug a chalky pink tablet from his pocket and forced a smile as he ate it. His urge to run was strong. He would have stood up and left, had he anywhere to go.

"You know, it occurred to me earlier that I know you from work, but I don't think I actually remember your name," Max finally said after a few seconds of emptiness he had spent flicking his vision from one set of eyes to another. The room turned around him, leaning off its axis. He sank deep into the sofa and felt, more than he saw, a hand placed gently on his knee.

"I have been crucified with Christ. It is no longer I who live, but Christ who lives in me. And the life I now live in the flesh, I live by faith in the son of God, who loved me and gave himself for me."

Well, if I didn't feel weird before. . . .

"OK, what should I call you?"

"Whatever you want."

Max's stomach was turning. The Pepto had no effect compared to the withdrawal symptoms. His body was becoming heavy. The room was tilting slowly back and forth inside his head. Most of his surroundings were becoming dull and disconnected. Max was extremely aware that his clothes were touching his skin. He tried to loosen his collar and shook his shirt to get some air under it. It was not his clothes. It was his skin that was itchy. Max rubbed it softly feeling very aware of the deity, and his friend, who were both staring motionlessly at him.

Can he tell? His addiction to heroin was not a secret, but Max could feel the impending doom usually associated with his fear that people would find out. *He will find out that I do not deserve his help.*

His gracious host finally blinked, and then stood. He spoke softly without eye contact as he walked toward the kitchen. "Max, I want you to relax. Do you need some water?"

Max nodded his head softly, and let his eyes sink to the floor. He could no longer bear the weight of that gaze, and all that it implied. He felt the steps that ended in the kitchen, each slightly bending the floor. The sound of water hitting the glass was sinister. High-pitched at first, then fading to deeper sound at the top, slapping hollowly. The sharp, stinging *click* of the water glass being placed on the coffee table of the same material pierced through Max's head. It seemed to echo internally. He felt it ring from his ears, through his jaw, and into his teeth, which he pressed tightly together.

"Drink this. You're dehydrated."

Max looked up and started to ease his tension. Looking back was a quirky religious man who had done nothing but accommodate him. Max started to feel embarrassment. It washed over him like a cold wave. Sweat pooled in his armpits and trickled across his forehead.

This is a good man.

"I wanted to say thanks. For everything." Max was glad he had water, or he would have struggled with the words. He took a gentle sip. "It actually means a lot to me that you would help me out. I don't have much to offer in return. But if there's anything you need or anything I can do, just let me know."

"You know, there may be something you can help me with. Are you a religious man?"

"Sometimes." Max glanced up from his water at the crucifix hanging across the room. "I don't practice any sort of . . . um . . . rituals. Sorry, I don't want to offend."

"I want you to feel like you can say what you want. You won't offend me. God has done so much for me, and there are no words that can take that back. Do you pray?"

Max thought about the evening prior, and the confrontation he had had with his dreamcatcher. "On occasion. I speak with my ancestors. I don't think they hear me."

"They hear you." His hand was back on Max's knee. "Tell me this: do you believe in God?"

"I guess so. On some level, I do. Not that I know anything about it. Him. I also think that a lot of religion has been proved wrong. Right?"

"Some consider science and religion to be opposite. This could not be further from the truth. Many great scientists were, and are, deeply religious men. Some say that the pursuit of science is really the pursuit of God, the theory being that we will one day find questions that cannot be answered through experimentation, but can through prayer."

"Above my head, man." Max embellished his own laughter, fighting hard against his discomfort.

"You believe in God, but you don't practice religion. How can that be? How can one exist without the other?"

"I don't know, man. I have never really given it this much thought."

"If you believe in God, but practice no religion, you are acknowledging that He exists, but placing no value in gaining His favour. Does that make sense?"

"I-I guess I get what you're driving at."

"Good. Will you repent?"

"What do you mean?"

"Will you turn from your sinful existence? Will you give yourself—your mind, your body, your soul—to the Lord?" It was asked passionately, without raising his voice. The words were not heated or furious like a southern preacher. He was calm, confident, warm.

"Do I have to decide right now?"

"You may continue down your current path. You may continue your sinful and self-destructive behaviour. You may also take my path. That is the Lord's path. And on that path, you will find contentment. You will find salvation."

Where's the path to the bathroom?

Max's initial instinct was to make light of the overbearing request. He decided against it. "It's a lot for me to think about right now."

"Very well." A warm and intimidating smile crawled from one corner of his mouth to the other. He paused, as if calculating for a moment, before speaking: "You will be saved."

Max tried to hide his shiver. He was at a loss for words. He finished his water and leaned back in his seat, nodding softly.

"Under this roof," his new friend continued, more authoritative than before, "you will obey the laws of the Lord. And while you stay, you must accept the Lord's judgement of your actions. You will, while you stay, begin to make right the wrongdoings of your life. In time, you will find the light. Is that agreeable?"

"Yes . . . um . . . whatever it takes, man." Max decided that, in the morning, he would find a new place to stay.

His friend retired to his bedroom without a word. There was no second bedroom in the apartment, so Max assumed that he was sleeping on the couch. His new smartphone was surprisingly intuitive. He dug it out from his pocket and sent a message off to his other new friend, the green-eyed woman whose name he didn't know.

"It's Max from NA. I got a new phone. You won't believe how my day went."

He was asleep before he saw if she replied.

XII

If she didn't pry, he would not bring it up—that segment of a conversation that opened a door to his past. Their guests had left, and Roman knew that uncomfortable conversation was impending. He had hoped to bury it, that memory, way down, in a box in his mind, to fester. For not as long as he had hoped, they had cleaned in silence. A few plates in the sink were transferred to the dishwasher. Less cans than they would normally deal with were stuffed into the overflowing recycling. Roman brought it outside and, upon returning, was met with the looming question.

"Are we going to talk about it?"

Fuck.

"No," Roman replied quickly, hoping to squelch the prospect of a mental cavity search.

"I wasn't really asking."

"Why can't we just talk about when we're having kids or some other awful thing?"

"We can do that, too, but I really wanted to know what they were talking about earlier. Is it something bad?"

"Yes," he snapped. It was not real anger, but feigned, and poorly. "It's something bad. I really do not want to get into it."

"You can't be this closed off. If Anthony can know, and Sam can know, and *Sacha* can know, why can't I know?" He liked her tone. It was one that demonstrated how deeply she cared, and how well she knew him. She was firm and assertive, but with an underlying humour. She would not be offended if the conversation never happened, but she would be satisfied if it did.

"I will make you a deal. This whole thing hits a little close to home for me. I am a professional, and I can deal with it. When it blows over, or when we catch the guy, or when we drop the case, I will talk about it. I'm not some kind of pussy or anything, but, for right now, give me a little space for this one, OK?"

"Fine." She pouted playfully, thinking that some truth serum might do the trick. "Can I get you a beer?"

"No, thanks. I've had too many. Need to work in the morning." Roman had just sat down and opened the list of streaming services. He was already sporting the soft and goofy smile that one often has after the right number of drinks.

"Who even *are* you?" She brought one anyway. He took it without question. She sat at the other end on the couch and laid her feet across his lap. "Now, you were saying, earlier . . . about kids?"

"One day. Not today."

"When?"

"I'm too exhausted for this. Let's just watch some crap and fall asleep."

"That's the answer, isn't it? You are always too exhausted. You work all day, putting in insane hours. You come home both mentally and physically exhausted. You bottle it all up and shut down."

"What do you want me to do? It's a hard job."

"Is this really what you want? You want to work every single day? You want to be stressed out? You get three weeks of vacation every year and you spend them calling and texting Moussa about the work you left behind. You probably have forty years left, maybe ten good ones. Do you want to retire and wonder where the time went?"

"So, I should quit my job? That's what you want?"

"We have no debt. We can coast on fumes to pay off the house. You make enough playing poker to retire, if that is what you want. Write a book. Start a business. Live for yourself. How many years have you served? You spent six in the army and almost ten as a cop. Is the world a better place because of it?"

"No. Not really," Roman laughed. *Poker.*

For a few minutes, they sat in silence. Kim searched for a show or movie. Roman drank.

"And if we are going to have kids," Kim broke the silence, "let's do it soon. I don't want to be raising a teenager in our sixties."

"I'm going to catch this guy. When I do, I'll take some time off. Real time. And we can have this conversation again."

XIII

Max was awakened by his new roommate stirring in the kitchen. The sharp, metallic sounds of drawers opening and closing combined with the shuffling of their contents to drive daggers deep into his head. He could feel it in his teeth. His skull felt, hopefully for the last time, too small for his brain.

"Man. Are you looking for something?"

He did not know what time it was. The lack of natural light peeking through the curtains gave him the impression that it was late, or early. His new roommate did not reply or even acknowledge the question. Max sat up, rubbing his eyes. They burned from the dried sweat on his hands, and he immediately regretted it. The condescending Jesus was blurry when Max looked up to make eye contact. He buried his face in his hands and pressed on his temples, in a desperate attempt to alleviate the pain, which seemed to press outward.

"Any chance one of those drawers have Aspirin?" Max asked desperately, squeezing his eyes shut.

"I have to step out," his new friend finally replied. "I need to get some supplies, and then I'll come back for you." The redheaded God Boy slammed the last drawer shut and walked briskly out the door. His urgency was more than evident, yet he maintained a walk, like a man late for work. He locked the door behind him and silence swept over the apartment. Max was alone. He looked up and lost a stare down to an inanimate object.

I don't feel alone.

His eyes drifted slowly around the room, looking for the clock, the rhythmic mechanism of which was the only external sound aside from his own breathing. Inside his head, blood thumped through constricted veins, and his ears whined. The latter was common among retired heroes. With what strength he could muster, Max raised himself onto sore, shaking legs. He crept weakly across the living room into the kitchen. He moved slowly, because he was aware of how fragile his stomach was, and he did not trust his balance. He lowered his head into the sink and ran cold water through his hair.

At least I didn't have to crawl this time. Small victories.

He laughed to himself—just one hard exhale that gently vibrated in his throat—and the sudden flexion of his abdominal muscles churned his guts enough to force a dry heave. The cold water was extremely refreshing on the back of his head. Max heaved again and, this time, not dryly. He rinsed his mouth and turned off the tap.

After unsuccessfully perusing the kitchen for Advil, Aspirin, or Tylenol, Max turned his attention to the bathroom. He mulled over the possibility of masturbating to relieve his headache, if only for a few minutes. He then rolled his gaze back to the wooden representation of the Christian saviour, whose eyes seemed to follow him around the room.

"I wasn't going to do it." He pursed his lips. "As if thinking about it is so bad." Max spoke aloud to break the silence more than he did to tempt a response. "And if you don't stop with that judgey attitude, I'll put a paper bag over your head."

With the tap off, Max was alone with the chirping of the clock and the horribly overwhelming crucifix.

And a brand-new smartphone.

It was sitting on the coffee table. Max wondered if there was a response from his new green-eyed, drug-addicted friend.

I have got to start remembering people's names.

Max briefly forgot his withdrawal and was genuinely excited to see if she had returned his message. He delayed gratification, the way one would pause before checking a lottery ticket to imagine what a wonderful life may lie ahead.

A weird couple of recovered drug addicts.

A darker thought occurred. His phone had not alerted him. There might not be a message waiting. Could she have relapsed? Or maybe she had decided to ignore him. She might not be at the meeting on the following Sunday. She could be avoiding him. He felt he was driving himself insane. If she had not responded, he may not be able to handle the rejection. The thoughts spun around in his mind, a twisted carrousel of self-doubt and inadequacy. Max filled a glass with cold water and regurgitated it as quickly as he swallowed it. He washed his face and hands in the running water and pushed his long hair back behind his ears. He scanned around the kitchen for a hand towel, moving slowly to avoid disturbing his empty, delicate insides.

The hollow clicking of the unseen clock was interrupted by his new phone exploding in vibration. Without a case and resting on the hard surface of a glass coffee table, it created a thundering sound against the quiet backdrop of the apartment. The upward-facing screen illuminated. It brought a genuine smile to Max's weathered face.

She is the only one with my number.

Max abandoned his search for a hand towel and quickly wiped his hands across the rough surface of his jeans. A lump in his back pocket caught his attention. He stood frozen in place. It was not joy that gripped him, but fear. He had not been strong enough to flush the stamp bag that morning and would not be strong enough to do it now.

He dug in his back pocket and retrieved the tiny, misshapen bag. He placed it gently on the counter. Max ached. Every nerve in his body was screaming in pain. He felt weak. His knuckles would hardly bend, and his fingers lacked the required dexterity. His hands trembled weakly. He pressed down on the bag with his right thumb and peeled it open with his left, spilling its contents onto the counter. The counter was cold against his cheek, which he pressed flat on the surface and closed his right nostril with his thumb. He inhaled forcefully through his left.

Straight to the brain.

Max shivered with anticipation. He rolled backward onto the floor and slammed into the stainless steel stove across from the sink. He closed his eyes and tried to fight back the tears. It was a fight he could not win. The clock was visible to him now. It hung on the wall to his right, clicking aimlessly away. Max took notice of the time.

Two days. You made it two fucking days.

It was quiet enough to hear the key slide smoothly into the lock. He listened to it turn and release the deadbolt. From his pitiful seat on the kitchen floor, he raised his head and made eye contact with the entrant. Max's eyes were met not by the warm and welcoming ones he expected, but by ones so cold and still that they may have been dead.

There was a sinister way the man moved into the kitchen. His steps were slow and calculated, and his eyes were fixed, as though they were carefully measuring every breath and heartbeat of his quarry. Through his nose, he was breathing deeply, slowly, forcing his lungs to fill to capacity and empty completely. His arms neglected to swing with the motion of his steps, and it was from that absence of natural synchronicity that Max inferred the finality of the situation.

Held in place by panic, Max stared back and studied the disconnected man who he used to call a friend. He no longer felt any pain. His skull eased and returned to its original size, relaxing the pressure inside his head. He watched helplessly as the man between him and the exit retrieved and casually donned black leather gloves. The twisted knot that had stretched from his ribs to pelvis eased and numbed. Max let out a deep sigh of relief.

My gun.

"Are you going to kill me?" he asked, already sure of the answer.

The man, who had now covered his face with a medical mask answered through it: "Yes."

Slow is smooth. Smooth is fast.

He stood up easily. His legs felt as if they had regained their strength. Max turned his back on the kitchen and faced the coffee table and started to walk. He moved calmly, presenting his motions as random and wandering. He approached the end of the couch where he had slept for an unknown length of time and could see the handle of his Browning. He raised his head and made eye contact with the crucified son of God that was hanging over him. He did not have to speak any words to thank his saviour, and looked back down at the gun, preparing to end his ruse.

Max felt he was justified. He had confirmed verbally that his life was in jeopardy, but still imagined how hard it would be to defend himself in court. His history of petty crimes and substance abuse would paint an ugly story. Even in self-defence, he would still serve a prison sentence. Max wondered if there would be a rehabilitation program, and if he would be allowed his phone. He wondered briefly what conversation they may have had if he answered his phone when she called. He wondered if it may be the best thing for him to serve a few years and come out with a fresh start. He thought of the eyes that were looking down on him.

Is this how you do it? I repent? I offer you my soul and, in return, you save me, in this life or the next. You present me with a choice. A cursed and sinful continuation of life, or a gamble at some kind of deathless death? What lies before me—should I take your hand? Is it eternal damnation, some fiery, torturous eternity? Some horrible fate more obscure than what the greatest poet, using the wildest mind-altering drugs, could ever hope to imagine? Or, in my wordless thoughts, could I break even? Could I walk beside you in the Kingdom of Heaven? Some paradise of comparable artistry, if such a place even exists? Or do I just go dark? Do I just end this miserable existence that I created?

Does it really fucking matter?

It called to him. His new phone sat on the coffee table and under it, on a small shelf, the grip of his Browning was visible, beckoning. Such complicated system, it was, elegantly designed to fit in one's palm. The cool metal, with its weight and power, felt like a natural extension of his own arm. What an ultimate equalizer it was, an impossible amount of potential energy, so easily released. The bringer of death. The creator of peace. Safety. Life.

"Maybe we can come to some kind of agreement."

Monday

"First you take a drink, then the drink takes a drink, then the drink takes you."

- F. Scott Fitzgerald

I

For the second time in as many days, Roman would visit St. Joseph's Basilica. And it was on his second attempt that he managed to parallel park the dealership loaner next to a curb on the southern side of 100th Avenue. It was a short walk to the church. Roman internally blamed his subpar parking ability on the cold weakness that follows a night of heavy alcohol consumption. These were his last few moments of serenity. He reclined the seat and lowered the visor to cast a shadow across his tired eyes.

He had Alka-Seltzer, one of the few things he had grabbed from the car he had dropped off, and he crushed one into a bottle of overpriced drive-thru water. He sipped his coffee and listened to the fizzing.

Fucking idiot.

Roman mouthed the words as he thought them, referring to his hangover, and lit a cigarette. He smoked and drank with his eyes closed, flicking the ashes unceremoniously out the window. When the tablet had finished dissolving, he took two Peptos and downed the full bottle of water. He chased it with his last sip of coffee, and savoured the combination. For the better part of the morning, he had been dwelling on the thought that if Moussa's local mosque hadn't caught fire the night before, he would have slept in and sent his partner to reinterview Father Edmund.

Satisfied that he had wasted enough time, Roman exited the

car and proceeded toward his destination. The heat from the weekend had dissipated. It had rained the night before, and fresh clouds were blowing in from the east, promising more of the same.

Fishing is the least.

Despite the weather, Roman had opted out of a jacket. The coolness would prevent perspiration. Traffic was light—both the street and foot varieties—which made the walk more relaxing. With no one to dodge or shoulder through, he enjoyed his own easy pace. With only a few blocks left to walk, he stared blankly at the orange hand across the street.

"Morning, detective!" an unseen man spoke from behind him. The voice was familiar, and not welcome. Roman considered ignoring him, but when the man stepped into his peripheral, he decided that would not be an option. He pursed his lips inward and looked over, more with his eyes than his head. Roman opted for a nod rather than a vocal response, the least he could get away with.

This fucking guy.

"I solved your problem," he started. "We met yesterday. Waiting to give confession." The man had a proud smirk across his face. There was a friendly thing about how he carried himself. Roman thought it may have been his slightly slumped posture, or the way he held his hands downward, arms fully extended. The man was wide-eyed and hopeful, which reminded Roman of an excited dog. He seemed to not be put off by Roman's appearance, a wrinkled and untucked shirt, his unshaven face, the smell of gin sweat drying in his armpits. The overall image was less than impressive: that of a hungover detective with a loaded gun on his hip. In any case, the friendliness was contagious, and Roman knew they were going the same way. He lit another cigarette to hide his breath and offered the pack up silently. The man waved it off.

"You solved my problem? What problem is that?"

"Before I get to that, I wanted to ask you something. Do you know, as a smoker, what advantage you have over everyone else?"

Roman shook his head blankly and spoke through a squinting smile, "No."

"Most people wonder, and some of those people even spend hours thinking about, how and when they are going to die. You already know how you are going to die." He paused for a response that did not come. "It's suicide. You know that those cigarettes will kill you, and you smoke them anyway."

Roman started to respond: "OK, well—"

"—And suicide is a mortal sin." The man lowered his voice to a serious whisper that was somehow still affectionate. "That means you go to hell."

"A mortal sin?" Roman asked, after exhaling smoke over his shoulder.

The man responded with a head nod, aiming his eyes to the side and upward. He seemed a little less confident.

"I'm a cop," Roman continued, feeling like he had the man in a corner. "You know that. I like to believe that I do good things in my work. I don't carry this gun because it looks cool. My job is dangerous. I'll ask you this. If I die at work, knowing that I could be killed any day doing it, is that considered suicide? Or, in other words, if I die protecting the innocent or fighting evil, will I go to hell?" The light changed, and they resumed their walk to the church.

"There is a place, just up ahead, where answers to those kinds of questions can be found." The young man seemed overly pleased with himself, and Roman wondered if he actually believed that smoking a cigarette would condemn him to eternal damnation.

"Just so happens that I'm heading there now."

"But the real reason I stopped you, Detective, is that I wanted to say that I solved your problem."

"And what problem is that?"

"The solution. Is order."

"Yeah, you're going to have to give me some more detail."

"It is the order of the universe. The answer that you are looking for is not in the physical or scientific proof that God exists, but in the *order* of His creation."

Roman didn't speak. It was an easy technique he had learned to keep people talking. It worked.

"Your car is parked where?" the man continued.

"At the dealership, getting the air conditioning fixed."

"Exactly, and where else?"

"What do you mean?"

"I mean what I asked, Detective. Where else is your car parked, aside from at the dealership?"

"I'm not following."

"Is it here? Right in front of us as we are walking?"

"No." Roman had to fake his annoyance, as he was genuinely interested in the direction the man was going. That is if he were actually making a point.

171

"Could it be? Maybe in a few steps, could we find ourselves bumping into it."

"No."

"Why?"

"OK, well, I know where it was when I saw it last. I know where it was headed. And I drove here directly from that location. I would say that it is a physical impossibility for it to travel here in time to block our path." Roman was proud of his answer and impressed with his own articulation. He started to forget that he was nursing a hangover. A combination of caffeine and acetylsalicylic acid create that effect.

"OK. That's a very intelligent answer if you are restrained by the physical limitations of our transit system. Now tell me why it cannot just cease its existence at the dealership and commence existing here, on our path. Or tell me why it cannot just exist in two places at once."

I'm not stumped.

"I lack the education to understand the physics of why that is not possible. I would have to defer to the writings of men much more intelligent than myself, who could explain why things happen the way they do."

"Ah. There it is. You would have to defer to the writings of men who have spent their lives defining how things happen in their observations and, using those observations, make accurate predictions. Those men who are highly intelligent can break down what we know to be physically possible. They can define it. They can put it on paper. But if presented with the question of something being impossible, the answer is still the same. Your car simply cannot exist twice. And that is the great answer, is it not? At the very bottom of every scientific question, and at the very end of every debate on the subject, the order of the universe confirms the existence of God. Without God, by whose authority can we argue that it is impossible for your car to just *be,* in front of us, now? I don't mean by some device or mechanism that has not yet been invented. What I am saying is that for us to be able to make predictions based on observations, some force has to maintain the integrity of those laws."

Roman did not respond. He blamed his loss of words on his compromised mind. They walked in silence.

After a few minutes that should have been more uncomfortable than they were, they arrived at St. Joseph's and ascended the stone steps. When Roman turned to look square at the religious man, he noticed for the first time that the left side of his face was bruised heavily.

"What happened to your face?"

"I got jumped." He looked Roman straight in the eyes. "You know, for a man who doesn't believe in God, you spend a lot of time at church."

"You got jumped?" Roman focused on the first three words and ignored the hasty attempt to redirect the conversation.

"Yessir." His voice didn't waver, and his expression was equally steady.

Roman sighed, knowing that would be all the available information about the purple, swollen face staring back at him. "Is it sacrilegious if I put my butt out in this planter?" He pressed it into the soil as he spoke.

"That isn't between you and me, Detective. That is between you and Him." He pointed skyward.

"I'm investigating a crime," Roman explained. "That's why I'm here so much. You might be able to help, since you probably spend most of your free time here. Do you happen to know anyone who seems dangerous? Someone whose religious ideals seem at all . . . extreme?"

The colour drained from the man's face. Roman watched him fight, weakly, to hold his mouth still. The young man's face held fast, as if his timing were broken, needing to reply but lacking words.

You do know something.

"I wouldn't be the right guy to ask, Detective." The words doubled out of his mouth.

"Why is that? Who should I ask?" Roman had returned to his detective mode and was watching the man's mannerisms become increasingly uneasy.

The smile was fake. Roman could see that. But his answer was not. "When I feel lost in a problem, I ask Father Edmund. If that fails, I pray for answers."

"You do, eh? I'm going to give you a card. If you think of anything that I should know, I want you to call me."

"I will. Thank you." The man took the card and started to leave. He moved as if he had forgotten how to walk.

"I didn't catch your name!" Roman had to raise his voice.

"I didn't give it!" he shouted back from the bottom of the steps, nearly running.

II

There was an eerie greatness to the hollow building. With the sky overcast, the low-hanging fixtures were not enough to fill the room with light. Sinister shadows were cast upward in strange and overlapping patterns. The door was heavy, oak or maple, and the hinges screeched when Roman let it close behind him. The locking mechanism scraped easily into place under its weight, settling with a metallic thud that rang off the walls and back. The vast emptiness and slow echo of his footsteps triggered an unsettling feeling, a dizziness that Roman could not shake. He took a seat in the pews near the entrance and lowered his head to gain his composure. Starting from his agitated stomach, a poisoned weakness crawled through his body and rippled to his extremities. Almost subconsciously, he placed a sweaty hand on the grip of his issued 9mm to reassure his safety. He slouched deep in his seat and eased his head backward to marvel at the stained glass that towered above him. It occurred to Roman that the intensity of the architecture was to represent God and his strength. He felt pathetic in the massive church.

You want me to know my place.

The moment was disturbed by Father Edmund hurriedly pacing down the aisle. Roman had had a short-sighted hope that he would be stood up. If that were the case, his due diligence would be completed; and a few more minutes alone would have been good for the hangover. The approaching steps relieved him of that fantasy. He rolled forward, rubbing his temples, and made eye contact with the priest, who took a seat beside him.

"Fa—" Roman cleared his throat. "Father."

"Detective." There was a genuine unease in the priest's voice. Roman noticed, but pretended not to, and turned on a recording device. He placed it in the space between them and robotically started their interview.

"I understand that confessionals are confidential. I want to remind you that you are not incriminating anyone. Any information that you provide will be hearsay and not used as evidence. This conversation will be recorded for internal use only. If we choose to proceed with charges against a suspect that you identify, you may then be asked to testify for an official record. Do you understand?"

"Yes detective, but should we not do this somewhere more private?"

Roman scanned the massive room and shrugged. "More private than this?"

"You would be surprised. My office. Please."

Roman casually placed a Listerine strip on the roof of his mouth as he stood. The walk to the office was arduous—not physically, but mentally. Small talk was not Roman's strong suit, but he did feel it was necessary to keep the priest calm, so that he might speak freely. The lingering effects of the previous night did not help.

"Do you ever think about lighting this place better?"

"Aside from the obvious financial strain that would place on us, many members of our congregation like the way the natural light displays the stained-glass windows."

"What if you have to give a service on an overcast day?" Roman gestured upward. The priest shrugged and smirked at the detective. The casual motion was what Roman was looking for.

We are friends now.

The priest's office lacked the magnificence that Roman had beheld a few minutes prior. The space from which the church was managed was no larger than a spare bedroom in a modest house, and was decorated with all the charm of an accounting firm. The underwhelming nature of this office, like the overwhelming nature of the nave, Roman figured, was by design. He was sarcastic in his own thoughts.

So modest.

After resetting the recording device, Roman prompted the priest to begin. He sat silently and took fake notes. It was a skill he had developed from years of experience and, as he had predicted, the priest quickly forgot that he was being recorded. He told his story in a non-linear fashion. As he organised the events in his mind, he doubled back and retold the events several times. Roman did not jot down any notes until the priest had completed his entire thought and would scratch off parts that the priest retold. The notes would later be thrown in the garbage. The priest sang like a canary.

As Roman expected, the meeting was short. Father Edmund spoke about a young man who had given a confession the day before. The man had implied to him that he was considering committing a violent crime and said that it would not be the first time. The details were vague, and Roman was not sure if that was because the priest did not have specific details or because he was withholding them. He hoped for the latter.

"Father, I have a few quick questions for you."

"And I hope that I have the answers."

"You mentioned that the young man was someone that you recognised."

"Oh yes. Aside from attending Sunday service and giving routine confessions, he takes advantage of a program that helps people with a troubled past get back on their feet."

"With jobs and apartments and stuff?"

"Exactly."

"Do you happen to know his name?"

"Off the top of my head, I do not. I'm sorry."

"You keep some kind of record of these people? A file that we can review?"

"We do. I'm sure of it. I haven't been especially involved in this program specifically. But let me see what I can find. Do you mind waiting?"

Yes.

"No, take your time."

Roman could see the pain in the joints of the elderly priest as he fought himself from the chair and into the hall, leaving Roman alone with the sound of air recycling through the vent and a clock ticking behind him. There was a voice message on his phone stating that his Toyota was ready to be picked up. He had no new text messages, and reviewed the same Facebook posts that he had seen several times that morning. A burning sensation crawled up his esophagus and forced a painful burp, which Roman exhaled through his nostrils. Either his skin had grown clammy in those few minutes, or he had only just noticed it. His mind was beginning to cloud. The caffeine from his coffee was wearing off, and his hangover was fighting its way to the surface. He rose to his feet and breathed deep to calm his stomach, hoping desperately that there was a water cooler in the hall.

He did not make it that far and was met at the door by Father Edmund, who was re-entering the room with a thin folder. He placed it on the desk and opened it to reveal a single page, which looked like a poorly-written resume. There was a colour photo paperclipped behind it. The important detail for the detective—the one that the elderly priest had set out to retrieve—was not there. In its place was an obvious alias, at the top of the page.

"There's no name?"

"The nature of the program is to give people a second chance. An alias is not uncommon. Sometimes those with a troubled past want to remain anonymous. We allow it."

Roman could feel the gin sweat beading on his forehead, which was a blotchy mess of pasty white and blushing red. "You somehow get these people a job and a place to stay, without their name?"

"Sorry, Detective, I don't run the program. I believe that we just set up the interviews and they give their names to the company. Sometimes these people really do not want to reveal their past to us, and we try to respect that."

Roman paused and closed his eyes, fighting the dreadful feeling of being powerless. His mind was clouded. That was his own doing. The priest was becoming defensive, which would do him no good. After a few seconds, he spoke again, in the friendliest tone he could muster.

"Is there someone who could tell me more about him? Like where he works? Or lives?"

"Samantha runs the program. She could probably help. I'll get you her number."

Roman took the picture from behind the partially-completed resume. An obvious realisation clicked in his head, and he blinked twice, slowly, in disbelief. He pinched his eyes and sat down to calm the spinning of the room. He forced himself to relax and study the printed, smiling face of the young redheaded man in the picture. That same man who had just lectured the detective on religion and refused to give his name. Roman crushed his teeth together.

"Do you need her number?" the priest offered for a second time.

"I have it. She's my cousin. Are you sure this is the man who gave that confession?"

"Absolutely. One hundred percent." He shook his head to reinforce his sincerity.

"I'm keeping this picture." The detective did not make eye contact as he took his recording device and marched out of the room. He gave the priest no option to protest.

Outside, the sky above the church was clearing, allowing the sunlight to dry the puddles and worms that Roman had skipped around earlier. The forecasted rain hung low, still, ominously billowing in the nimbostratus clouds to the east. He was a few feet from the door, examining the picture and reliving the conversation he had on those steps. His breaths were as deep as his thoughts. Could he have handled his two conversations differently? Could he have spoken for longer? Annoyed—with himself more than anything—he started toward his rental and immediately returned to retrieve two cigarette butts from the planter beside the door.

III

With the sky clear, and the sun once again pounding relentlessly, Roman made his way back to the loaner. It was in bad form to run down a residential street with a visible service pistol, so Roman opted for a less offensive power stride. He arrived with a familiar sweat pattern under his arms and down the centre of his back. He threw himself into the driver's seat and slammed the door with such ferocity that he was sure he heard the internal components shift out of place. After settling for a moment, he reopened the door and vomited, forcefully, the cocktail of hangover cures he had spent the morning ingesting.

Feeling better, he closed the door more softly the second time. The picture was held tightly in his left hand, and had been since he first snatched it from the priest's office. He held it up against his steering wheel and took a picture that he immediately texted to his best friend's fiancé, his cousin, Sam.

"I need to know everything about this man. Name. Where he works, lives, anything."

He shoved his phone into his pocket, and immediately felt it vibrate. He pulled it back out with short-lived excitement. Captain Massey was calling. He paused before answering, dreading the conversation he had expected to have had in the office that morning.

"Captain," Roman answered, trying to sound as straight as one could when their stomach couldn't handle coffee.

"Where. The fuck. Are you?"

"Downtown. I just got a good lead on this double homicide."

Not really a good *lead . . .*

"Triple homicide. Oh, and you just got a lead? That's great! You know what I have?! A dozen fucking reporters knocking down my door. A third body in as many days. And my two lead detectives MIA. So why don't you pull your head out of your ass and get down here, so I can replace it with my freshly polished boot?!"

"Yes, ma'am!"

Roman's phone blew up with two more messages before he moved the car. The first was from an unknown number.

"You want out? BPW2."

To that, Roman did not respond. Instead, he deleted it. The second was from Sam.

"He is from the program. I told you about him. Really nice guy. I honestly don't know his name. Got him a job as a road worker, I think."

Roman hammered the car into gear and started toward the precinct.

IV

The exercise helped, but did not completely relieve Sam of her hangover. Kim had noticed. She was sluggish, walking instead of running on the treadmill, and lifting less weight than normal. Despite her plea for a late morning and a few more hours of sleep, Kim, her best friend of many years, had dragged her to the gym. It was the best cure, Kim had told her, aside from chasing it with a Caesar or mimosa. That would be their second stop today. Sam had not worked since Anthony's business started making good money, and Kim, with her commission-based income, could take whatever time she wanted. Today was a recovery day.

First out of the shower, Sam pulled her bag from the locker and placed it on the bench, digging for her phone. There was one new message. Her cousin, Kim's boyfriend, Roman, had messaged her twice. Expecting a personal insult to which she would think up a clever reply, Sam was surprised to see the picture of a young man that she recognised, with a plain request for information. Not just the man whose picture she saw, but the photograph itself, was familiar. Sam herself had taken the photo for his file. It was explained to the man, whose name she could not remember, that the photo was for employment applications. Studies have shown that a resume with an attached picture led to more interviews. She replied and sat on the wooden bench, still unclothed, but covered by a towel, contemplating the privacy of the program. The privacy that made the program so successful was now compromised. She knew Roman would not have asked if it had not been important, part of some investigation about which he would not speak. She still planned to stew on it and lose sleep.

"That thing is a death trap!" Kim was wandering over, drying her hair.

"What is? Sorry? I'm still a little foggy."

"The step there, I tripped going in and coming out." She indicated, with her chin, the elevated step that separated the pool and shower area from the changeroom.

"I think the design is to keep water from flowing into the changeroom." She said flatly, disinterested.

"It's like the pattern of the tiles or something. You can't see what's going on. Could trip and hit your head."

"What? Like you want them to remodel the whole place because you can't watch where you're going?" Sam still spoke flatly. Internally, she questioned the tone of her own voice and harshness of her words but decided that Kim would attribute it to the hangover.

"Just saying. Someone is going to get hurt." Kim dug her bag out of the shared locker and moved to the far end of the bench, turning so that she would not be fully exposed while she dressed. Had she dropped her towel in a direct line of sight, her friend would likely just turn her head, but she decided to spare her. The discretion was more for the sake of her friend than her own bashfulness. "I have a weird question for you."

"Fire Away." Sam, still dealing with a knot in her stomach and an uncomfortable chill, hadn't moved.

"Well for starters, are you OK? Like, I knew you were having a rough morning, but you look like you're in some kind of pain."

"Just a hangover. We had a few more after we left your house. Anthony is still in bed. Poor guy was out cold when I left the house. It's just hitting me really hard for some reason."

"Us, too. I had a couple. Roman drank the better half of a bottle of Hendrick's, and all those AGDs."

"He's been going a little hard, eh?"

"He is just stressed from work, I think. That's the other thing I was going to ask you. You or Anthony—I can't remember—said something about the case. How it might be getting to him?"

"And?"

"Roman wouldn't talk about it. I mean, I'm sure it's not a compromising secret or anything. I just feel like there is something that I should know. Especially considering the way he's been lately. Drinking, like you said."

Sam had started to get dressed as well, modestly, like her friend. "That's a story. Fuck. I'm surprised he didn't tell you."

"Just, like . . . why is that a secret?"

"It's about his older brother."

"He told me he had no siblings."

"He doesn't. Not anymore. They were close. Really close. Sergei was like a second father to him. Maybe six years older? Their dad worked out of town. A lot."

"And Sergei died?"

"I'll tell you. Promise you won't make a big thing out of it to Roman." Sam was mostly dressed. "Him and I haven't even talked about it in like five years."

"Sure. Of course," she lied. Kim had every intention of bringing it up to Roman, after she got him good and inebriated.

"So, Sergei had a bullying problem. It started off minor. Like it usually does when they are young. Some of the guys started calling him 'Sir Gay.'"

"That's stupid."

"Kids, right? God, if he had had a better role model, someone who he could really talk to, it could have been different. But this really bothered him. Someone should have told him not to let it be known how much it hurt, because if it stings, it sticks."

"He was?" Kim was at a loss for words, and apprehensive to dig through her vocabulary. She could see that the story bothered Sam to tell.

"He was. Eventually, he goes to talk to his father. This had been an issue for years. Roman was too young to know what was going on, and I was probably like five. Their dad was a good man. I swear to it. But he was raised in a different time, in a different part of the world."

"I'm guessing he was not OK with it."

"Not even a little bit. He was a Catholic. Really old school. We aren't too many years removed from trying to beat people straight or treat it with an ice bath. Sergei kept it together fairly well, for a while. From what little I can remember, and from what I gather, no one really knew how bad it had gotten."

"It's not a condition."

"Not Sergei, the kids in high school. Once it actually came out that he was gay, it did not go over well. And you have to remember this was a different time. Like, over twenty years ago. People weren't as understanding as they are now."

Kim opted out of explaining that she was aware how much Western society had evolved, and decided to press the story. "Did he kill himself?"

"No, but eventually, he might have. Most of his friends abandoned him. He was driven into a bit of a depression." Her eyes had not yet begun to run, but had a shine that would betray her attempt to conceal those emotions. "Then, it starts getting ugly. Sorry, but my story might have implied that Sergei was soft. The exact opposite was true. He was big. Over six feet and stocky. He stood up for himself. A lot. You can imagine. A kid like that, backed into a corner, every day. He didn't have a lot of support. Name-calling turns into arguing, and arguing turns into a fight.

"Now, a lot of this is hearsay but, from what I've been told, Sergei would win more often than he would lose. One on one, he could take just about any guy his age. And when he won, Sergei really won. Maybe it was a way to blow off the steam, or maybe he blacked out. Maybe, deep down, he thought that if he laid a beating on someone every once in a while, they would leave him alone.

"Either way, teenage boys in the nineties really didn't like getting beat up by the gay kid. Furthermore, those same boys, going home to their parents all smashed up . . . you know, 'the gay kid did it.' I'm not saying it was all because of that. But more and more, complaints started coming in about this big, violent Ukrainian. The school gets involved. They want him suspended. And Sergei's old man—Roman's too, let's not forget—was far from supportive. I think, once or twice, he laid a beating on Sergei himself. Kid was getting it on all sides.

"One day, Sergei doesn't come home. It's a Friday. Dad is out of town. Mom either doesn't care, or just thinks nothing of it. He doesn't come home on Saturday, either. He would've been seventeen at the time, so no one even starts looking for him until probably Sunday. No one thinks to notify the police until Monday morning."

"Did they find him?"

"Roman, walking home from school that day—"

"—No." Kim, at this point, was as visually upset as Sam, covering her mouth with her hands.

"Yes. He had cut through the forest. It wasn't the fastest way, but the most scenic. He found him tied to a tree—stripped, beaten, and three days' rotten. And spray painted on his chest was, 'God hates fags.'"

"It was the kids at school?"

"Probably. They never arrested anyone. No clues, no witnesses. They ended up calling it a fistfight that got out of control."

"Jesus."

"I know. Ice cold, right? Never wants to talk about it. Anthony knows. Some of their older friends know. I think that's why Anthony has really been keeping an eye on him these last few days. They've been friends for a long time, and he is genuinely worried. Just the nature of the case he's working—and you've probably seen it, too. It's really bothering him."

"Let's go get some drinks."

"Agreed."

V

There was an impressive abundance of reporters. Roman counted less than a dozen, but with each sporting their own camera crew and van, the parking lot was a pandemonium. Some familiar faces stood at the entrance, to keep business flowing. Like a herd of pigs fighting for their slop, the journalists would crowd the doors and harass any officer trying to enter or exit.

Animals.

Roman slipped in through the back without being detected. Focusing straight forward, he marched through the precinct to the captain's office. At every turn, business would slow and eyes would follow him. No different than the vultures outside, they wanted to know. There was no dull roar in the bull pen as he crossed to her office, just the superficial motions of fake work. He entered without knocking and closed the door behind him, expecting to see his partner getting roasted. They were alone. One file, and nothing else, was at the centre of her desk. She opened it without a word and fanned the pages in a subtle attempt to remind her detective that the documentation was thin.

"You better have some good news."

"I have a lead," Roman said as he sifted gently though the pages, hoping desperately for a memo from the forensic team. He was not so lucky. "They're backed up in the DNA lab?"

Her silence was more powerful than any words. He did not

have to look up from his reading to know that her unblinking, steel-blue eyes were burning a hole through his forehead. Her dark blonde hair would be pulled back in a tight bun, with not a single loose strand. A cold, flat expression would be carved into her face like marble. He did not have to look to see, and would never admit that it was fear that gripped him. Time passed quickly as he flipped through the pages, catching up with the information that she had undoubtedly reviewed. From his peripheral, he watched her slowly tapping and turning her pen. First on the heel, then she would flip it over to the tip, sliding her fingers to the desk. She did this with metronomic consistency. Roman could once again feel the gin sweat creeping onto to surface of his forehead. With his experience, he could feel that it was more diluted than earlier that day. He wondered if she could smell it. Roman snapped a piece of gum straight from the package into his mouth and chewed for a moment before he spoke.

"Did you review the toxicology?"

"I have," she answered with an inflection in her voice that implied to Roman that she, too, saw the potential.

"Ketamine. In both victims." His eyes were still on the page. "It's interesting to me that neither victim had a lethal dose."

"What does that tell us?" She was softening. Roman could hear it in her voice. Roman knew that as frustrated and angry as she was, her professionalism would not be compromised by her emotions. He pressed through like a defenceman who had made a bad play. The game would continue. Play forward. Work through it.

"Well, both these men were beaten to death. Still, pending the autopsy, of course. But I saw the bodies. There were obvious defence wounds. Both of them"—Roman flipped back and forth between the pages— "were given enough ketamine to knock them out, or at least sedate them, without killing them. If it were just one of them, we could throw it away as a coincidence. But this is precise." Roman worked hard to maintain his composure. The stress of the day was catching up with him. Each passing minute represented lost time. His knee was dancing involuntarily under the table. He would be pressed for time and moving quickly after he left the office, but could not allow her to sense the tension in his voice.

"And you are getting at something?"

"Yeah. If he just happened to bump into one guy in an alley, fine. But both victims, back-to-back. The second guy was dragged. We know that. I'm thinking he drugs them and then moves them."

"And then he—or she—carves them up to make some kind of religious point?"

"They were both homosexuals. We can deduce that much. Otherwise, we have no motive. That, I think, is the religious point. But what is more important to me is that . . . if he could drug them with that kind of precision, why not just kill them with ketamine? There is no shortage. Move a dead body and cut it up in the alley? Wouldn't that be easier? No. I think that he wanted them to suffer. He wanted them to die painfully. He, in my opinion, cared so much about that part that he actually made this harder on himself."

"You should maybe go look at that third body."

"Is it at the scene?"

"Morgue. It was found behind Eden. It's a strip club."

"I know what it is."

"You said you had a lead?"

"I spoke with a Father Edmund. He's a priest from St. Joseph's downtown. He had a confession from a young man. No name, but he said the guy admitted to committing some violent crimes and planned to do it again. Average build and young. I'm thinking nineteen to twenty-five. The only distinguishing feature he could come up with is that he has noticeably red hair. I did some digging. Turns out he is a road worker. I'm going to talk to Fat Frank. Get him to work on finding this guy."

"That's a weak lead, Detective."

"Do you think so? I mean. . . he gave a confession that was so concerning to the priest that he called me in. Guy is obviously religious. An able-bodied young man. I forgot to mention, he is part of some kind of a second chance program at the church. That's why he didn't give his name. My bet is that, if we find this guy, he will probably have a file. We cross-reference his DNA with whatever we dig up from *three* crime scenes, we'll get a match. I'd bet on it."

"From what I hear, you would bet on a lot of stuff."

"Have you seen my partner? I haven't heard from him all day."

"He called me just before you got here. There was some kind of issue at his mosque. He seemed really bent up. He's taking the rest of the day off."

Roman replied with just a head nod as he moved for the door.

"One more thing."

"Yes?"

"We have issued vehicles for a reason. Stop driving your own car."

"Yes, ma'am. Starting tomorrow, I promise."

VI

The logical path was from the precinct to the dealership, before heading to Eden. Roman wheeled the loaner Toyota off the street so quickly that he heard the suspension bottom out going into the parking lot. Time was a factor. The tires squealed as he curled into the customer parking area, forcing the antilock brakes to engage as he stopped. He checked his watch and powered across the parking lot and through the service bay door. The nearest advisor was on the phone, and Roman moved to the second, again stepping as fast as possible without running. From nearly three strides away, he launched the loaner keys onto her desk, and was speaking before she flinched at the impact.

"Roman Owen, picking up a 2017 Camry. I was told its ready." Her eyes were wide—a natural reflex induced by the impact on her desk. "Yes, I called you. If you have a seat, I'll get it pulled up," she responded after a long second and in an overly fake, obviously upset customer service voice.

"No. Thanks. I'll just pay and go. I can find the car."

Then, speaking slowly, in a desperate attempt to cause no further offence, she explained, "Your car is still under warranty. There is no charge. Just a fan that needed to be replaced. We also ran it through the wash and vacuumed the inside."

Realizing then that it was the stress of the day was catching up and that he was projecting it on an innocent and friendly low-level employee, Roman calmed himself. "That's great. Thanks. Sorry about the attitude. I'm having a day."

"No offence taken. Just need you to sign." She had the paperwork printed in a hot minute, which he signed without reading. The only significant information was the total due: $0.00. The advisor passed off the attitude as another customer who had been expecting a hefty bill for a minor repair and attributed his change in tone to receipt of the good news. *Free repairs tend to have that effect*. She pulled the keys from the dealership copy of the invoice and handed them to him.

"Where is it parked?" he asked.

There was a brief pause as she considered the absurdity of the question.

I could have had it pulled up.

"We park them to the west of the building," she answered, indicating with her hands which way to walk.

"Thank you."

Roman turned and resumed his time-sensitive power march to find his girlfriend's car. He checked his watch twice as he walked. Less than two hours. As he approached the west of the building, he hit the panic button and heard the off-key screaming of the car alarm from just a few rows over. He gracefully shuffled between the first two rows with a motion that resembled more of a skip than a step, always aware of the pistol on his hip that might break a mirror or scratch a vehicle. He subconsciously rested his dominant hand on the grip, a drill that was engrained from years of repetitive motion under pressure. He allowed the alarm to sound for longer than necessary, the unpleasant, loud noise replacing what would be his own voice if he were to allow himself to audibly express his current frustration. He turned it off only just before he swung himself into the driver's seat.

It was clean. The fabrics were recently vacuumed, and the air was fresher than it had been when he dropped it off. The aroma was soothing and, for the first time that day, Roman breathed easy, allowing his heart to settle—and his mind with it.

I'm in control.

Curiously, he inspected the car from his seat, stretching around to locate the source. It was not because the scent disturbed him, but more to satisfy his natural inquisitiveness. He did not locate the freshener but, if not for that artificial scent and the inspection that followed, he may not have noticed fresh damage to his headliner. On the passenger side, where the door meets the roof, the fabric was pulled loose and hanging. He considered letting it go. He was pressed for time, and they would surely deny it. He was sure, without a doubt, that the damage had not been there when he dropped it off. They had cleaned it, inside and out. He put the car in reverse, backed out so that he was facing the street, and drove slowly toward the stop sign that would be his point of no return. When he arrived at the stop sign, he paused. A gap in traffic approached, with ample space to fit the small Toyota—especially with his impeccable timing.

"Nope. Don't care." He spoke the words as if he were speaking to the polite service advisor who had done nothing to receive his previous attitude. "You don't get off that easy."

Roman put the car in reverse and ripped a quarter turn to the west before shifting, as calmly as he could, back into drive. He drove slowly and under control, trying to calm the rage that was growing inside. It was a known fact to those of his generation, who were born after 1981 and before 1996, that rudeness and raised voices would get you no further than the same words spoken politely, respectfully. He drove the car to the bay doors and parked it, blocking any vehicles that might enter, yet leaving enough space for him to leave without getting boxed in. He strode casually inside, pacing thoughtfully and passively, to the same young lady who had handed him his keys.

"Can you come with me for a minute?"

"Come where? Sorry?" She was confused, and rightfully so. He had not yet explained the situation.

"I want to show you something, right here." Roman indicated toward the bay doors that he was blocking. The implication was that business would wait until he had he had been resolved.

"Everything OK?" The man cutting in was Roman's age, give or take a few years, clean-shaven, with a short-sleeved dress shirt tucked in and a plain tie that was same colour as the store's logo. His name tag was brass-coloured, and too distinctive to be temporary. The man's eyes darted noticeably from the detective to the car and back.

"You're a manager? Come with me," Roman demanded. The man followed and subtly motioned for the young lady to stay at her desk. They arrived at the car, and Roman calmly opened the passenger door and pointed at the damage.

"I see. What can I do for you?" he asked. There was an

inflection that Roman took to mean that he would not readily own up to the damage.

"Well, it's simple. I dropped this car off early today for an AC repair. This didn't look like that." He was pointing with his finger nearly inside the newly-formed hole, as if to imply the manager would be too incompetent to notice if he had not. "Now, I'm picking it up, a little pressed for time, and I find this damage. I can't deal with it right now, but I want it on record so I can have it repaired when I come back." This tone was one that Roman had mastered. He was completely calm and polite, but broke his speech in just such a way that his anger could not be mistaken.

I can be mad. Let's do this calmly.

"We fixed the air conditioning. I think we just replaced a fan. We wouldn't have caused this."

"Well, you fixed the fan. You also cleaned the car. I understand that you *believe* that you couldn't have caused it. But you did. So why don't you take out your tablet, or phone, or camera, or whatever the fuck you want, and document this? That way, when I return for an oil change or some shit, you will repair it without a fight. Comprendes?"

The manager looked at the issued pistol and scanned upward at the wrinkled, untucked, and half-buttoned shirt loosely worn by the detective. He compiled that with the sweat stains and aggressive posture before him, and determined that he could not win the argument, nor could he afford to let his business wait while he tried.

"Tell you what. Next oil change, I will get this fixed." He took a quick picture with his cell phone. He then smiled and winked. "I'll fill your tank, too. Bring it back empty."

Roman didn't respond immediately. He took a mental note of the name etched into the brass plate above the man's breast pocket and walked around to the driver's side.

"Sorry for giving you guys so much attitude. And thanks, but I don't need any free gas."

Roman pulled the car slowly out of the parking lot and onto the street.

What the fuck, man. Relax. Seriously. You're being an asshole.

VII

"I just feel like it compromises our integrity." Sam was sipping her Caesar, chasing away a hangover that reminded her that her thirtieth birthday was rapidly approaching. "He didn't want to give his name to the program, and we are going to snake around behind him?"

"I don't think Roman would ask unless it was important."

"It doesn't matter how important it is. If the guy came in one day and said he was going to attack someone, or burn down a building, or like, intentionally crash his car, we could justify it. Roman sends me a text message and what? I just forget what it's all about?"

"He is your cousin. You know it will never come back to you. Do you actually *know* the guy's name or anything?"

"I don't. We don't keep it if they ask us not to." A tray of appetizers was placed between them, along with two side plates and silverware wrapped neatly in paper napkins. After asking for another round of Caesars, she continued: "We could find him. I'm not a total moron. I know where he works."

"And would that even be so bad? To tell them that much? If he is a real suspect, they could get a warrant and force you to release any information that you have."

"I don't *have* any information, but I remember where I got him the job. It was only a few months ago."

"Did he tell you what it was for? Is it something to do with the murder that he is investigating?" Kim's glass was empty. She bit off a chunk of pickled asparagus.

"You know that he can't tell me." Sam caved and started at the spring rolls. Kim, who was starving and only waiting to be polite, followed suit and started picking at the plate between them.

"He *can't*." Kim covered her mouth as she spoke. "*You won't.* I think that's the difference."

"His obligation is legal. Mine is moral. That's the difference."

"And what if he is the murderer? What if your moral obligation slows police down, and more people get hurt? Is that better?"

"What if he is not? Maybe he is connected. I don't know. What if he becomes a suspect, and the police track him down using information that only I know? What if he gets away? What if there is not enough evidence? Maybe I don't want to put myself in the middle of it. Especially when the information that I have was supposed to be confidential."

"So, what you are saying is that maybe your moral obligation is not the only thing that is keeping you quiet. Maybe it's some kind of self-preservation. Is your own safety more important than a stranger's?"

The patio air, which had been hot and dry when they arrived, was becoming humid. An earthy, musky scent wafted in on each cool gust, and drew their attention to the looming darkness to the east. Although still distant, it promised to deliver a storm in the evening. When the second round of clam-tomato-and-vodka drinks was delivered, Kim asked for the bill, and paid with an easy tap of her credit card.

"You could call it in anonymously."

"Would that make it OK?" Sam asked with a snarky, friendly tone. "It would not clear your conscience if you were truly worried about divulging somewhat private information. But how would it sit if you had information that could put a dangerous man in custody? And you kept it to yourself? What, truly, is your moral obligation?"

"I guess if I call it in anonymously, it can't get traced back to me. Maybe I can pretend that I know him through work. I'll just say that he is acting strange and seems particularly interested in this string of murders."

"Would you include that lie in your next confession?"

VIII

Across the street from Eden, Fat Frank was having a coffee in a familiar Canadian establishment when Roman arrived. Not a word, but a glance, was their only communication while Roman stood in the line. It wasn't hatred or a lack of respect that generated the tension between them, but a mutual distaste for their pairing. Roman, who had worked with and trusted his partner of over three years, was not warm to Frank's investigative style. To Roman, there was an art to solving violent crimes, a way of placing and understanding the wickedness of a murder. From his walkthrough of a scene, he preferred to draw on instinct and assemble events that were most probable. His new counterpart, Fat Frank, exploited an innate ability to delegate, and would close cases from the comfort of his office chair. Seeing him in the field was rare, and today was one of those exceptions.

"Have you spoken to Moussa?" Roman broke the ice and took a seat across from him.

"No, but from what I hear, he is taking a personal day."

"I dug up a lead. Really wanted to run it by him, but the guy is MIA. Triple homicide, and he takes a personal day. I guess you will have to do." There was humour in his voice that was not lost on Fat Frank.

"What do you have?" he asked with a forced, friendly smile.

"Check this out." Roman placed his phone flat so they could review the picture together. "I bumped into this guy twice. Really nice little guy. Loves God. We had a couple talks about religion. I got that feeling, though."

"Which one is that?"

"The one that solves murders. You wouldn't know."

"Watch it. I get the job done as good as anyone." Both were happy to see their lack of experience together would not impede their communication. No idea was a bad one, and talking through bad ideas bred good ones.

"So, I get that feeling," Roman continued, "and I ask the guy his name. He basically runs away. I talk to the priest at his church. Priest says he could be dangerous. Says he is planning on committing *more* violent crimes. I said *more* because he also told the priest that he has committed violent crimes in the past. There is a lot more to it but, for now, I'm going to say this is our best bet."

"And who is this guy?" Fat Frank drained the last of his coffee and inspected under the lid to confirm it was empty, which puzzled Roman.

Is it hiding in there?

"Don't know. No name from the priest, either. Here's what needs to happen. I'll text you this picture. He is average height and build and works road construction. We have to find this guy. Word on the street is that you are good at finding people. I'm also going to give you my cousin's number. She knew him. We need his name. I'm sure she'll help any way she can. I guess she knew him through the church or something."

"Got it. One thing, though."

"What?" Roman was already getting up.

"I'm not simply good. I'm the best at finding people. Don't forget it."

"I'll put your name in for the award. Show me where they found this body."

*   *   *

"The guy has a pattern."

"Oh yeah?" Fat Frank barely looked up from his phone.

"He wants these bodies to be found, but not before he's had time to get out of sight. Anything out of the ordinary this morning?" Roman was scanning in all directions.

"It's an alley with a body in it. Forensics already picked through. I don't know what you are looking for."

"Neither do I."

It had only been a short walk down another dirty alley before Fat Frank and Roman stopped at an unremarkable scene. The barrier was still up, and an officer was watching the area from his undercover car, just outside the police tape, to their south. The car was facing north, shading the driver from the sun. The visor was down, and his face was hidden by reflective aviators. *Probably sleeping.* The alley, which was the parking accessway for the rear-facing garages of the houses to their west, was separated by a nine-foot fence from the strip club. Eden Exotic Entertainment faced east onto the busy 97th Street. The street ran north and south, parallel to the alley which was visible across the strip club parking lot. Roman stared through the chain link fence at the empty parking area and pondered on what use it might have. He wondered if their patrons drove themselves without a plan for a safe ride home, or if they enjoyed the entertainment sober.

What am I looking for?

The back, west-facing wall of Eden was two storeys and featureless, flanked on both sides by deciduous trees that would provide cover from any curious bystanders. Roman paced carefully along the fence line between the trees and noted that the space between the building and fence would be adequate for dragging a body, but the feat of hoisting one, whether conscious or not, over the fence would be Herculean. With a decisive motion, he grabbed the bottom of the fence and pulled it upward in a spot bisecting two posts. He then moved to another section and attempted, again, to pull it out of position, this time with more ferocity, giving it several violent tugs.

"What the fuck are you doing?" Fat Frank spoke up, having not moved since indicating to Roman where the body was found.

"What I'm doing," Roman answered while pulling on the third and final section of chain links with no success, "is actual detective work. Something that you usually pass on. And that is why you couldn't solve a fucking puzzle." Roman released the fence and exhaled forcefully.

"What did you solve? Is that a good fence?"

Roman didn't answer immediately, and continued his inspection of the fence northward, looking across the parking lot, before finding the second-layer clue. "That"—he pointed east—"is that I'm looking for."

"What?"

"That sign. In front of the strip club."

"Oh yeah?"

"What does it say?" Roman asked, as if testing Moussa's temporary replacement.

Fat Frank squinted his eyes, then opted to put on his glasses, which were hanging around his sweaty neck. "Ladies' night. Sunday."

"Right."

"So what? You think our killer is female?"

"If Sunday is ladies' night, that means six out of seven days are men's night. What do men go to the rippers to see?"

"Titties?"

"Yes. So, then, what do woman go to the rippers to see?"

"Penises?"

"Exactly. I'm guessing this third body was carved up with anti-gay religious shit like the first two?"

Fat Frank cleared his throat and shifted his weight. The overexertion caused by standing for more than a few minutes was testing his patience. "Yes. I think so"

"Our boy is getting sloppy. He is leading us. This is what he wants us to think: victim three shows up on Sunday night and enters the club. Has a great night, man meat on display, maybe has a few drinks, and leaves to go home. He walks outside and runs into our murderer, who is on a killing spree targeting homosexuals. He either tempts him into the alley or jumps him. Doesn't matter. Maybe he drugs him inside and grabs him as he is stumbling out. Doesn't matter. He wants us to think that he met the guy here killed him in the parking lot and threw his body in the alley. But there is no *fucking way* that he got the guy over that fence!"

Fat Frank wheezed in response, as if getting some words out might kill him.

Roman continued. "What I'm thinking is that he brought the guy here, planning to shove him between the fence and the building, but someone—doesn't matter who—was parked in that lot. So, he whips around to the other side and dumps him in a panic," Roman finished, and exhaled heavily. The two detectives were equally out of breath.

"Not bad, Roman." Fat Frank wiped sweat from his forehead using a what looked like a filthy handkerchief.

"That is why you get off your ass and walk through the crime scene. You guys talked to the people that live here?"

"Obviously. It's an alley blocked by garages. It wouldn't be out of the ordinary for someone to come through here at night. No one had anything to say."

"We ask around at this club yet?"

"No one is there until four o'clock. Opens at six."

"I'll come back at four. I have somewhere to be right now. You head back to the office. Maybe sit down or something. If, by any chance, you see or talk to my partner, tell him what I said."

Roman had to run to make it to Kim's Toyota in time. He checked his watch and peeled out of the parking lot.

IX

May have ruined my headliner, but they did a bang-up job on the AC.

There was one other customer when Roman entered the generic establishment, impressed, as always, by the way they were able to capture the local sports bar/pub atmosphere and franchise it. It was not for the quality of food or service that he figured it was successful, but the consistency of cold beer, fair prices, big screens, and comfortable booths, of which Roman took advantage, sliding in sideways so that he could see the entrance and, from the corner of his eye, the larger fellow with a newspaper and a warm beer. The man's beer, Roman knew, was served in a frosted glass, another consistency that surely contributed to the success of the franchise. In the middle of the day, a man with a thawed glass, sitting alone in the corner diagonally opposite from his own booth, was surely security for the other members of his meeting. He checked his watch and saw that he was on time, which was more than what could be said for Sacha.

His server, who was also the bartender, sauntered over and took his order, which was for two pints of Rickard's. Those, too, arrived before his old friend. Roman checked his watch again and had a healthy swallow of the rich, dark ale, noting that the ogre across from him had still not sipped his beer, nor turned the page of his newspaper. Roman tapped the grip of his pistol, which he would normally not bring into such an establishment, but he had been burdened today by a feeling of impending doom. It was hidden beneath a windbreaker across his lap, and Roman was sure that it had not been noticed by the private security. The familiar feeling eased the tension in his mind.

"I think we both got stood up." The music was quiet, and Roman only had to raise his voice to a comfortable mezzo forte for it to carry across the empty room.

The man didn't respond.

"We both know why you're here." The humour had left Roman's voice. He had another swallow and continued to taunt. "Are you from England? Is that why you drink your beer warm?"

"Is everything OK?" the waitress stepped in.

"It's fine. We're old friends. Just a game we play sometimes. Don't worry about it."

The door finally pushed open. In walked his old friend, Sacha, and another man, who Roman did not recognise. The unknown man was taller than Sacha but shorter than Roman, with a high, peaked, receding hairline, befitting an eastern European. It was hardly noticeable with his hair trimmed so short. The man appeared to be in his mid-forties, wore tight-fitting jeans that had never seen a hard day's work, a black V-neck, and a cheap leather jacket with a modern style popped collar. Roman hated him. He knew nothing of the man beside the way he walked and dressed, but there was a queerness that he could not place. As the man approached Roman's booth in Sacha's wake, the still silent security moved seats so that he could no longer be seen from Roman's peripheral without turning his head.

"Detective Owen," the man stated as he squeezed in beside Sacha.

"I don't think we've been introduced. Who the fuck are you?" Roman made a subtle point of not confirming his identity, knowing that, with Sacha there, it was not necessary. There was always a possibility that the conversation was being recorded.

"Let's say I'm a friend that wants to make a deal."

"Of course, but, before we get to the wheeling and dealing. . ." Roman turned around in his seat and raised his voice to the goon. "Hey, lurch. Get the fuck out."

The man did not reply or look up from his newspaper.

"I'm talking to you, asshole. Drag your fat ass out of here so we can have a meeting."

The waitress, understanding the weight of the conversation, stood quietly behind the bar drying glasses. She noted the nearest exit. The man who had not yet spoken peaked up from behind his newspaper to make eye contact with the nameless man in Roman's booth. He was given the OK with a subtle head nod, and walked casually out.

"I will break down what our 'deal' is going to look like for you." Roman held up an index finger and tapped it. "One. You are going to forget who I am"—he turned to Sacha—"both of you. Two." He tapped his middle finger, extending it alone, and directing the gesture at both Sacha and his employer. "If you ever contact me again, I will kill you. Both of you. Got it?"

"No."

"No?"

Sacha had still not spoken, and Roman figured that he would be keeping his mouth decisively shut.

"I don't agree." The man's accent, unlike Sacha's, was real and thick. "I will tell you the deal. You have two options. You can pick. You gunna tell me what I want when I want. And you gunna do what I say, when I say it. Or you gunna pay me back. You got boat. You got truck. You got house. You think that was free? You wanna not be my friend? Fine. But then, you gunna pay back. All the money I loan you. All of it."

"Maybe I didn't make myself clear, you little shit. We are not having a negotiation. You did not *loan* me anything. I let you run your little business. You paid me. Now, you've pissed me off. And you are going to fuck off. And if I see you again—"

"What you gunna do?" the man cut him off. "You gunna shoot me? Here? You gunna arrest me?" The man presented his wrists sarcastically, mocking Roman. "You know who I am? No? So, what you gunna do? What I say is what you gunna do."

I'll kick him in the balls under the table. When he curls forward, I'll grab his collar and drive my right fist into his temple. I'll stand up and hit him again. Then, I'll press his face against the table and put my pistol against his cheek. Little fucker will panic. I'll shove it so hard the metal will break his skin. He will probably cry. Wannabe little gangster. Sacha will sit there with his mouth shut. I will threaten to kill him. I will yell and he will beg. I will tell him to get the fuck out of this city. I will warn him that, the next time we meet, I will kill him. He will piss his pants. I will shove my pistol in his mouth. I will make him promise to never contact me again. He will struggle to answer while he gags on the barrel. I will remove the pistol and, with the same hand, still holding his head with the other, probably by his hair, I will elbow downward with all of my weight. His cheekbone or orbital bone, depending on my accuracy, will crush under the blow. He will scream in pain. I will tell the bartender not to say a fucking thing. She won't move. She would have already called the police. I will leave in a hurry.

The rage pulsated inside Roman's head like a sealed can heating inside a fire, expanding until the pressure burst it open, violently. "Shut your fucking mouth, you Ukey little fuck! Do you even know where the fuck you are?! This isn't the Ukraine. I'm a cop, you asshole! I will get you deported so fucking fast. You can go back to that Russian shithole that you came from, but not before I cut your balls off and feed them to you!" Roman stood and grabbed the man around his face, squeezing his cheeks into his teeth. "Last chance. I'm warning you!" He released the man and with the same hand flipped Sacha's almost full beer out of his hand and into his lap. He then open-palm smacked the nameless man across the back of his head. "Smarten up. Both of you."

Roman left without another word.

X

"Are you the coroner?" Roman asked. He was the only other person in the office aside from the teenage receptionist.

"Medical examiner," he answered flatly. His tone and mannerisms were obnoxiously uninspired, like the corpses that the man spent his days dissecting.

Roman deduced from that tone that the mistake had been made before. He still did not know, or care to learn, the difference. "Sure. Sorry. What time is the autopsy?"

"Already done."

"That fast?"

"Three murders in three days. Captain Massey had it rushed."

"You rushed it?" It was his final attempt at lightening the mood.

There has to be some kind of soul in there.

"Was that an attempt at humour?"

Nope.

"I guess it doesn't take long to determine cause of death if his skull is bashed in."

"You can have a look at my report if you want. Not a hundred percent of the COD."

"Where is the body? Has it been identified?"

"Not yet. You can take a look at it, if you want."

"Please."

"Follow me."

The medical examiner led Roman from the lobby, which was decorated to be less offensive than the hallway, which was hidden by a pair of swinging doors. The faint touch of embalming fluid and cleansers that Roman picked up on the back of his tongue upon entering the building was immediately overpowering when he passed the threshold. The two walked in silence, which was a relief for the detective, whose heartrate had only slowed to normal moments before arriving. His breathing was deep and deliberate. His hands were nearly shaking from the incident that had immediately preceded his drive to the morgue. The air tasted stale and uncirculated. It was the sharpness of the smell that he found unbearable, not the volume, like wet paint in a basement. He followed the medical examiner around a corner and down concrete steps. This far from the office, there was no need for ornamentation. The residents there were not concerned with such things.

Their steps echoed crisply off the walls, through cool air, as they passed into the fluorescent dungeon. To his left, he glanced, quickly, through a circular window on another set of swinging doors, to reveal a cleaning team preparing for another examination. The temperature dropped again as they passed into the storage room. It was not so cold that their breath was visible, but comparable to the maximum power of Roman's recently-repaired air conditioning. The medical examiner moved with a sense of purpose that was appreciated by Roman, whose time, he felt, was fleeting. He checked his watch and saw that he was ahead of his constantly-developing schedule. The man whose name Roman did not bother to learn picked a thin file from its place on the wall of square metal doors. He passed Roman the folder and, without a word, released the pressure latch and pulled the door open. The chemical smell filled the room and drew a quiet but violent gag from the seasoned detective, who turned his head and buried his face in his elbow.

"You OK?" It was the first inflection in the voice of the medical examiner, who, until this point, had been as cold as his patients. It was humorous to the man that what others found so repulsing was a casual part of his day.

I'm hung over.

"I'm fine. Never get used that smell, eh?"

"We only just finished with this one. It fades quickly, but I'm not used to the air without it."

Gross.

"OK, let's see what we have here." Roman motioned with his hand that he had regained his composure and opened the file to review its contents. He perused the pages as the examiner slid the corpse from its freezer. "You have COD listed as asphyxiation?"

"Tentatively, yes." The examiner was fiddling with the zipper that sealed the transparent body bag.

"And burns? From a taser?"

"I'll show you once I get this open. Not an issued taser like the one you use, but it is an electrical burn—and very severe. I'm thinking it's something that someone rigged up. But I guess that part is for you to figure out. You want my opinion?"

"That's . . . why I'm here." He paused like a Jedi, mimicking the accent. The joke was missed, which amplified Roman's internal laughter.

"I think someone caught him off guard. With a homemade taser. Probably immobilized him for a few seconds and put a bag over his head. Plastic, so he couldn't breathe. He had some bruising and lacerations, but they are a couple days old. He is small, too. Skinny. Like a drug addict. We sent his blood to get tested."

"OK. Let's see what we—" Roman stopped midsentence to process what was resting before him. He stared silently for several seconds, until he felt his legs weakening. The room tilted on its axis and Roman grabbed for the wall, connecting with his hand just in time to stop himself from falling. The twisted knot in his stomach that had all but faded cramped and rolled until he gagged. The gin sweat returned, and poured through his skin, which he could feel losing its colour. He intentionally slowed his breathing, and considered that he had not eaten since regurgitating his breakfast near the church. The thought drew attention from his balance, and he collapsed to a knee. The room was receding from his view. He placed his free hand on the ground.

"Detective?" The voice was distant and muffled, as though spoken from another room.

Don't pass out.

"I'm fine." His own voice was booming and clear. He wondered if he had yelled. He forced several large breaths into his lungs.

"Are you OK?" The examiner's question filled the room and pounded hollowly off the metal surfaces.

"I'm fine." He was. A few more heavy breaths and he could feel the room returning. The last wave of sweat was as cold as ice, and the rush of blood to his extremities overwhelmed his hands, which tingled almost painfully. He rose back to his feet, still leaning with one hand on the wall of freezer doors.

"Sorry, Detective. I didn't think you would be so put off by a body. I assumed I didn't have to warn you or—"

"—It's not that." *I'm hung over.* "I know this guy. I *knew* this guy."

"I'm sorry."

"No need to be sorry. We haven't spoken in years. It just caught me off guard is all."

"Do you want me to get you a glass of water?"

The thought of ingesting anything in an atmosphere that reeked so incredibly of cleaning agents was so off-putting that he flexed his mid-section. A sour, hot liquid crawled up the back of his throat and dried on his tongue.

My breath must be foul.

"No. Thank you. Fuck. It's just . . . this was a good guy, you know."

"If you don't mind my asking, where did you know him from?" There was a genuine concern from the examiner, who would normally only see such reactions from family members who were brought to identify the recently deceased. They would not have accepted the death of a loved one, and would be surprised to see that their identification of the body was hardly more than a formality.

"I don't mind. We, uh . . . we used to . . ." Roman was rubbing his eyebrows as he settled himself. "He is an old army buddy is all. Borderline hero, in his prime. Fuck. Can you email that file over to my office?"

I have to eat something.

"Already done."

"Thanks. I can show myself out."

"Of course." The examiner, being experienced with such things, exited quietly.

Roman stood over the body and inspected it carefully from head to toe. As promised, there was a severe burn between his neck and shoulder. A sloppy inverted cross, carved offensively into the man's chest, was still visible, despite the coroner's cut-and-sewn 'Y' shape. On the bottom of his foot, as Roman suspected, he found the short form of another Bible verse. He took a picture of both with his cell phone. The man's eyes and cheeks were sunken. His hair was long. It had been neatly buzzed down to his ears the last time they had spoken. The skin over his pelvis and ribs was pulled tight, with nearly no muscle or fat to hide the bones. Even without a medical degree, Roman could see that most of the bruising was at least a day old. He was rail thin, and horribly aged, but there was no doubt in Roman's mind that he was looking at Dolphin Max Cardinal.

RIP, brother.

XI

After completing his rapid circuit around the north side of the city, Roman found himself pounding across the parking lot in front of Eden Exotic Entertainment. Had the body been discovered on the east side of the fence, this would have been considered part of the crime scene. The same undercover car, with the same useless officer, had not moved and watched over the scene to prevent any disruption. Once given the all clear, they could pack up the tape and allow public access.

During the day, the club was quite unremarkable. It was a dark two-storey building with no descriptive features aside from the name of the establishment under a set of lights that would draw in street traffic. Roman was surprised to find the door unlocked, but assumed the manager would be there, getting set up for the quieter Monday night crowd. He let himself in and had a mild déjà vu feeling caused by a smell similar to Evolution Club, which paired horribly with the well-lit daytime strip club. Dark lights and alcohol, Roman deduced, must be the only way the patrons could manage to spend any time here. For money, the employees could do the same.

After walking alone past what would have been security and coat check—another easy grab into the loose wallets of those that would fill the place on a busy night—he wandered to the main stage. It was a glossy peninsula, with trees of easy, spinning chrome, that stretched out into an ocean of chairs and tables, all facing inward. An upper level surrounded the room. In three locations, a heavy velvet rope and three steps separated the "perve row" and cheap customers from those willing to pay a massive markup on Grey Goose to have it poured by a scantily-clad teenager. Roman wandered around, surprised that he had not been interrupted, and pondered the irony that the more expensive seats provided the worst view of the entertainment. The opposite of what one would expect at a sporting event.

The lights would have been dimmed in the evening. All eyes would have been on centre stage. An eyedropper with liquid ketamine, or even a small tablet, could easily be dropped over the edge or slipped in deftly without the knowledge of security. A grown man, perhaps his Jesus-loving suspect, could drag a heavily intoxicated man, Max Cardinal, outside, without arousing suspicion from security. They might even be relieved. One less asshole to deal with while horny women poked at their muscles and begged for their contact information.

It's what he wants me to think. I'm being baited.

"Woah! STOP! What the fuck are you doing?!" The voice came thundering across the room. Roman was not surprised, and waited patiently to be confronted. A massive man with a shaved head and trimmed goatee was barrelling toward him, shoving aside chairs and tables that were in his path. The man wore tattered jeans and a black bowling shirt embroidered with the same red logo that was on the street side of the building. His arms were thick and tattooed. His stomach stretched his middle buttons. He was enraged. His eyes bulged forward, and his teeth were presented like those of a dog protecting its dinner. As the likely result of a sodium-heavy nightlife diet, his skin was flushed in a deep red.

Roman was seasoned in his timing, and stood stoic until the last second, like a matador preparing to sidestep a charging bull. He casually turned his body so that the issued 9mm came into sight and, at the same moment, flipped open his wallet with his off hand to reveal his badge. The bar manager shrank internally. Roman could see it in his body language and in his eyes. Roman knew that in an establishment like this, there was more than enough illegal activity to incite the worst fear with the simplest of gestures. He placed the badge back inside his pocket. The manager continued his attempt to evict Roman, now crippled by the cyclone of possibilities rolling in his mind.

"What are you doing here?" he asked, attempting to sound intimidating. "We aren't open."

"I know that. I'm Detective Owen. Let me start by saying that you aren't in trouble."

"If this has to do with that body you found, I already told them today that we know nothing about it." He could hardly breathe. His chest rose and fell with panic and, despite standing still, his heart rate continued to rise.

"I know. I just wanted to ask you a few questions. Maybe you can help."

"Don't want to be rude, officer, but I don't make a habit of talking to the police."

"Why is that?"

"Honestly, I just don't want trouble. You know what kind of

place this is."

"What kind of place this is?" Roman baited him with a simple mirroring technique.

"Not like that. I'm not saying that it's some kind of place. Wait, how did you get in here?"

"Door was unlocked. Sorry, I didn't get your name."

"Dave. So, you just let yourself in?" The manager realised now the building was private property and, despite being an officer of the law, Detective Owen had no right to be there.

"I won't waste too much of your time. I'm looking to confirm whether or not two people were in here last night."

"Can't do that. In fact, I think I would prefer if you left. We don't open until six."

"You have cameras, and you scan IDs here. You would have to. Can we make this easy? Can I review those?"

"You know what? No. I'm actually going to ask you again to leave. I can't show you that without a warrant."

Roman started for the door.

Fucked this one up.

"Do you mind if I have a talk with some of your dancers?"

A disgusting smile spread across the bar manager's face. "My dancers dance. They don't talk. Especially to the police. But if you do want a dance, come back in the evening. Just don't forget to drop off that gun and badge." He followed Roman to the door, and made sure to lock it this time.

Now there's an idea.

Roman sauntered easily back to his car. He sat down with a

clever smirk, pleased with the idea that had been inadvertently given by the early life heart attack of a club manager. He picked up his phone to make the call, but saw he had two missed messages.

The first was from Fat Frank: "Got some info for you."

The second from Captain Massey: "Call me."

He opted out of a reply for the time being, and chose Anthony from his contacts list. He called and Anthony answered almost immediately. "What's up, cheese tits?"

"You have anything planned for tonight?"

"No. Why?"

"We're going out."

XII

Roman's phone rang. It was Captain Massey and he begrudgingly answered. "Yes, Captain?"

"Where are you? I told you to call me." Her voice was stern with a hollow crack that implied desperation.

"I have one more interview and I'll head back to the station."

"We got a name and address for your suspect."

"For who?"

"The road worker. The one you told me about. Fat Frank got it. We need you down here."

"I'll make it quick." Roman hung up without waiting for a reply. Rick Van Pelt's wife had already been interviewed by his partner the previous day. They had not met this morning to compare notes and Roman's trust in Moussa was dissolving. He could not remember the last time they went a full workday without communication. He hurried up the steps and tapped gingerly on the door. Despite the haste with which he had to conduct the follow-up interview, he forced himself to downshift as he was interviewing a woman whose husband had been violently murdered the previous day. He could hear footsteps approaching through the door and used a few waiting seconds to get a quick look at the neighbourhood. It was quiet. With full-sized detached houses this far from the highway, he imagined the constant motion of children playing in the street. Across the road, a woman inside her car was scrolling through her phone. He could feel his age. Children didn't play in the streets anymore. Parents were afraid to let them roam, and the developing minds were perfectly content when glued to an addictive feedback loop of flashing colours. The door opened behind him, and he turned to meet the red, swollen eyes of a woman freshly widowed.

"Good afternoon, ma'am. I am Detective Owen. We spoke on the phone."

"Of course, come in." She pushed open the outer screen door and motioned for him to follow her into the house. "Can I get you anything?"

"No, I'm OK. Thanks. May I?" He indicated with an open palm that he wanted to sit.

"Please make yourself comfortable."

She sat across in a worn armchair beside a box of tissues and a garbage can. He sat on the couch, making sure to stay upright and forward, resting his elbows on his knees. "Let me start by saying that I am deeply sorry for your loss. We are doing everything in our power to get you closure. Are the kids home?"

"They are both upstairs. You know how kids are with their technology these days. Do you have any leads? Or, or clues?"

"I am really sorry, but I cannot discuss the details of the case until we have more definitive answers. What I really wanted to talk to you about was the interview that you did with my partner."

"OK." She seemed a little uneased by the direction.

"What kind of stuff did you talk about?" It was a follow-up technique that had proved to be useful in the past. Despite disappearing in the middle of a triple homicide, his partner was competent enough to comfort an interviewee and allow her to speak freely. Asking her to summarize the previous interview could bypass the tension.

She wiped her nose and the tears that were filling her eyes. "Well, he just asked me if we had any enemies. It was a strange question, given our history. We got past that, and he asked me about where he liked to go, and who his friends were. And he didn't seem really interested in my responses. He asked me about our relationship and that part was hard."

"Why was that part hard? Can you tell me about your relationship?"

"I can try." Her mouth trembled as she worked to get the words out.

"Take your time."

Hurry. Please.

Roman's phone was ringing silently in his pocket. He ignored it.

"We didn't have a great relationship, to tell you the truth." Her constant wiping of her nose and eyes couldn't handle the load and tears were crawling down her cheeks. "We would fight a lot. When we got married, everything was great, and then we had the kids. I think it was my fault, really. I put on some weight, and I was never able to get rid of it. Our sex life had all but stopped. Then after a while we would just bicker. He wasn't an awful man. He worked hard. I just could not seem to keep him happy. We tried things, in bed, you know. Tried to keep it interesting. But didn't work. When I say it, I mean—"

"I don't really need to know that part."

"I'm sorry. If you don't stop me, I will just go on and on. I can't imagine this is really relevant. I said a lot of this to Moussa when he came by yesterday."

"Sometimes, the most minor detail to you could end up being the detail we need to pivot an investigation. Do you happen to know where he was headed the last time you spoke?"

"He was heading home. I expected him in less than an hour, but he was never one to show up on time. To tell you the truth, I think he may have been cheating on me."

"You haven't been watching the news?"

"No. I can't handle it right now."

Roman paused for thought; experience had taught him that better words, spoken slowly and carefully, were more effective than filling the room with noise. His phone buzzed in his pocket. He hid the frustration as best as he could. "I'm sorry." He pulled out his phone. It was riddled with messages, some scathing, from Fat Frank and Captain Massey. "I'm really sorry, but this is urgent. Can I come back tomorrow when I am not so pressed for time, and we can have a more detailed conversation?" Roman would break the promise and not return the next day.

"Of course. Any time."

"Thank you. I will call before I show up." Roman let himself out, ensuring not to leave an opportunity for an embrace. He jogged down the steps and toward the car, noticing as he dug for his keys that the woman across the street was still scrolling her phone. She looked up and made eye contact. Like a deer in the headlights, she froze. *Let it go.* Had she been doing nothing suspicious, his presence should not have alarmed her, but there she sat, expressing fear through her motionless eyes. Roman stepped around his car and walked across the street to her driver side window. She rolled it down.

"Are you Detective Owen?" she asked without hesitation.

"I am. How did you know that?"

"Are you the detective on Rick's murder?"

"Yes. Is there something I can help you with?"

"I was wondering if we could have a quick talk."

Roman checked his watch. He squeezed his teeth together and forced himself to sound relaxed. "Sure, I have a few minutes."

Quickly, please.

"Do you want to sit?" She casually hit the unlock button.

What the fuck.

He walked around and got in, taking a subtle photo of the license plate as he passed around the rear bumper. *Twenty-seven.* Roman chose an exact age as it would be easier to remember than a range. She was thin, yet healthy, with mid length auburn hair that was pulled back in a messy bun. Her makeup was layered too thick, blended poorly around her artificially blushing cheeks. Roman guessed that she had not yet been burdened with a professional job.

She wants to be a teenager.

"Can I start with your name?" Roman asked.

"What happened to him?"

"If you watch the news, you probably know as much as I do."

"He was murdered."

"Murdered?" Roman mirrored.

"I saw on the news. The story is about, well, homosexual men being killed by some kind of zealot?"

"Zealot?"

"Like a religious fanatic. It doesn't make sense to me."

"Why is that?" Roman was fighting his impatience while trying to maintain some level of tact.

She stared straight forward with her hands on the wheel, as if searching for words that didn't come.

Roman tried again, "How is it that you know Rick?"

"I am a friend."

"Is that why you are waiting outside of his house?"

"We were close. He came to me for support. Are you going to find out who killed him?"

"We are doing everything we can. What kind of support?"

Again, she stared forward, expressionless, and did not answer.

Roman could hardly settle his bouncing knee. He checked his watch and pursed his lips before speaking with a well-practised, friendly tone. "Are we talking about financial support? Or emotional support?"

"Emotional. He wasn't happy. With his marriage. His wife. His life in general." She was gently shaking her head. Her eyes were glossy and reflective.

"I want to continue this discussion, I really do, but I happen to be in a hurry this afternoon. Is it possible that you follow me to the station, so we can have a more detailed interview?"

"I would love to, Detective, but I also am pressed for time." Her bottom lip was quivering softly.

"Maybe we can schedule something. For when you have more time to talk." His phone was vibrating relentlessly in his pocket. He pressed down on it, as if that would stop it.

"I don't think that is a possibility. Like I said, I am short on time. I think I made a mistake coming here."

"I'll tell you what. Here is my card. It has my cell phone number. If you find a spare minute and want to chat, I want you to call me. OK?"

"For sure. I will." Roman considered asking for a piece of ID but thought better of it. He could run the plates at the precinct and did not want to push. He got out of the car and squatted down beside the open window so that he could see her.

"I didn't catch your name?"

"Jamie."

"Jamie, what is the best phone number to reach you?"

She did not answer. She kept her eyes forward, started the car, and drove away.

XIII

"It is a 2015 Honda Civic. Black. Owned by a Miss Jamie Doigle. Female. Brunette. 163 cm. 53 kg. Born December 12, 1994. Current address on the driver's license does not match the registration, or the Equifax."

"You pulled her credit?" Roman was surprised that he had gotten so much detail from a license plate. It had been only fifteen minutes since he texted it.

"Yeah. There's a reason people talk to me when they want to find someone. I don't fuck around."

"Phone number?"

"Several. Based on the credit bureau, she keeps them for about as long as it takes to get cut off."

Roman ran his fingers through his hair and rubbed his temples. "And my other guy?"

"Boss has that one. Good luck, by the way." Fat Frank was more than pleased to tell Roman that Captain Massey had the file, and she was not in a good mood.

"Thanks." Roman was not excited to see the captain in a bad mood for the second time in one day. The dread was buried in curiosity. He had to know what they'd dug up on his zealot. He was the only suspect, although Jamie Doigle was not making a great case for herself. He entered without knocking and sat across the desk, rubbing his hands together like a child on Christmas. "What do we have?"

"We got an anonymous call this morning. Someone that works with our prime suspect says that he has been acting strange, going on about this triple homicide. They didn't go into any huge detail, but suggested we look into it."

"Did they give a name?"

"No, but they did say where he works. Frank did the rest. His name is Paul Derocher. He works as part of a road crew. A flagger, to be precise."

Roman grabbed the file without asking. "Anything else? Woah." Roman was surprised by its girth. "This is thick."

"Tell me about it. Guy has been convicted twice. Involuntary manslaughter and second degree. Both times as a minor. He had a real rough childhood. Both parents were active members of the Canadian Forces. They had him in some kind of Catholic all-boys' school after he burned a kid alive. No motive."

"Burned him alive?" Roman spat.

"The report says that he lit the kids' tent on fire and stood there watching him die. There was a second boy in the tent who survived but trust me. You don't want to see the pictures." Even the stoic Captain Massey expressed gawking distaste for the story. "He couldn't attend public school and ended up in some Catholic private school."

"That's probably where he went all loopy. About religion and all."

"While he was in there, he attacked another student and killed him. He had issues with violence the entire time, too, constantly getting in fights."

"What happened after?"

"Juvenile detention until he reached the age of majority. His father was KIA in Afghanistan during his second trial."

"Did he ever get treatment? For mental health or anything?"

"They tried. It's all in there." She nodded toward the file in Roman's hands. "They couldn't diagnose him. He was violent when he was violent, but pleasant and friendly in therapy. I would guess bipolar or something, maybe schizophrenic but I'm not the doctor who talked—"

"It's neither," Roman cut in while reviewing the file. "It's the religion."

"Come on, Roman, you're speculating."

"No, I'm not. Are we still doubting our motive, our current one? Think about it. A hunter has no problem killing a deer or a moose but loves his dog. A rancher can have thousands of cows butchered and would have his heart broken over a horse. Why? It's because we humanize what we love, and dehumanize what we hate. When he, Paul, decided that one of these guys was gay, they became some kind of abomination. They were no longer *he* and *she*. They became *it*."

"Let's not get ahead of ourselves. Put some more energy into it and come up with a full profile."

"Agreed. Can we find out where he was being treated, and if he is still being treated?"

"Frank is working on it. Not looking good."

"We should try to get eyes on this guy. I'll review this file after work before I head to the peelers."

The Captain displayed no reaction to Roman's attempt at humour. "The body you identified today."

"Cardinal."

"He worked with Derocher. Same crew."

Roman had to pause to process. A dark thought was churning in his mind. The kind that would keep him up at night. It was the kind of idea on which one might dwell for years. He pushed it aside. "Has anyone been to Derocher's house?"

"Undercover. On standby. You spoke to him. What's your feeling?"

"To be honest, he doesn't seem stupid. Fairly well spoken for a young kid out of juvie. Here's what I think." Roman took a pen from the Captain's desk, a disrespectful action that she would address later, and quartered the blank side of one of the pages. "Two possibilities on top and two on the side. Four possible outcomes. One. He is not the murderer, and we bring him in. We scare away a possible lead. Frustrate ourselves. Two. He is not the murderer, and we don't bring him in. Nothing happens. Three. He is the murderer, and we bring him in. Do we have enough to convict him or even hold him? Guy gets wise and disappears. Lawyers up. We may be fucked. We would be betting on a confession, but I don't think he would be easy to crack. Four. He is the murderer, and we don't bring him in."

"It seems like you are leaning to option four. So, we just let him run rampant?"

"We get eyes on. Stake out the house, or apartment, and watch him. Best case scenario, he tries for four in four days, and we bust him. Case closed."

Derek Lukachko

"Are we are ruling out the possibility that he may just know something. Option three. Maybe he has information that could be valuable. We let him roam, don't bother questioning. Follow him around and wake up tomorrow with another body. Maybe we bring him in, and he sings."

"Not this guy. I don't think so."

"Your call, Detective. Do not make me regret this."

"You won't. Here is what I want. Is he in a house or apartment?"

"Apartment."

"Even better. I want three undercover units watching the building. Hard stake out, two-man teams. No one goes in or out without us knowing. I want the same thing at St. Joseph's."

"Which is?"

"Church. His church. We talk to his foreman or boss or whatever he has. I want to know if he shows up for work. Does he have wheels?" Roman was flipping through the folder.

"Pickup truck."

"Let's flag the plate. Make and model. See if we can find him. Last thing. Airports, busses, trains. If this guy goes on a trip, we have to know."

"That is a lot of resources."

"That's my judgement. You can make the call. Before we talk about bringing him in, let's see if we can find him."

"You have my support. But I don't want to dump all this energy into this and come up short. We may be way off."

"What else do we have?" Roman asked rhetorically. "We have

236

to make it abundantly clear that no one moves on him until we give the go-ahead. If we spook this guy and he takes off, we are back to nothing."

"Are you taking the apartment or the church?"

"Neither."

Roman took the file and left the office.

I saw him the day before and the morning after he killed Cardinal.

XIV

Kim was curled up under a blanket when Roman called. She had the late afternoon to herself and was slowly working her way through a bad book by a good author, stopping at irregular intervals to check and update her various social media outlets.

"Hey, what's up?"

"Why do you sound upset to hear from me?" His voice was dry and lacked the commanding depth that mirrored his personality.

"Well, concerned more than anything. You don't usually call me in the middle of the day."

"I wanted to say that you are right."

"About?"

"I'm done with this."

"Are you now?" she asked with feigned comical disbelief.

"After I finish with this case, I'm going to call it quits. You're right. I just can't do it anymore." He had the image of Max's body burned into the back of his eyelids.

"Are you feeling OK?"

"I'm having a weird day and I'm not sleeping right. After this one, I'm done, with all of it." If Roman had his way, she would never know what "all of it" really meant.

"You sure you're not just hung over? Sam was in fairly rough shape this morning."

"Maybe. I don't know."

"Have you given any thought to what you are going to do?" Roman could hear from her tone that he was making no progress trying to convince her that he was serious.

"No. But another thing, after work Anthony and I are going out."

"Where to?"

"Eden."

"The strip club?"

"That's the one."

"Can I come?"

"Nope. I'm going for work."

"Work?"

"Work. It's not like I want to go."

"You are going to the strippers, on a Monday, with your friend Anthony, and I can't come because it's for work?"

"Yes."

"You're lucky I trust you."

XV

On the first pass they saw that parking in what should have been a nearly deserted lot was not an option. Roman and Anthony circled around the block and considered parking in the alley. The police tape was removed, and the alley was alive with intoxicated men and women exploring the area. Some were wandering around in a haze, pretending with their friends that they had some level of the expertise required to piece together a crime that had not yet been solved. Others were simply enjoying the ambience. All were ignorantly unaware of how close they were to the garages to the west. The club had only been open for a couple hours and the party had spread outside. One assembly of three young men worked as a team to climb over the fence. The second waited on top and passed two liquor bottles to the first man over.

"Won't be long before someone calls the cops. This is way out of hand."

The irony was not lost on Anthony, who burst into violent laughter, "Yeah. I wonder if there are any cops around, eh? Tell me again what we are doing here."

"I don't know why I didn't expect this. I am here to work. You just, I don't know, watch my back."

"And the great Detective Owen is going to crack the case by going to a strip club. How you convinced Kim to let you go to the strippers on a Monday, I will never understand."

"I told her it was for work. What did you tell Sam?"

"Told her I was going with you to the Eden. Let's just park a couple blocks from here and walk."

"These people are fucked." Roman pulled ahead and saw that one street over was completely empty, as it would be on a Monday evening in a residential area. They easily parked the Ram and started walking. The noise from the alley was carrying well over the houses, surely waking the residents. "I don't know if I told you, but I personally identified the third victim."

Anthony stared inquisitively at Roman before responding. "This one? From the strip club?"

"This very one." He pulled a nearly empty pack of cigarettes from his pocket and gave one to Anthony before he continued. "I almost passed out when I saw him."

"How did you know him?" Anthony lit his cigarette, took a long drag, and exhaled over his shoulder.

"We were in the army together. Way back in the 'all or nothing' days."

"Man, if this case wasn't hitting close to home before. Fuck. You all OK and everything?" He took another shorter drag and pushed it out through the side of his mouth. They arrived at the corner and turned left toward the club.

"I'm fine, fuck off. It's just weird, you know?"

"Weird how?" Anthony's normally playful tone was throbbing with genuine concern. Roman felt it and worried he was getting too heavy.

"Nothing crazy. Just last time I saw him, the guy was leaving the army with aspirations. Athletic. Young. Too smart for infantry. To see him lying in the morgue like that, all strung out and frail. It's not him. Like it is him, but it's weird how you think you know someone. Like the guy who he was to me must have been wildly different than who he actually was."

"I read a book about that. I can't remember the name right now."

"Wait. Anthony." Roman paused to think like he was solving a riddle. Anthony stared at him, unblinking and heavily focused. Roman finally continued, "Since when do you know how to read?"

"Fuck you!" He punched Roman hard in the front of his shoulder, aiming between the pectoralis and deltoid to cause maximum pain. "I can't remember the name right now."

"I know the book. It's Italian. The basic concept is that if you only see someone for two hours a day, five days a week, you only know that portion of the person. To someone who sees him during a different two hours, he may be a completely different person. I barely knew him, honestly. The guy he was to me is mostly a fabrication. I fill in the gaps to create a full person. I guess I never really asked him, and he never really talked about it. I didn't even know he was gay."

"That's kind of what I was getting at. I may not have used so many words, but you're right. You didn't know him that well. Just what you remember. I said it before, and I'll say it again: Don't get your head all wound up in this case. Seriously though, what are we going to do about this line?" They had arrived at the club, and the chaos had not subsided. The lineup, which would normally be just a few people, stretched to the sidewalk and grew less organised farther from the door. The two bouncers were far too worried about managing foot traffic to deal with anyone climbing on or over the fence into the alley.

"They were not ready for this."

"How could they be?"

"Two days ago, when I talked to the owner at Evolution, I warned him to prepare for it. Told him that crowds follow death. I also met the polite young man who runs this fine establishment and he seemed more concerned with chasing me out of the building, so I gave him no warning."

"Probably in there right now scrambling to get more girls and more security here as fast as he can. But seriously, we aren't waiting in this line. I'm not eighteen. Let's just go to the pub down the road."

"Fuck that. Follow me." Roman dug in his pocket and took out a billfold. From the centre he carefully removed two fifties and folded them in his palm.

Like you are supposed to be here.

He walked with an unbroken stride to the front of the line, cutting directly in front of a young lady who, from the way she was dressed, could have been a patron or employee. While she was digging in her knock-off Gucci for an ID that may or may not exist, Roman leaned into the bouncer and opened his palm for a handshake that sandwiched the cash. Roman spoke directly into his ear to be clear over the background noise. "Dave is expecting us. We're friends of his. Two fifties. One for you and one for your friend. Or both for you, I don't care." The bouncer tapped him on the shoulder with his free hand and gave a head nod to his counterpart, signalling that they were being granted access. As he passed into the building, he overheard a stirring that was surely caused by a testosterone-pumped teenager, amped up about seeing the injustice of the doorman.

After an expensive and mandatory cover charge, Anthony immediately grabbed them two overpriced beers and found a table. "Pretty lucky we were able to find a table. Cheers."

Roman had to strain to hear through the background noise and his own tinnitus. "This place is chaos. I was honestly hoping for a quiet Monday night."

"At the stripper's?"

A familiar face caught Roman's eye from across the room, and this time his approach was much less aggressive. The manager weaved easily through the crowd and tables, sweating not quite profusely, but enough to shine under the flashing lights. Through the heavy drumbeat of whatever new-age pop music was playing, Roman could hardly make out the man's words. "Did you name-drop me to the bouncers to get in?"

"Yeah. We met today. You told me to come back with money."

"Are you fucking serious? What are you doing here?"

"Having a good time. A few drinks and enjoying the entertainment. I would prefer to not make a problem. Your security is clearly overwhelmed. Have you seen what's going on outside?"

"I got more guys on the way, but if you aren't here to harass my business, I'll leave you alone."

"Deal. You want a drink? You look parched."

"What?" The manager's hearing was likely more damaged

than Roman's after years in the industry.

"Parched. Like thirsty. I'll buy you one." Roman took out his billfold and raised his head to look for a server.

"First one is on the house." The manager easily waved over one of the shot girls. "What are you having?"

"Patron, if you're buying. Anthony?"

Anthony, who was more interested in the selection of private entertainment options, answered, "Whatever you're having."

"Two Patrons."

"Three," Dave corrected. After a quick shot and a shake of hands, the manager decided to leave them alone. The same could not be said for the young ladies who had likely taken notice of the wad of cash that had briefly been on display.

"How are you doin', sweetie?" The first of possibly many women closed the distance in a hurry. Like sharks with blood in the water, they had watched the men since their arrival. The shot of Patron with the manager might as well have been chum. She pressed against Roman and wrapped an arm around his shoulder. She was short and pale, with a copious amount of some drugstore perfume. On a good day, she might have been a few inches over five feet. Her waist was petite and she had ample hips and bust, creating the sleek hourglass shape that so many strive for. She wore three articles of clothing, one of which was a set of heels that had her balancing uncomfortably on the balls of her feet.

Carefully ignoring her breasts, which were conveniently at eye level, he responded casually, "I'm well. How are you?"

"I am having a great time." She put her left hand down the

front of his button-up dress shirt and gently tickled his chest with her nails. "Do you want a private dance?"

"That depends."

"On what?" She smoothly threw her left leg across his body, landing in a full mount or straddle position.

"It depends on how long you've worked here."

Puzzled by the question, she guessed that her answer should be a short or long. "It's my first day!" She answered playfully, with a giggle that could not be any less natural.

"That won't do. Are you sure you haven't been here longer? It doesn't seem like your first day."

"Does it really matter?" She began gyrating suggestively in his lap.

"It actually does. Be honest." Roman's voice was friendly enough, but he fought hard against the urge to let it slip into a playful tone that would be much more comfortable.

She stopped her motion and looked him square in the eyes. "Eight months. Is that good enough?"

"Perfect. Let's go." She took his hand and led him from the table. He flicked his gaze around and shot a quick wink to Anthony, who hardly seemed to notice with all the attention he was receiving.

Around the corner and down a hallway, Roman found himself entering a semi-private room, sectioned off by three walls and a curtain. The room was empty, aside from a mirror in the corner and a padded bench. The walls were decorated with a bold, tacky design, similar to what one would expect to see on a bus seat, and for the same reason. She turned him around and gently pushed him onto the bench. He fell into the seat without a struggle. She turned her back on him and swayed slowly with the music, which was audible, yet less offensively loud, from the main stage. Reaching graciously up her back she grabbed at the strings loosely holding her top. She sat down gingerly on his lap and placed the garment on the bench beside them.

"Woah. Hold up." Had he been paying attention and not digging in his pocket for the wallet-size photos, he may have become aroused. "Grab a seat."

"Sorry, what?"

He patted the empty space on the bench beside him. "Just sit down for a minute."

"O-K," She obliged, more sheepishly than he had anticipated. "I still have to charge the same rate."

"All good." Roman pulled two twenties from the outside of his billfold and handed them to her. "How much time does that buy me?"

"About five minutes." She crossed one leg over the other and rested easier in her seat. Her sensitivity to her own nudity had long since worn off, and she showed no interest in redressing.

"Good. That's all I need. You said you've been here for eight months. Were you telling me the truth?"

"Give or take."

"How is your relationship with the Sunday night entertainers?"

"The magic men?" she asked with a sour tone.

"Sure. Whatever you call them."

"They're OK. Most of them are hot AF. I tried to tease one into asking me out when I was new and got harshly rejected. Turns out he likes D more than V."

247

"Are they all gay?" It was not part of his investigation, but more of a scientific curiosity.

"Some of them. Not all."

"If I asked you who worked last night, could you tell me?"

"I could find out. But I won't tell you." She stuffed the two twenties into the tiny purse that Roman had not noticed her carrying. "And you're just about out of time."

That wasn't five minutes

"Fine." He retrieved his billfold and pulled two fifties. "Here. Can you find out now?"

"They don't take money for sex."

"It's not sex I'm after. Can you make it happen? Names and phone numbers."

"Are you a cop?"

"It is a myth that police have to disclose that if you ask. But, yes, I am a cop."

"Oh, snap!" Her eyes lit up brighter than they had been in years. "Are you that detective?!"

"I don't know who *that* detective is, but probably, yes."

"Oh, damn." Her voice receded from the fake bubbly tone that she had practised into a more natural Alberta accent. "You think one of the dancers did it!?"

"No. I just want to know who was around last night. Think you can help me with that?"

"It'll cost you. I can get you three names and numbers of the boys that work Sundays. I can't guarantee they will answer, and I will clear it with them first."

"How much?"

"Hundred each."

"Fine." He pulled six fifties from the centre of his billfold, which was becoming less impressive in a hurry, and handed them to her. "Don't let me down. I'm not going to wait in here all night. Can you bring me the info to my table?"

"No. Dave is going to be pissed if he finds out. I'll text them to you. What is your number?"

After exchanging contact information, he stood up to leave. "One more thing. Do either of these men look familiar to you?" Roman passed her the two pictures, holding them casually between his index and middle fingers.

Less than twenty-four hours since one of these guys killed the other.

She stared quietly at them, holding them curiously close to her breasts, which were still uncovered. From his angle he could look down past her hands and see the hard corners of the photos passing close her skin as she breathed, less than an inch above her nipples. After a few seconds, he noticed goosebumps beginning to form and raised his eyes to hers. Despite her occupation, Roman felt guilty for staring and was slightly embarrassed to see that her eyes were no longer on the photos but staring back at him. "Are you fucking serious?"

"What?"

"I have no idea who this one is." She handed back the picture of Paul Derocher. "But this guy is a regular. Is this who got killed in the alley?"

"You know him?"

"He is a regular. I think his name is Max. He started showing up a few months ago. Had some money to throw around."

"You work on Sundays?"

"No. Maybe I don't know exactly what is going on, but this guy came in here. A lot."

"It seems strange to me that a gay man would spend a lot of time in a strip club on nights when the entertainment is entirely women."

"If this guy was gay, someone forgot to tell him." She handed back the photo and placed the neck loop of her untied top over her head and turned around. "Can you tie me up?"

Roman carefully tied a shoelace bow and patted her on the shoulder. "I guess it is possible that he was a bisexual."

"Maybe. But he sure loved the ladies."

Roman found his own way back to the table where he had left Anthony and found a new party of young assholes. In his brief absence the bar had become significantly more crowded. Roman wondered if Dave, overwhelmed by the lineup of money that was desperate to get inside, had decided to loosen the capacity restrictions.

"Roman!" he heard the voice and spun dumbly to locate its source. One of the unfortunate side effects of military service is hearing damage, which, when uneven, causes an impairment in one's ability to locate sound. "Roman! Up here!" Anthony yelled again. He turned and saw his friend, alone, sitting at a VIP table with a bottle of Tang10, tonic water, and a two empty glasses.

This fuckin' guy. Asshole doesn't even like gin.

"What are you doing?" Roman asked after ascending the stairs to the ultra-exclusive upper section of the club.

"Man. If we're going to go out on a Monday, let's go all in."

"You think I'm drinking that whole bottle?"

"Just have a couple. Don't be a fag."

Roman's phone vibrated, and he was happy to see that the message came from the newest number in his contact list. He opened it and was surprised to see a picture. The photo was a nude woman, lying on her back with her head hanging over the edge of the bed. She had one arm across her stomach and the other holding the camera at an angle specifically chosen to hide the upper half of her face. Her mouth, painted with red lipstick, was open wide and smiling, revealing straight white teeth and a tongue that was sticking out seductively, as if to catch a snowflake. Her legs were lifted vertically, one bent with a small gap between her thighs. It could have been a picture of any woman if Roman didn't have such a recent and vivid memory of her. A text followed up the picture.

"I think you paid enough to deserve this."

"You are a clever girl. You should go to school."

"School isn't cheap."

"Hey, man." Roman tapped Anthony on the back as he was pouring their drinks. "Just a few and we'll head home. OK?"

"Sure thing." The clear liquid splashed up this inside of the glass as Anthony poured enthusiastically.

XVI

With all the balance he could muster, Roman almost entered his home quietly. The difference in elevation to which he had become accustomed in three years had not changed. His ability to judge it blindly had. Like his judgement, his balance was impaired by the drinks that had flowed more easily as the night had progressed. He fell loudly into his hallway, dropping his keys and phone, which crashed across the floor.

"Shut up! You fuckin', keys."

He climbed to his feet and, after centring himself, closed the door softly. He braced himself on the back of his couch as he entered the living room and kicked off his shoes. He then performed an exaggerated tactical roll over the couch, landing in a half-sitting position. He flipped the TV on and turned it to a sports channel—it did not matter which one—and reduced the volume to nearly silent. Beside his TV, in the corner of his living room, was a half-sized black fridge. It was within his ability to walk over, but in an attempt to let his girlfriend sleep, he crawled across the carpet to retrieve a bottle of Hendrick's, a glass, and a can of tonic water.

In the centre of his own universe, Roman stared blankly through the flashing colours coming from his television screen. He mixed a strong drink with the expensive gin. Upstairs, hopefully still sleeping, was his girlfriend and soon to be fiancée. He imagined her curled up inside a mountain of blankets, cocooned and warm.

A few houses down, and illuminated by the soft glow of the streetlights, his friend was entering his own home much more gracefully than Roman. The Hyundai Elantra Roman had hired through an app on his phone was already making a turn to vacate his quiet cul-de-sac.

Across the city in a safe residential neighbourhood his truck was parked against the curb. The alley, less than a football toss away, was flooded with the flashing red and blue lights of squad cars that had finally arrived. The crowd outside of Eden, which had spilled earlier into the alley behind it, dispersed like startled cockroaches.

North of a home improvement retailer and over a fence, three undercover cars were waiting stealthily for any sign of Paul Derocher. Coming in or out of his apartment by way of alley or road, he could not go unnoticed. It had been suggested by Fat Frank and approved by Captain Massey that a silent drone, equipped with infrared and thermal optics, would patrol the area. Two more undercover teams worked in shifts to watch the area around St. Joseph's Basilica, Paul's last known location. Every bus station and the international airport had their systems primed to flag Paul's ID if he tried to leave the city.

In her home in St. Albert, Captain Massey turned sleeplessly, hung up on the loose net that had been cast and the abundance of resources that had been allocated to the investigation. She checked her phone for updates and was disappointed. The media had been alerted and, despite all efforts to avoid leaks, they had more information than what was intended. Major broadcasters ran fear-inducing stories. The citizens of the city watched, horrified, from their homes, or partied hopefully around the released murder locations.

Roman sipped his drink. He sank back into the couch, listening to the ringing that reminded him of his ever-worsening hearing damage. His heart beat steadily against the inside of his chest, pushing thinned blood through his over rested muscles. He hadn't exercised in days. His eyes were fixed without focus through the TV screen. Behind his blank stare he was internally reviewing the horrific image of Max Cardinal, rigid and frail on the cold steel. He could still taste the air. The memories of that chemical smell, that bitter taste, would be forever bound to that moment. He had not received a phone call or text message from the office or his partner. No communication meant that no one had eyes on the target. If the pattern continued, there would be another body in the morning.

The sky was starless. The air was static. The dark clouds that had been easing their way toward the city now shrouded it, snuffing out any light that was reflected off the moon. When the storm finally broke, there was little warning. An experienced fisherman or sailor may have docked, but an interchangeable resident of the great oil city would be caught easily. The temperature dropped rapidly, and the first few drops were scattered, fat, and random. With a few ugly and powerful gusts of damp wind, the hard rain finally fell, flooding the alleys and gutters. It pooled in the uneven asphalt that was caused by the ever-fluctuating temperatures and blinded those who were staring through windshields, whether moving or stationary. An expensive surveillance drone was forced to the ground and recovered by its pilot.

Roman drifted to sleep on his leather couch, drink in hand. The stress of the day cycled repeatedly in his mind. Every event occupied a few seconds before another, seemingly more important memory, stole his attention. Each fading thought started differently, but ultimately ended the same.

Where the fuck are you?

Tuesday

"I am trusting in the Lord and a good lawyer"

- Oliver North

I

By several minutes, she entered ahead of him. He was parked so that the rising sun would silhouette his van, rendering him all but invisible. The door closed behind her, marking the start of his window. Unlike others that had moved to a scanner and turnstile, WE Fitness employs a receptionist to track its members as they enter and exit. He was a member. In previous visits, he had noticed how loosely they watch the door, yet he never expected to use that information.

There were five of them when it happened. Two middle-aged women from separate cars had a brief conversation in the parking lot before heading inside. He would have passed it up if not for the three younger men, all arriving together, who converged with them on the door. The first woman waited as the second held the door for the first young man. He, too, waited patiently as his two workout partners passed in, followed by a man who dressed unrecognizably in a mismatched track suit, large sunglasses, and a faded Edmonton Oilers ball cap. Unbeknownst to the five that created his Trojan horse, the last to enter had plans to take a life. It would be the fourth in as many days.

The women broke off from the group and struck up a conversation, which was likely structured around daily pleasantries and weather, with the receptionist. Behind the three men, who had no interest in his actions, he made his way to the left, where he would change from his outdoor shoes. His heart rate increased, as did his breathing. He felt a cool rush of sweat trickle out through his pores. It was possible that he could be recognised, despite his clever disguise. Hiding in plain sight was his bet. Aside from dressing slightly differently than usual, he had shaved his three days of facial hair into a goatee and dyed it.

The three men who provided his camouflage walked to the receptionist to check in. He followed a few paces behind, watching carefully from the corner of his eye for an opening. She turned her eyes slightly to review something on the computer screen, and he broke from the group and started toward the changeroom. He walked casually, ignoring the adrenaline that was pulsating through his veins. He did not turn back to see if she saw. If she did, he hoped, she did not care.

He would never know how successful his first phase had been. In the changeroom, he considered three possibilities. The first was that he'd entered the gym unnoticed. The second was that the receptionist saw him, did not recognise him, and did not bother to stop him. The third, and worst possible case, was that she saw him, recognised him, and signed him in. Although dangerous, the third scenario did not imply absolute failure. He circled the changeroom, reconfirming what he already knew. The EXIT signs were not illuminated from behind, and there were no emergency lights. He noticed this first during a short power outage nearly six months prior. At the time, he did not consider the information to be useful, only that the fine for improper lighting in the event of a power outage was likely small enough that management never bothered to install a backup generator. He had been swimming at the time and had to find his way to the lockers in complete darkness.

The pool had large, west-facing windows. Due to several requests from its members, the gym had the blinds closed. In the afternoon, light from the setting sun could get through. This early in the day, he bet that, with the power out, it would be as dark as the changeroom. After ensuring that new lighting was not installed and that the changeroom was empty, he checked his watch and changed from his tracksuit into a pair of swim trunks. He did not remove his socks. He shoved the tracksuit into the bottom of the bag and retrieved a set of latex gloves and night-vision goggles. The NVGs were easy to acquire. It was an impulse while online shopping and plain curiosity that had made him click "Buy Now." He had only used them once before. He kept everything inside the bag so they were easily accessible, but not visible to anyone who might enter.

The entrance to the pool was through the changeroom. He looked quickly over his shoulder for any obstacles that could disrupt him during the short distance he would have to travel blind. Aside from an awkwardly placed step dividing the tiled shower location from the carpeted changeroom, he was clear. It was no more than thirty feet. If he followed the wall on the right, he would pass the sauna. The wall on the left had a large opening with showers. He opted to follow the right if he got lost. So, he waited, keeping his eyes on the changeroom door. If another person entered it would not compromise his plan. It would only add another factor that could work against him.

He stared at his watch. The seconds ticked down. He struggled to maintain the steady pace of his breathing. His vision narrowed. In the final seconds before passing through the Rubicon, he considered alternate scenarios. He could run. He could leave the building and get in the van. He could drive away and leave behind what he'd worked to protect.

But how far could I get?

He carefully separated the latex gloves and stretched them over his hands. The last second on his watch dropped off, and he paused the timer to prevent the audible signal. The lights snapped out, and, with them, the calm background music of the gym. It was replaced immediately by the unsettled groans of early morning gym-goers. He darted quickly to the changeroom door and closed it softly. He locked it and spun around. Thirty feet plus the distance to his bag. He grabbed the NVGs on the way and turned them on. He wasted no time and took long and powerful steps, clearing the changeroom in a few silent seconds. As he passed into the shower area, his foot caught the elevated barrier and he sprawled forward. The NVGs bounced off the ground in front of him. He crawled blind on all fours, thrashing furiously back and forth on the wet floor to feel for them. He could attempt to complete his task blind, which would create new complications, but he could not leave behind the serialized NVGs. He crawled around, turning left and right, and then slammed headfirst into a tiled corner edge of the shower area.

"Fuck!" he cried in frustration. He reached up to feel for blood but thought better of it. His eyes fought impossibly to adjust to the darkness. As they did, he noticed a small green light on the ground. The goggles had powered on, and he crawled over and pulled them over his head. He kept one eye shut and allowed his other to adjust to the brightness inside. He was still completely blind and switched on the IR flashlight. The entire area became immediately clear. He spun briefly to look for the corner where he had hit his head. Impaired by a lack of depth perception and colourblindness, he forfeited an attempt to search for any DNA evidence that he could leave behind. He pushed open the door to the pool area and lifted the NVGs off his face. He opened the previously closed eye, which would still be adjusted to the darkness, to test the visibility. It was as dark as the changeroom. He pulled the goggles over his face and confirmed that no potential witness was in the area.

Like an apex predator hunting an unsuspecting prey, he approached her. She was climbing cautiously from the pool, testing every step for grip before moving her next limb. His socks had a thick sole, and with the faint sound drowned out by the gentle lapping of the previously disturbed water against the sides of the pool, he knew she could not hear his carefully placed steps. He circled around her, his breathing shallow and soft, looking for the best direction of approach. At the top of the ladder, she stood with her feet in the water, holding onto the handrails. He maintained his distance. She was athletic and shorter than average. There was no doubt that he could do it. It had to be quiet. Although time was a factor, he could not risk giving away his presence. If, even for a split second, she became aware of the situation, she would scream. He would not take the risk. He slid a step closer, just out of arm's reach.

I can't do it from this angle.

She stood on the top step, seemingly paralyzed by blindness.

Have I come too far?

The seconds were agonizing.

I could leave.

He looked back at the changeroom door.

No one knows I'm here.

He backed up and started for the door, keeping an eye on her. She squatted down and up, testing the strength in her legs, and then lowered herself down into the pool. He stopped, watching for an opportunity. She was nearly shoulder deep.

I can drop on her if she lets go of the ladder.

The small light would give him away in the dark, so he was not wearing his watch, yet he could feel the seconds falling off and closing his window. He stood still, fighting to control his breathing and losing strength in his legs.

Give me a reason.

She rolled her shoulders and started quickly up the ladder. She climbed out and started toward the towel rack. He closed the distance, still taking soft and deliberate steps, and moved between her and the pool. He braced himself with a low, wide stance and reached a fully extended arm over her shoulder, cupping her mouth. With all the force he could squeeze from every connecting muscle, he pulled her backward, thrusting his hip low into hers. Her feet squeaked as they slipped from the wet surface. For a moment she was airborne. Her legs swung upward toward the ceiling. Her torso was flat, parallel to the floor. Her arms reached forward, grasping at the emptiness for balance. His grip softened through the motion, and she inhaled sharply. Her lungs filled with a high-pitched wheezing sound as she processed the attack. Her exhale would have been a scream. The killer drove her downward as her body rotated backward. With her weight and his downward force, the back of her skull impacted the uncompromising tile floor. It was from the sound, not the visibility allowed by his NVGs, that he was able to confirm the effectiveness of the impact. Like dropped melon, the back of her head met the tile with a hollow, popping sound. His stomach churned at the noise. It was far more barbaric than he had imagined.

Her limp body fell to the floor awkwardly. He knelt beside her and watched her chest rise and fall unevenly. Her head had impacted inches from the edge of the pool. Had he moved on her a second earlier, she would be awake and fighting him in the water. He grabbed her by the ankles and spun her around so that she was lying lengthwise on the edge of the pool. With one hand under her shoulder and one under her thigh, he rolled her into the water. She was heavy. She did not struggle for air. He watched for less time than he planned, but for long enough to ensure she would not wake up.

He turned and walked evenly toward the changeroom. He used a comfortable pace, focusing on each step. He was on the backside of a mountain, escaping with time to spare. Seconds counted less than mistakes. He shuffled through the shower area and into the changeroom. The door was still closed and locked. He peeled off his wet socks and swim trunks. He stuffed them in the bag. He donned his pants and indoor shoes. He zipped the top of the track suit up to his neck to hide his bare chest. He left the goggles and gloves on until he got to the changeroom door. Then those too were unceremoniously shoved in the bag, which he zipped closed.

He opened the changeroom door with his sleeve and stepped out into the main gym area. It was dark, but with some visibility from the windows and scattered cell phone flashlights. Only minutes had passed since the power went out. Members were gathered into small groups, discussing whether to stay. The more enduring ones continued to train. Employees, working hourly, debated lazily about what to do. Despite his racing heart, he moved casually to the front. The room was dark enough that he could skip the sunglasses and hat, which at this point felt like overkill. He grabbed his outdoor shoes and stepped into the sunlight, fighting the overwhelming urge to break into a run. He did not stop to retrieve his device, which he had used to kill the power. It was homemade and not traceable.

As he walked from the building, the image of her chest rising and falling swirled in his head. The sound of the impact against the tiles echoed in between his ears, causing the same awful sensation in his stomach. He tried to hide his gagging as he climbed into the panel van. His eyes welled, and his mouth sank. He turned on the engine and pulled out onto the street. As he drove, he painfully relived those few seconds. The sound of her feet slipping. Her last conscious breath startled and gasping. The soft feeling of her mouth against his gloved hand. The worst was the dead weight of her body, that only seconds before had felt so light, as he rolled her into the water. Each fresh and horrifying memory repeated in turn until he turned off the street and into a parking lot around the corner. He took several heavy breaths before punching blindly into the dashboard of the van, screaming with fury. He cussed wildly, throwing several heavy blows until the touchscreen cracked. He felt no pain in his hand. After exhausting himself, he leaned into the steering wheel and cried. He shook and sobbed for several minutes until he gained enough strength to drive again.

The employees of the gym did nothing about the power outage for nearly twenty minutes. After emergency services were called, it was ten minutes before they arrived and another fifteen before they found the body. As planned, no one had seen or noticed the killer.

II

The song was soft and cheerful when he first heard it. It was distant, as if playing quietly in his mind. He shifted his focus to locating its source and it easily amplified. He pressed harder, deep within his memory, to locate its origin. It was artificial, with a soft, humming harmony, followed by a metallic melody. The sound grew and quickly became overpowering. He tried to dial down his focus, but he had lost control. Each wave increased in intensity. It pounded wildly, repeating its torturous beat. It was a song that was incredibly fresh in his memory and lost at the same time, like a simple forgotten word. The agonizing scream of electric chimes blended seamlessly into the last few seconds of his dream, and he was briefly aware that he was asleep. Chased away were random images that would soon be forgotten.

My phone. Fuck off.

He relaxed in his seat. From the smell and feel of the leather he could tell, with his eyes closed, that he was in his living room. He let the phone run its course, ignoring whatever responsibility was prying for attention. He opened his eyes slowly and let the last undisrupted memories tell him why he was not in his bed. The answer was there, he just had to dig. It does not impair your ability to remember, just the process by which memories are formed.

Gin. Asshole doesn't even like gin.

The phone rang again. If it was the same person calling, the length of time between calls implied a high level of importance. He looked at his watch and decided to let it go to voicemail. In front of him, on the glass surface of his coffee table, was a bottle of Hendrick's, which was depressingly approaching emptiness. *I'll have to get more today.* Beside it, there were two cans of tonic water. Being one who mixes them strong, Roman figured he had done most of the damage to that bottle last night. It was still sour on his breath and tight in his head. Silently, a top-ten countdown listed off achievements of great athletes. Curious to see what exact moments were being counted, he searched for the remote. It was on the floor between his feet with the batteries scattered. "Fuck that," his voice squeaked out dryly. The repetitive song originating on his kitchen counter ceased.

After failing the first attempt, Roman forced himself onto his feet. He combed his fingers through his hair, tugging softly, as he walked to the kitchen. The noisy culprit had been placed neatly beside his keys and wallet. In between the phone and coffee maker, he found two full glasses, one of orange juice and the other of water. Two tabs of Alka Seltzer and a note had been placed beside the water glass. "Coffee is ready to go." An empty mug occupied the single cup section of his coffee maker. He hit the 10oz button to start the machine and then dropped the two tabs into his water. Checking his phone, he saw two missed calls from captain Massey.

Can you fuck off already?

He also received a text message from a contact labelled "Cindy." He opened the message and saw three names and phone numbers followed by a message. "Told you I would come through."

He scrolled up past a long conversation that had started with a nude photo. The original conversation, which they'd had in lieu of a private dance, was not a memory that eluded him. He drank the juice with one breath and scrolled to the bottom of the conversation, screenshotting the three names and numbers that had cost him nearly $500. He watched the dissolving tabs bounce in the bottom of the water glass and then deleted the conversation, and the nude picture with it. He then blocked the number, deleted the contact, and cropped the photo of the contacts so that only the three names and numbers for which he paid remained.

He swirled the water glass to force the sediment from the bottom and then drank deeply. His coffee, which had brewed in under a minute, was still blisteringly hot, and he chased each sip with the water. He then sat back down on the couch and redialed Captain Massey. His eyes burned dryly. He covered them with his hands, resting his elbows on his knees, and left the phone ring on speaker.

Don't answer.

On the second ring, she did. "Are you serious?"

"What?"

"How many times do I have to call you?"

"I was in the shower. What do you want me to do?" He cleared his throat, which still produced a pre-pubescent-sounding squeak with every second word.

"Whatever. Don't make me call you twice. He's here."

"Who's there? Moussa?" Roman asked, still groggy and trying to understand the faint but noticeable alarm in her voice. "Good. Lazy fucking asshole."

"No, and I'm not sure Moussa is the lazy asshole between the two of you, but that's a different conversation. Paul. Paul Derocher. He's here."

"Sorry, what?!" Roman felt immediately more awake. "He's where?"

"Here. At the station."

"Why? Who grabbed him? We made it strictly clear that we were watching. Was he caught in the act or, or what?"

"He came in. He wants to confess."

"Are you fucking with me? No."

"Yes."

"You want me to believe that the man killed three people, and just walked in and said, 'I'm here. I did it'?"

"Right up to the front desk and dropped his ID. He said he wanted to confess and that we know what for."

"He's arrested? Jesus, fuck. That was easy."

"Not arrested. He hasn't made a statement."

"Why not? Get someone in there and get it out of him. Like, did a fish just jump into the boat? Smack him with a bottle and wrap this up." Roman was fighting between disbelief in the fact that Paul Derocher had walked into a police station to confess and that an office of trained detectives had not taken his statement. Mixed feelings of joy and rage.

"We tried. Obviously. And I'm not appreciating your tone. More to follow. He dropped your business card on the desk with his ID and stated that he would make a confession to you and no one else. He went on to say that if the next person he spoke to was anyone but Detective Owen, the only word we would hear ever from him was 'lawyer.' So, if it pleases you, get the fuck down here and take the boy's statement." She never raised her voice. Her inflections did more than volume ever could.

"I'm on my way." Roman drained his coffee in a single gulp and did the same with his water. He ascended the stairs, sniffing his armpits, and into his ensuite. He layered his deodorant on thick, showered in body spray and grabbed the bottle of mouthwash. His plan was to rinse his mouth several times on the drive. His pistol was on his dresser, still holstered on a belt with a pair of pants. He changed quickly and ran out the front door. Upon arriving at his driveway, he cussed in frustration with a crescendo that emptied his lungs. His impaired mind remembered only in that moment that his truck was parked a block from the strip club. He hopped across two lawns, trying to avoid a full sprint, to Anthony's door. It was unlocked and he entered without knocking.

"Asshole! Get up!"

"What the fuck?" His friend called from his bedroom. "Go home, you prick. What time is it?"

"I need a ride. Now." He lowered his voice slightly, but it was still loud enough to express his desperation.

"What, why?" Anthony emerged at the top of the stairs in plaid pajama pants and a plain T-shirt.

"It's a whole thing. Guy wants to confess. We have to go."

"Confess to what? Who?" Anthony's friendly tone hadn't broken, nor had his persistent lack of vigour. He spoke slowly and charismatically, intentionally frustrating Roman. "Can't it wait? Let me at least make a coffee."

"The fucking murders that I have been investigating. My truck is at the strippers. You have to drive me to work."

"Fine." Anthony yawned, starting to make his way down the stairs, "Wait, what? There is a guy who wants to, um admit, confess? To those murders?"

"Apparently." Roman felt that he could not express well enough the gravity of the situation. Anthony stared into his thoughts, looking deeply confused, as he walked without focus down the stairs. He looked at Roman, questioning the situation before Roman continued. "I know. It makes no sense. But time is a factor. Come on."

"All good." He yawned again. "I'll drive you."

III

It was quieter than it had been the day before. He marched silently through the building. They watched. He pressed his eyes to the floor. There was no fake work to imply disinterest. His new reputation preceded him. He was a fabled champion who had left a business card, and with that short conversation, successfully encouraged a serial killer to walk into a police station. They stared in awe, afraid to interfere. Around each corner it burdened him. Had he known which words were spoken to incite such peculiar behaviour, he would not have felt like such an imposter.

This makes no sense.

He could feel their contempt as he passed by. Unchanged and unshaven, he did not live up to the conquering hero that was expected. Each in turn was agitated by the fragrance that wafted behind him. The undeserved silent ovation ended in his wake. The last office before the hallway was that of Captain Massey. The lack of sleep and residual effects of alcohol weakened his resolve. The situation overwhelmed him. As if walking through a dream, he questioned the legitimacy of every passing scene. He followed the hallway without a briefing and quickly found himself on the hidden side of a two-way mirror.

It won't be him.

It was. Roman looked through the window at the relaxed eyes of the young red-haired man. The lone officer to Roman's left, assigned to watch Paul Derocher, shifted his gaze between the two. Only one could see the other, but they appeared to be in a stare down. The look on Paul's face was unsettling. He was calm and collected. He showed no signs of fear. He had swelling around on the left side of his face. Roman studied the damage, assessing the healing process. As if he could sense Roman through the glass, Paul stretched his lips into a thin smile and then turned his gaze to the door. After a few seconds, he returned it to the mirror.

Fucking creep.

"Roman." It was Captain Massey's voice that broke the silence. He turned, and at the end of the hallway she stood with a thick file. In only a day it had grown from a pathetic stack of three sheets to a bulging mess. "If you are done with the pleasantries, I would like to review some information with you." Her monotone sarcasm was familiar to Roman, and implied good news that was too sensational to be spoken outside of closed doors. Before following her, he stared one more time into Paul's eyes, trying eagerly to get a read.

He closed the door behind himself as they entered her office. "Sorry it took me so long to get here, Captain."

"It may have worked to our favour." She placed the file between them but left her hand on top with her fingers splayed.

"How is that?"

"When you told me that you were going to the strip club yesterday. I didn't think in a million years that you were telling the truth."

"I was working."

"You smell like you were working."

"I wanted to see if I could get the contact information for the previous night's entertainment. Apparently, it's only men on Sunday nights. The entertainment I mean."

"I feel like you could have figured that out."

"I'm not finished. I wanted to know if Max and Paul were seen on the night of the murder. The manager had no interest in giving me any ID records or footage without a warrant. The most recent victim—"

"The one that you identified?" It was not really a question, although she presented it as such.

"That's the one. I knew him many years ago. I never had any idea that he was gay. And it just so happens that he was a regular and on nights other than Sunday. Either he was not gay, or he was bisexual. Seems weird right?"

"That is incredibly underwhelming, considering we have your primary suspect next door, waiting to confess to the murders."

Roman made an expression which suggested that he was ready to let it go. "This file is thick. More than yesterday."

"When he showed up here, we entered his apartment."

"You entered Paul's apartment? Without a warrant?"

"You know, while you run around putting emphasis on the sexuality of our victims and conducting routine interviews, I actually do real police work. One thing that I can do is get warrant." She took her hand off the file. Roman snatched it with a playful, mocking gesture.

"Anything in there?"

"They found heroin on the counter. We had Cardinal's blood

tested and confirmed that he was a user."

"Ketamine?"

"No. We also found a garbage bag containing clothing and an Afghanistan Campaign Star."

Roman looked up from the file. "Cardinal's?"

"Likely. And a Browning 9mm on the floor."

"Registered?"

"We aren't that lucky. We did have it tested for prints."

"And?"

"He must have been sweaty the last time he used it."

"Derocher?"

"It was recovered in Derocher's apartment, yes. The last person to handle that weapon was Cardinal."

"Jesus. We have to sweep for a DNA sample."

"Forensics is going through the building, but you know as well as I do that he was there. Based on the age of the print, and the uncleaned heroin on the counter. This could be the last location where he was alive."

"We're thin on this one, Captain."

"We also found a phone."

"Derocher's or Cardinals?"

"Can't tell. We gave it to the tech department to see if they can unlock it."

"What kind of phone?"

"iPhone. Why?"

"Take it to the morgue and see if you can unlock it with his corpse. Has the weapon been fired?"

"Jammed."

"Typical. I really wish we had a DNA link."

"We have a motive. We have a likely suspect with a history of mental illness. We can confirm that they were in close contact right to the end. They knew each other through work. There's an unregistered firearm with the last victim's prints."

"Awe, come on. This is circumstantial. What do we think happened? Derocher doesn't shoot his victims. Two were beat to death and the last was tased and suffocated."

"Last time I spoke to your partner, he told me that *you* were very confident that the first two victims were alive when he moved them. We have no confirmation, no cameras or witnesses or credit card transactions that put the victims in the supposed locations of their deaths. Is it possible that at some point in his game, Derocher holds these people at gunpoint? Maybe Cardinal decided to not play along. Maybe he decided not to take the ketamine? *Maybe* it gets out of control and Derocher decides to shoot him."

"The ultra-reliable Browning misfires. Carinal disarms him, tries to chamber another round and the gun jams."

Captain Massey nodded in agreement. "Derocher tases him and decides to suffocate him before he regains control."

Roman thought for a few seconds before speaking. "Please tell me there was a misfired round in the apartment."

"No. Sorry. That would have been good, but it would also be easy to take just it on the way out."

"Why? Why take the round and leave the gun?"

"That would be a fantastic detail to get from Derocher's

statement. Speaking of that, in two or three days, I am confident that we can get a DNA match from the other bodies or crime scenes. But if we don't, we are going to need a really solid confession. I don't want 'I did it. I'm sorry'. We need details. He has to know exactly what happened. We need something that the media doesn't know. Don't ask him about the gun. See if he brings it up on his own."

"If the guy is here to make a confession, he will want to tell the story. I need a coffee, and a bagel or something."

"And a breath mint."

IV

He closed the door gently and took a seat across the table from Paul. As the room was constantly being recorded, the device that he placed on the table was for dramatic effect. Without saying a word, he opened and began silently reviewing the file. He sat back from the table, still upright, with enough space to open and flip through the pages without revealing the contents. Paul sat across the table and stared. To a less experienced detective, Paul's expression would have been blank and emotionless. In between pages, Roman peeked up and noticed his eyes were open wider than normal. There was a forced flatness to Paul's mouth. From farther away he could not see it. Up close, Paul was anxious.

"Detective Owen." Paul broke the silence. Roman had expected to wait longer. He wanted to hear the tone in Paul's voice before he began. There was a slight drop in the strength of his voice on the second syllable. Anxiety was confirmed.

"Paul Derocher." Roman spoke with his eyes still in the file. "How can I help?"

"It's DERocher, not DerochER."

"My apologies. Last time we spoke, you chose not to give me your name."

"I do not consider myself to be that man. Not anymore."

"Have you been read your rights?" He raised his expressionless eyes to meet Paul's.

"Yes."

"You understand that this conversation is being recorded?"

"I do."

"If you don't consider yourself to be Paul Derocher, what should I call you?"

Paul paused. He lowered his eyes from Roman's to his own hands. "Have you read the Bible?"

Roman looked at Paul's uncuffed hands. "Parts of it."

"Have you read Galatians 2:20?"

"You will have to refresh my memory." Roman remained flat and expressionless, portraying the idea that he was disinterested in Paul's confession.

"I am, in body, Paul Derocher. I can only imagine the horrible things you have in that file. I swear that I am no longer him."

"You understand that legally you *are* Paul Derocher?"

"Of course."

"OK." Roman spoke softly. He adopted a tone that would cause the least offence, mimicking what one would expect to hear on public radio: "You know, I wasn't here when you came in. I came from home, actually."

"Although this is your place of employment, I understand that you can not be here all the time."

"I don't want you to feel like I intentionally kept you waiting."

"I can tell from the way you smell that you did not take your time getting here. That I do appreciate."

"Why don't you tell me why we're here?"

"We are here because I decided to turn myself in."

"Excellent."

"Well, here I am."

Without a hangover, Roman felt he would be better equipped to manage the situation. He knew how carefully his words needed to be chosen. He could not lead the conversation. If the lab came back negative on a DNA match, they would be relying heavily on this confession. If Roman did lead the conversation, trapping Paul with a series of carefully placed tactics, it would be inadmissible as evidence. "What should I call you?"

"You can call me whatever you like."

"Can I call you Paul?"

"If you think it suits me."

"Well, Paul," Roman said, placing the file, closed, on the table between them. "I don't think that I have to tell you what is in this file."

"Maybe you should. Seeing as how I have not read it; I can not know for sure what is in there."

"Could you guess? What would you bet is in here?"

"I am not a betting man, but if I was to make a bet, I think I would be accurate."

He carefully studied Paul's body language. The way he sat, the way he held his hands, and the expression on his face told Roman that the young man was becoming more comfortable. Roman's hope was that Paul's comfort would be with him, and not with the interrogation itself. "You know, we don't always get everything right. Not at the beginning, anyway. We piece things together from the clues that are left behind. Is there anything that I might have in here that you want to clarify? Maybe something that we could've gotten wrong?"

"That depends."

"On what does that depend?"

"Since you are telling me that for all legal proceedings, I am Paul Derocher, I would wager that there is a very extensive history in there. A story about how I came to be."

"That would be a smart bet."

"So, like I was saying, it depends."

"On?" Roman's capacity to hide his irritation was dwindling.

"It depends, in my opinion, anyway, on how thoroughly you have reviewed that file."

"Let's assume that I have not reviewed this file in great detail."

"If you have not reviewed the file in detail, I would say that maybe you should. How could I correct misinformation if you are not misinformed to begin with?"

"You and I both know that isn't the case. I have in fact reviewed this file thoroughly. I assisted in compiling it."

"Can you tell me what you think? And if you say something that is wrong, I might correct you."

"Why am I here?" Roman decided to pivot the conversation.

"You work here."

"Why am I here, in this room, right now?"

"Because you gave me a business card."

"Why do you think I gave you a business card?" He allowed himself to express that he was becoming annoyed.

"You are investigating a crime, and you think I can help."

"Can you?"

"Yes."

"Will you?"

"Yes."

"Please, go ahead." Roman pushed the recording device closer to Paul, suggesting that now was the time to speak into the microphone.

"You know just about everything you need to know about me. It's all in that file. But I know nothing about you."

Roman noticed that the red-haired man had, for the first time since they met, acknowledged that he was Paul Derocher. "What do you want to know?"

"Do you believe in God?"

"I am not a man of faith. You and I have had this conversation."

"Twice. The sky, as it seems, is great and powerful. Through God, one might ascend through the clouds into His kingdom, correct?"

"Maybe according to you."

"No. Not according to me. When you lie in the grass and stare at the stars, it is down as much as it is up. The blueness of the sky is gone after a hundred kilometers. You are not staring, from a place of safety, into a universe of wonder. You are staring into the depths of an abyss, held in place, quite precariously, by a force that we cannot explain. Is it measurable? Yes. Definable? Understood? No. Without God's grace, you might drift for an eternity into oblivion, clawing desperately at the earth as it eases from your feet. There is a great amount of trust that you place into things so far from your own comprehension. That trust is your faith." Paul breathed heavily and shoved back the hairs that had fallen on his face.

"So what? If we gain a better understanding of gravity, you will renounce your faith? Is that it? The last piece of the puzzle?"

Paul slammed an open palm on the metal table between them, causing an echo in the small room that disturbed Roman's tinnitus. "You are still not listening. The fact that it exists in the first place, so absolutely definable and consistent *IS* the miracle."

"If you say so."

"Could you feel God when you entered the church?"

"Should I be able to?"

"When I step inside that building, He overpowers me. He overwhelms me. His greatness surrounds and penetrates me. Surely you felt something." There was warmth and desperation in his words. Unlike his earlier emotions, this display was undoubtedly genuine. Roman thought about Captain Massey's "bipolar" hypothesis.

Great actors train for years to transition emotions like this.

"If I told you that I felt God, His greatness, inside the church, could we get back to the reason why you and I are here?"

"That *is* the reason why we are here!" he yelled again. This time, the corners of his eyes started to pool with tears.

"I have never had a direct, religious experience. Have you ever spoken to God?"

"Those who say they have not truly felt the Lord are refusing, or plainly lying. You can say to me right now that you have not spoken to God, but I assure you that you have. He may speak through the mortal flesh of man, or through divine visions. His voice is quiet if you

283

choose not to hear and His signs are subtle, especially if you choose not to see."

"Have you spoken to God?"

"He has spoken to me."

"Has He told you to do things?" Roman knew he was pressing. He had drawn close to the line of questioning that might waste the interview.

"There are those who have received direct instructions from the Lord. Their stories are documented. For the rest of us, we follow those teachings in the Bible."

"Do you ever feel like those teachings leave a lot to be interpreted?"

The young man pursed his lips as he thought. His friendly stare grew cold. "Even the laws of man leave room for interpretation."

"But the laws of man can be reviewed and altered. We adjust them as we go and mold them to fit the needs of every man, woman, and child. Since the laws of the Bible are carved in stone, what if they were misunderstood? What if someone did something evil, but for reasons he thought were justified?"

"Evil? Have you done something, Detective, that others might consider evil, or bad, or wrong, but for a good reason?"

Paul's nostrils flared as he spoke. His shoulders raised and lowered with his heavy breathing.

Yes.

Roman decided to dial back the pressure. "I may have. I think that everyone does the wrong thing every once in a while. But I also believe that in doing so, most people are justified, or at least they believe they are justified. Those actions do not necessarily make us bad people."

"And that bad thing that you did, Detective—was it justified?"

He could feel the eyes on him. The entire interview had a live audience, watching silently from behind the mirror. He wondered if Moussa was there. "I believe that it was."

"Did you make your peace with God?" His breathing slowed, and Roman could see the calmness return.

"We have spoken, you and I, a few times now about my relationship with God. Do you think that I have made my peace?"

"We have spoken, yes, but I don't believe that you have ever really told me about your relationship with Him."

"It's not good. I can tell you that much. But that isn't why we're here."

"It is the only reason why we are here." His voice was rising again. "If the relationship is not good. Why don't you fix it?"

"I didn't come here today to discuss religion. I came here because I got a phone call that said you wanted to make a confession. You said that you would only do that if I was here. Is that correct?"

"I think that our paths were meant to cross. We met twice. It was on consecutive days at the church." Paul's eyes were glossed over and again it seemed he was losing control of his emotions. "That might not mean something to you, but it means something to me."

"Did you come here to confess to a crime? Or did you come here to waste my time? So far, you have more than accomplished the latter."

"I knew you would catch me. After we spoke the second time,

I knew."

"You know what I think? I don't think you did it. I think that you brought me here to talk about God. You wanted to play a game with me and pretend that you are some kind of saviour."

"I will make you an offer. I will tell you what I have done, but you have to swear on your soul that you will go back to the church and make your peace with God."

"Deal."

"Swear it."

"I swear."

"Let Him hear it."

"I swear on my soul that if you tell me what you did, I will make my peace with God."

"I did it. You showed up and told me that you were investigating it. You knew. I could see it. You knew when we spoke that it was me."

"What did you do?" Roman was leaning forward on the table; he had abandoned all tact and was prying with sincerity.

"I burned it."

"What?"

"The mosque. I burned it down."

Roman shot a quick, confused glance at the mirror behind him before returning to his questioning. "What else did you do?"

"I don't know what you mean." Paul leaned back in his chair, as if punched by the question.

"To Max. Tell me about Max Cardinal." Roman was pressing hard, speaking firmly and quickly. Paul was squirming.

"I don't know anything about him."

"Don't lie to me."

"I took him in. He had nowhere to go."

"And then what happened?"

"Nothing. I left him in my apartment. He was strung out."

"Did you kill him?"

"No."

"Yes, you did. You killed him and two others." Roman opened the folder.

"No."

"We had a deal." He put a picture of Max, dead and stripped naked, on the table between them. "Tell me what you did, and you can go home. I just need to know what happened."

"No."

A knock interrupted them. Roman ignored it, but Fat Frank popped his head in. "Detective Owen. Captain needs to see you." He glanced over at Paul, who was sweating through his shirt, and back at Roman.

"Right now?" He held back his voice but showed with his eyes how angry the interruption had made him.

"Right now," Frank answered flatly.

He sighed heavily and stared unblinking into Paul's eyes. "I'll be right back." He tucked the picture away inside the folder and took it with him.

V

As he rounded the corner, moving quickly, he bumped heavily into a sharply dressed man moving in the opposite direction. The man's shoulder landed almost directly in the centre of Roman's chest. It was a deliberate impact. Roman could tell from the force of the impact that the shoulder had been thrust and the man's feet were planted. He staggered, losing his balance and twisting as he fell. The man caught him with a firm grip, one hand on his shoulder and the other under his arm. As he was pulled back to his feet, he prepared to shove the man back against the wall. He stopped when he saw that he was looking at his partner.

"Moussa. Where the fuck have you been?"

Moussa looked left and right down the hall and into the bull pen. His hands still held Roman in place. "We have to talk."

"No shit."

"Come with me." His tone was authoritative, and he turned to walk away.

"Dude. I need to see the captain."

Moussa stopped and looked over his shoulder. "You need to come with me right fucking now." He continued walking without looking back.

Roman followed, looking over his shoulder at Captain Massey, who was waiting in her office. She beckoned him with her index finger, as they were just outside of speaking range. Roman shrugged and indicated that he meant to follow Moussa, still not knowing what it was about. Moussa moved with a powerful sense of purpose, nearly knocking down two more people on the way. He stopped at the doorway to a small unused space, the kind that was free for use to anyone who needed it but not specifically assigned. Moussa pulled open the door and pointed sharply inside, stating nonverbally that he wanted Roman to enter.

"Man, what is this about?" Roman pleaded, trying to regain control of his partner. Moussa did not reply. Instead, he grabbed Roman firmly by his shirt, first with an overhand grip and then twisting to increase the tension. Roman placed his hand on top. "Settle down. What the fuck?"

Moussa thrust Roman through the door. He could have fought back. He had known his partner to be cold and unemotional, but there was something else. Moussa had his jaw clenched firmly and his unblinking gaze fixed. After being released, Roman spun and entered the room forward. It was a small, nondescript spare office. There was an outdoor window with broken blinds, a cheap table, and two office chairs.

Have I ever been in here?

"Is this your new office or what?" Roman asked playfully, trying to lighten the mood. When he turned to face Moussa, who had gently closed the door behind them, he was met with a heavy right hook across his chin. He fell backward into the table. Using a chair for balance, he managed to stay on his feet. He stood quickly and tried to return the favour. Moussa curled his forearm to the side of his head, easily blocking the punch, and then hit Roman again. This time it was a body shot directly in the solar plexus. Roman gasped and fell. He landed sitting in the chair.

"What the fuck is wrong with you?" he yelled in desperation.

"Wrong with me? Are you serious?" Moussa's normally soothing voice was raspy and broken. As if he could hardly contain his emotions. He faked a left jab. When Roman raised his hand to block it, Moussa's open palm smacked him across the face. Before Roman composed himself to stand, Moussa, using the same hand, delivered a vicious backhand across his temple, turning Roman's head. Roman reached with his left and grabbed Moussa's arm. He shifted his weight to rise and reached out to get a hold of Moussa's shirt, but was met with a left hook. He tried to duck the shot. Moussa's knuckle connected behind his ear. The placement of the shot drew Roman momentarily away from his consciousness. He fell to a knee and released his grip on Moussa's arm. Now out of breath, Moussa straightened his shirt and stood upright. Roman looked up at him, staring befuddled at the behaviour of someone who is normally so mild mannered. Roman used the chair and table to climb back to his feet. Upon arrival he was shoved back down. Moussa pushed him hard with both hands and Roman fell over the chair, landing awkwardly on his upper back.

Lying on his back with his feet planted on the floor Roman urged his partner. "Moussa, buddy, talk to me."

"You are a stupid fucking asshole. You know that?"

"I don't know what you have been up to all day, but—" He adjusted his jaw painfully, gripping it in his hand. "Ow, fuck. But we got the guy. He is in the interrogation room. He said he burned down your mosque, too." Roman rolled onto an elbow, propping his torso up on an angle. "Are you going to let me up?"

"I don't know why I'm doing this. Probably because I consider you a friend."

The rage seemed to have subsided, but Roman opted out of standing without permission. "You have a real funny way of showing it." He waited for an explanation that did not come. He shook his head gently and felt around for bleeding. "We'll have a few beers later and talk about it. For now, though, I have to get back in that interrogation room. And the captain needs me for something."

Moussa reached into the inside pocket of his blazer. He retrieved a small envelope and placed it on the table. He then left the room without a word, closing the door gently. The small panel of glass that allowed visual access to the rest of the office was covered with blinds. No one would have seen what had transpired. Eventually, Roman rose. He studied the envelope that had been taped shut. He picked it up and could feel something small and hard inside. He shoved it his front pocket and left the room, rubbing his chin.

VI

"That was a hell of a weird tactic, Detective."

"Door open or closed?"

"Closed."

"I had him, why did you interrupt me?" Roman closed the door behind him, isolating him and his boss in her office. It pained him to imagine that behind one soundproof wall, his prime suspect was sitting alone in the interrogation room. She had a stern look on her face. She was trying to hide her emotions.

"Sit down. Please."

"Hey, I know that was a little unorthodox. But, come on, the guy could get up and leave. If he wants to play this 'Messenger from God' crap, we have to let him. It worked." He didn't sit. Instead, he stood leaning forward with his hands on her desk. His heart and mind were racing equally.

"How do you figure?" She shook her head softly, distantly, as if she did not care to hear the answer.

"I know he didn't come all the way clean, but he admitted to arson. We can hold the guy now. It can give us time to build an effective case. It actually works out better. If he lawyers up heavy, we have no obligation to disclose anything about the murders. He can build the best defence in the world on that arson charge, and in the meantime, we continue our investigation."

"Roman."

"Captain, I'm telling you. Let me finish it. The guy is ready to pop, he's teetering. He could close off or break down any second. We can't leave him like this. Right now, he probably doesn't even know how fucked he is."

"Roman. Sit down." He sat, and she continued. "I think that you are a good detective, and I do not want you to think this has anything to do with my opinion of you."

"We are saying the same thing." He forced his voice to be steady.

"Someone else is going to walk in there now and scare him into a lawyer. And if we let him sit quietly, he might come to his senses."

"Roman, I am going to take you off this case." He could hear the pain in her words. One of the strongest people he knew could hardly keep herself together.

"What are you talking about?!" He pressed his fingertips into the side of his temples. "Why? One day ago, we had nothing. Now we have a fucking maniac, a radical fucking extremist sitting next door, trying to confess." He slammed his hands on the desk and his volume increased, "And you won't let me talk to him. And I'm the person he wants to talk to! With all due respect, what the fuck are you talking about?"

Her own fingers were steepled, pressing into her lips. She had waited quietly for him to settle his tone. "When you leave my office, I want you to go down to the weapons locker and turn in your sidearm."

"What the fuck is going on?"

"You turned your phone off to conduct that interview,

correct?"

"Yes. Obviously. Why?"

"Turn it on, please."

"Fine." He held the power button until the screen lit up. He threw the phone across the table to her. "It takes like ten seconds to fully power on."

"I don't need it."

"Then why? I don't mean any disrespect here, but can you tell me what is going on?"

She turned her head to search for words. "I am really sorry that I have to have this conversation with you."

"Look at me, Captain. How long have we worked together? Whatever it is, just fucking say it."

"I am placing you on administrative leave. With pay. Indefinitely."

His phone buzzed repeatedly on the desk as it alerted him of missed calls and messages. He ignored it. "I know I haven't been my best lately." She stared silently as he ranted. "I drink a bit. So what? We are rocking this case." The memory of his most recent meeting with Sacha popped into his head. He had carefully hidden the sidearm during most of the conversation.

The waitress. Did she call 9-1-1?

"Where would we be? Is there something you need to tell me? Something that I could clear up?"

"Check your phone."

"No. Fuck that shit. I have always respected how direct you are. So be direct with me."

"You are being placed on administrative leave." She cleared her throat. "After you leave my office, you will turn in your sidearm, and you will head to this address."

"For what?"

"Alberta Medical Examiner. You need to identify—" Her voice cracked. "It is really just a formality. You need to identify another body."

"What body?"

"It's Kim." Roman noticed for the first time that her eyes were red and glossy. Her lips were pressed forcefully together.

Roman stared silently at her, searching for words and trying to process what she had said. He understood her anguish. She had struggled to tell him. His phone buzzed on the desk. "No," he replied.

"Yes."

"How?"

The words came easier. "At the gym, WE Fitness, I believe. There was a power outage. She slipped getting out of the pool."

"She slipped getting out of the pool? And, and died?"

"Yes."

They didn't speak. Instead, they sat in silence. Roman eased back into his chair, lowering his eyes to his hands. He pressed his lips together in a feeble attempt to disguise his feelings. Captain Massey turned in her chair, staring out the side window of her office. She wanted to let him stew on the information he had just received without being disturbed. He chewed the inside of his lip and then pointed past her and through the wall behind her. "What time did he get here?"

"It was an accident unless we receive some new information. They are saying that when the power went out, she slipped exiting the pool. She hit her head and fell back in the water. Pending the autopsy, they are saying she dro—"

"That is not what I fucking asked. What time did he get here?"

"Roman."

"Stop doing that."

"What?"

"Stop saying my name. That little psycho asked for me. He said that he specifically wanted to talk to me."

"Don't jump to conclusions."

For the first time in their working relationship, Roman yelled at his boss. "Don't fucking talk to me like that! We both know what I am asking, and I know damn well that you already know the answer. You've been my friend for nearly a decade. So, stop being Captain Massey for one minute, and be my fucking friend. For one goddamn minute, Julie!"

"Yes."

"Don't fuck with me."

"Yes. It is possible."

"Little freak." Roman stood up from the desk and turned for the door.

"Stop!" Her voice did nothing to slow him down. She got up after him and chased him out of the office. As she rounded the corner to the hallway, she could see his right hand resting on his sidearm. He was moving fast. In a few steps, he would be at the interrogation room.

He wrapped all four fingers around the grip, resting his index finger on the trigger guard. With his thumb, he released the mechanism that holds the issued handgun in place. As he grabbed the doorhandle with his left hand, her weight, led by her shoulder, slammed his arm into the side of his body. Her momentum pushed him past the door, and she wrapped her arms around his legs, between his hip and knee. They fell into the hard-tiled floor. Captain Massey landed on top. She quickly straddled him and adopted the "full-mount" position. With both hands, she pinned down the arm that was holding his pistol.

"Let it go," she instructed him firmly. He released the gun. "Back up!" With one free hand, she waved off the officers that had quickly closed in on the commotion and with the other she took control of the issued pistol. "Detective Owen," she said, her voice lowered to a friendlier tone. "I am not going to report this incident. You are on administrative leave. Moussa can handle this case moving forward. You have just lost your girlfriend. I understand. You have to go home and take care of that."

VII

Worried that it could draw attention, Roman put the empty holster on the passenger seat. After leaving the precinct, he had used a ride share app to get back to his truck. From what he could see, the power was still out. The front door was blocked with police tape, and a few uniformed officers were loosely scattered. He watched for a few minutes as they went about their business. Aside from the tape, there was no system of control measures in place.

He slid casually from the truck and started for the door. He had parked with a reasonable standoff to not draw attention, but close enough that it could be noticed that he did not arrive on foot. He marched toward the door, ensuring that he did not make eye contact. He was sure that they would see him and hoped that they would recognise him as a detective and not question his presence. That fantasy was ended just a few strides from the door.

"Stop. Can't go in there." The young officer had his face half stuffed with breakfast. He wiped his hands as he approached.

Roman paused and took out his wallet. "Detective Owen, homicide." He flashed his ID.

"Homicide?" The officer looked to his own partner for support. The other officer shrugged. "I didn't know this was a murder. Really?"

"I'm in a hurry," Roman stated as the man stepped casually between him and the door.

The officer gently placed his hand on Roman's chest, a

technique known as contact control. He was not physically restricting Roman's movement but suggesting that he would. He used his other hand to hit the talk button his radio and leaned into the microphone on his shoulder. "I have a Detective, uh, what did you say your name was?"

With a smooth grace that did not imply danger, Roman placed his own hand over the officer's. He smiled artificially, and then snapped his gripped closed. He pressed his own thumb into the back of the officer's hand and twisted his wrist around. The powerful motion forced the officer's shoulder to drop slightly and his forearm to become fully supinated. It was painful. "Listen. I don't know how long you've been a police officer, but I am going to give you some advice. When a homicide detective shows his badge, the last thing you should ever do is step in his way and place your hand on him. I am only going to say this once. Stand the fuck down. Or you will spend the rest of your career giving out speeding tickets." Roman released his grip.

"Let me see that badge again." Roman showed it to him and stared at his eyes while he inspected it. "Go ahead. Sorry for the misunderstanding."

"No problem at all." Roman brandished that same artificial smile as he walked by.

He had been correct about the power. Flood lights made it possible to see clearly in the main area. It was complemented by natural light spilling through the windows. Another strip of police tape blocked the entrance to the women's change room. No attention had been paid to the men's, which he used to make his way into the pool area. The blinds had been fully retracted, and no artificial lighting was required. A familiar-looking photographer made his way around, snapping various photos. Two non-uniformed officers were having a conversation at the edge of the pool. A dried blood stain was circled and, beside it, a number card had been placed. Roman felt his stomach twist and his legs lost their strength. He took a few short breaths before he spoke, projecting his voice across the room. "Doug, you lazy fuck. How are you?"

"Roman Owen," an old friend responded. "I'm really sorry, man." They exchanged a quick chest-level handshake, hug, and backslap. "Are you holding up OK?"

"I just found out. I was working a case and—"

"The gay killer, or whatever they're calling him."

Doug's partner wandered off, his radio squawking loudly. Roman watched, slightly concerned. "We have the guy in custody right now. He—"

"I heard he just showed up this morning," Doug interrupted him again. "Walked right in with your business card and said he wanted to confess." Excitement grew in his eyes and tone. "I have been around a long time and never heard of something like that. You're, like, a legend as of this morning."

"Maybe we don't talk about that right now."

"Hey, sorry, man. I sometimes forget how desensitized I am. What brings you here? I mean, I know what brings you, but, like, what can I do for you?"

"Help put my mind at ease. What do we think happened here?"

"Sorry. Well, it looks pretty straightforward. I guess the power goes out. We are thinking she falls and hits her head. There was an impact injury on the back of her skull." Doug spoke carefully, using a practiced tone that was meant for the families of victims. "She then fell in the water, either conscious or not, and was likely not able to get back out. Tentatively, we are calling it a drowning. Pending the autopsy."

"She just fell?"

"Slipped, most likely. Freak accident."

"Is there security footage?"

"Yes, but it isn't clear, can't see what happened in the darkness. If it's any consolation, someone is going down for this."

"That's for sure."

"I mean, with the power out, it is totally dark in here. Can't see two feet in front of your face. Total violation."

Doug's partner called from across the pool. "Doug, can you come here for a minute?"

"Be right back." He slapped Roman on the shoulder and turned toward his partner.

The two detectives spoke quietly while Roman wandered. He inspected the windows. He looked back and forth at the changeroom doors and then stopped at the dried blood. He stood over it, trying to imagine at which angle she would have fallen. From the pool area, a large window allowed visibility into the entrance and main gym area. He crossed his arms and studied the scene, knowing that he would not have access to the file after he left.

"Roman?" Doug and his partner meandered their way back over to him. "Are you currently on active duty?" Doug looked quickly at Roman's hip, noticing the missing sidearm.

"Technically, I am on administrative leave."

"I hate to do this, man, but you can't be here." He indicated with his palm toward the changeroom door.

"Look, I only need a few minutes. Let me have a look around."

"No can do. If Captain Massey shows up, or someone finds out I let you in here, it will be my ass on the line."

"I do not think she slipped and fell."

"That is not for you to decide right now. I know this is close to home and I can't possibly imagine how you feel, but it's protocol. You need to go."

"Right now," Doug's partner added and placed a hand on Roman's shoulder, pressing him gently toward the exit.

"Hands off." Roman snapped, and the detective quickly obliged. "Listen. Kim was a competitive athlete and swimmer. No way she fell like that."

"Roman." Doug cut in. "I am on it. Trust me."

"Did you get forensics in here? Black light? Check for bodily fluids? Come on. If you don't treat it like a homicide, you won't find anything."

"Forensics?" The partner again. "This is a gym. And a pool. Half that water is probably bodily fluids. The other half is chemicals. Chlorine and shit. Same as the showers."

"The power. How did the power go out?" Roman did not notice the volume of his own voice rising.

Doug answered this time, waving a hand toward his partner to suggest he should stand down. "We don't know yet."

"How many buildings lost power?"

"Just this one."

"That's not strange to you?" He was trying not to yell.

"We have not yet determined the cause." Doug kept his voice down, trying to de-escalate. "Probably a rat chewed through a wire or something."

"Probably a rat chewed through a wire or something? Fuck off."

The partner stepped in again. "That is enough! You are not here on police business. If you stay, you will be under arrest!" He again placed his hand on Roman's shoulder, pushing him backward toward the exit. Roman clenched his jaw as the man spoke. He stood firmly in place, not allowing himself to be moved. The partner pulled his weight back slightly and then thrust forward, attempting to put Roman off his balance. As the weight moved into him, Roman pulled his shoulder back and dropped it so that the partner's balance fell forward. He parried the thrust with his left hand and braced his right hand, forming a ridge from his pinky to his wrist. He extended his arm forward in a punching motion and connected the firm "knife-hand" with the partner's neck, directly where it meets the shoulder. The man crumpled. He was still conscious, but his balance and strength were temporarily lost. He landed on the seat of his pants. Doug grabbed Roman with both hands and firmly pushed him toward the changeroom. He went willingly.

Just before crossing into the changeroom, Roman yelled back at the partner who was collecting himself and getting to his feet. "I fucking warned you!"

VIII

He hung up the phone. The verbal lashing he had received from Captain Massey had been severe and well deserved. She had sworn to honour what she said when he was pinned to the floor, and he would not receive any penalization for drawing his sidearm. She did, however, state that he would receive a written warning about the altercation beside the pool.

"Fuck!" He slammed his hand into the steering wheel. He was parked outside the medical examiner's building. He tried to gather the strength to head inside. She was in there. He knew he would see her. Frozen, or at least chilled, like Max had been. She would be stuffed in a drawer. In a plastic bag. Laid out like a cat to be dissected in a science class. He was sure he would not handle it. He had taught himself to disassociate. He could see and deal with the worst things imaginable during the day. He would put those things in a box in his mind and close it, seal it with packing tape, and leave it for tomorrow. Seeing her in that drawer, cold and emotionless, how could he pack that away? He would go home to an empty house. Eat alone at an empty table. He would sleep in an empty bed. And Kim would rest in a drawer in the basement of this building.

His phone rang. It was paired to the Bluetooth in his truck. It was an unknown number, and he ignored the call, hitting the disconnect button on the first ring. After a few seconds, it rang again. The same number. This time, he answered, "What?!"

"Hey, Roman, it's Sacha."

"Fuck off." He hung up the phone. It rang again and he answered, "Seriously, fuck off. I am not in the mood for this right now."

"I heard what happened." Sacha got the words out quickly, so that Roman would hear before he hung up again. He paused for a response that Roman did not give him. "I heard what happened to Kim. I wanted to call and say that I am sorry." He dropped the fake accent.

"How the fuck do you know what happened already?" Roman had calmed his voice. It felt nice to hear his friend's natural accent come through without the fake Ukrainian.

"Word gets around. Look, I wanted to say that I am sorry about Kim. And I really wanted to say that I am sorry about yesterday. My friend, he's not exactly, uhm, nice, you know?"   "All good. I guess. But if that little fuck thinks he can push me around, he has another thing coming."

"Let's just forget about it for now. You want a beer? It's on me."

Roman looked at the building that he couldn't manage to enter. "Yeah. A beer sounds surprisingly good right about now. Where?"

IX

She dropped her coffee when she heard. When the reality of those words finally organised themselves into an image, and with the subsequent understanding of that image, she lost the unfocussed connection with her hands. First, her arm dipped and her grip weakened, spilling the hot liquid, unnoticed, on the fake hardwood. The mug fell second, shattering around her feet. Last, Sam hit the floor, landing awkwardly as her knees buckled. She did not fully lose consciousness, but her awareness and focus evaded her long enough to collapse.

The first call had been from her mother. That one, she ignored. The second call was from her fiancé, Anthony. The short break between calls, neither being precautioned by a more natural text message, and the infrequency with which the two tended to call, made her curious enough to answer. He had said it plainly, straightforward, as there was no easy way to sugar-coat the information.

"Kim is dead," he had said. "She tripped at the gym and drowned in the pool. I haven't been able to reach Roman. I might just drop by after work."

Had Sam maintained her physical composure, the conversation may not have been so short. When she found herself staring at the ceiling from a pool of cooling McCafé, she lifted her phone to her ear and said passively, "Yeah. Go see him. Thanks for the call."

For longer than she would ever admit, she lay on the floor, easing back and forth in her mind the finality of the conversation. Could she really have died? Could Anthony be wrong? Could the body be misidentified? It seemed too fast to have been authentic. She returned the call to her mother, confirming what she had been told, and then made a call to Kim's mother, who did not answer.

While cleaning the mess and reminiscing about the many years of friendship, Sam finally broke down. She cried quietly at first, and finished on the couch, wailing like a child. She was alone and expressed herself shamelessly.

X

"You were going to propose?!" Sacha choked on the Richard's before he spoke, staring down at the diamond ring that Roman had placed between them.

"Why is that such a surprise?"

"I don't know. It just seems, like, wild, you know?"

"Not really. How long were we together? Years? I was going to leave the EPS too."

"For real?"

"It's a really nice ring, eh? I wonder if I can return it."

Sacha briefly considered the likely source of the funds for a 'really nice ring'. "So sorry man. You really loved her."

The waitress came around with another round. Roman basked in the soothing sound the glass made when she placed it against the bare table. He easily poured the remainder of his first round into his stomach and handed her the empty glass. Sacha did the same. "So much. I honestly don't know what to think right now. Like I can't go home."

"You can stay at my place if you want."

"I don't want to imagine what disgusting diseases live in the corners of your shit pit."

"Fuck you."

"Rotten fucking pizza boxes and shit-stained bathroom. You're gross."

"I would tell you to suck my balls, but you would enjoy it too much."

"Do you even do laundry? Or do you just fold the dirty clothes out of your hamper and put them back in the drawers?"

"What am I, fucking royalty? I don't use a hamper. I don't even put clean clothes in my drawers."

"You are fucking weird, man."

They sat and drank quietly for a few minutes. Roman stared at the TV over the bar. "Hockey season soon."

"I'm pumped. It will be a good year for the Leafs, I think."

"Same as last year and the year before. When she comes around, let's get a spicy perogy pizza."

"Absolutely. Hey, weird question: what ever happened with that case you were working?"

"Oh, man. I don't even know anymore." He had a sip out of his fresh beer and savoured it briefly. "We got a guy. Everything adds up. I'm not working it anymore though."

"Like, closed case, you think?"

"Not yet. It will be, I think. I won't get credit for it, but that is the least of my concerns right now."

"You are off work, I'm guessing."

"Yeah, for now. I'm sure Moussa can wrap this one up."

Sacha laughed. "Moussa. He's that towel head you work with?"

"Settle down. You're in a public space. You want to talk like that, do it alone in your sad apartment."

Another few minutes passed, during which they did not speak.

When the waitress came by, they ordered another round and a pizza. The TV over the bar showed replays of McDavid and Draisaitl. "Think they made him the captain too young?" Roman broke the silence again.

"They did the same thing to Crosby. Won like three cups."

"Pittsburgh isn't Edmonton. It's not a hockey city. More pressure here. Didn't we already name a street after him?"

"No. The street was already called that."

"Well, we have a Messier, a Gretzky, and now a McDavid street. There's no Crosby Avenue in Pittsburgh."

The waitress served the fresh beers promptly. Roman was ahead of her pace and slid over his empty glass. Sacha finished his and did the same. "Probably about ten more minutes for the pizza, guys."

"Thanks," Roman said, forcing a friendly smile. Sacha twisted in his seat to watch her walk away.

"So, Kim had life insurance?"

"Sorry, what?" Roman turned back from the TV. Sacha did not. He stared uneasily toward the bar, his eyes darting unnaturally around the room.

"Like, you guys probably have a good policy, right?" Sacha turned briefly to make eye contact and then returned his gaze to the sports highlights. Roman watched him raise the glass and have a sip. It seemed awkward in his hand, like he had never made the motion before.

"Yeah, so?" He was stern, trying to catch a look at Sacha's eyes, which were more elusive than they should have been, darting between the table, his hands, his beer, the TV, and the waitress.

"Forget it. Sorry I asked."

"No. Not 'forget it.' Look at me."

Sacha complied. He looked guilty. "Never mind."

"I will not 'never mind.' Tell me what you were about to say."

He shifted in his seat. "Maybe there was a silver lining to all of this."

"A silver lining?"

He shifted again and looked around the room. "Like, I'm really sorry about Kim, but if she had a good policy, maybe you could use that to cover what you owe. Just a suggestion is all." "Some of what I owe?" Roman felt the corners of his mouth being pulled down. His eyes burned slightly.

"You know what I mean." Sacha drank deeply.

"Maybe you're right."

"I guess all I am saying is that everything could work out. You know?"

"I know." Roman tilted his head back and, in just a few swallows, finished his nearly fresh beer. "I am going to take a piss. Order another round." He placed the glass near the edge of the table where the waitress could pick it up.

"You got it, man. On me, remember?" His uneasy shifting settled, and he relaxed into his seat.

Roman shuffled out of the booth. Before heading for the washroom, he turned to his right and placed a hand on his old friend's shoulder, "You're a good friend, you know that?" He patted him on the back and stared down into his eyes. His right hand was resting gently on the table.

"Thanks, man." They stared for a second. Roman, bracing Sacha in place with his left, grabbed the handle of the empty glass with his right. In a swift and powerful motion, he punched the glass into the bridge of Sacha's nose. It shattered on impact, throwing shards into his eyes, and sprinkling more into his lap. Roman dropped the broken handle. He then shoved Sacha, who was struggling to get his weight out of the booth, back down. Roman delivered two more hard and precise punches, which were guided by the firm grip he had on Sacha's shirt. He ignored the wild blows that were thrown back at him. The waitress screamed from behind the bar. Roman ignored it. Sacha gave up on returning punches and grabbed onto the sleeves of Roman's shirt, attempting to immobilize his arms. Roman pushed his weight on top and forced Sacha down between the bench and table. Sacha gagged when he felt Roman's knee make a hard impact between his legs and scrambled to get the weight off him. Roman passed his flailing legs, placing a knee on Sacha's pelvis, and threw his other leg up onto the table. Using his weight and left hand, Roman pinned Sacha's right arm against his body. With a dominant position and weight advantage, Roman could easily manipulate the smaller man. He pulled the left arm up straight and bent it against the table. Sacha flailed wildly with his legs and pumped his torso in an attempt to make space. Roman forced Sacha's arm into the bend of his knee and held it in place with his right hand. He leaned his weight onto it and felt Sacha's elbow hyper-extend against the edge of the table.

"I'll break it," Roman warned. Sacha didn't respond. He squirmed wildly from underneath Roman. Roman leaned his weight harder against the joint, and Sacha screamed. "You ever want to use this arm again? Start talking."

"Fuck you."

Roman pressed his weight into the joint until he felt it crunch under his weight. Sacha screamed again. After the range of motion was maxed out by the position, Roman shifted his weight back to Sacha's chest, and removed the broken limb from the bend of his knee. He held it with his right hand and then placed his knee on top of Sacha's broken arm, pinning it to the table. With his now free right hand, he grabbed Sacha over the face, squeezing his fingers and thumb into his bloody cheeks. Sacha writhed and twisted. He pushed and pulled with his unbroken arm, which was still held in Roman's much stronger left hand. He jerked his head around and opened his teeth, trying to quickly snap at Roman's fingers. Sickened by the attempted bite, Roman drew his hand back and then dropped a heavy punch into Sacha's face. With the adrenaline, he was unaware of where he made contact.

"The police are coming!" The waitress yelled to them from the door before running outside. They stared at each other briefly.

Roman put his hand on Sacha's forehead and pinned his head in place. "I'm not playing."

"Suck my fucking balls." He spit blood up at Roman.

Roman curled his thumb down and pushed it into Sacha's right eye. "You ever want to see out of this eye again? You better fucking tell me what you know."

"I don't know shit. What the fuck is wrong with you?"

"You know something about Kim's death." Roman was speaking slowly through clenched teeth. "Last fucking chance."

Sacha stared up at him from his one open and bloody eye. Small shards of glass were mixed with the blood that covered his face. Roman shook his head gently and then pressed his thumb down hard. Sacha screamed and kicked. Like crushing a rotten tangerine, the outer membrane of the eye eventually broke and the soft inside offered no resistance. Roman's thumb slid into the socket. He pressed and twisted until his entire thumb was inside Sacha's skull.

XI

He didn't bother to wash the blood off his hands until he was home. His house was empty and clean. The modern grey and white décor, which had been so carefully chosen, burned his vision. It had been so important to match the counter with the backsplash, and perfectly complement the colours with a bluish accent wall. It was all so hollow now. The central air hummed gently, and the filter in his tank pumped almost silently. He walked into his living room and stripped to his underwear, throwing his clothes unceremoniously into a pile at the top of his stairs. He rinsed his hands and face in the kitchen sink, basking in the cold water. The sudden change of temperature did not sharpen his senses as he had hoped.

In his underwear and socks, he paced aimlessly around his house, lacking the sense of purpose with which he usually moved. He let his eyes rest closed, opening only for short periods to change direction. By depriving himself of the most important sense, Roman hoped for an epiphany that would not come. He paused and opened just one eye to observe the lack of depth perception. Sacha would see this way for the rest of his life. After a short transition from amusement to disgust and back, he resumed his incessant slow march, dragging his feet across the carpet. From the pile of clothes, his phone rang. The sound was distant, as if drawing from some other reality. He stared at it. He hated it. When it stopped, he closed his eyes and resumed his journey.

At the next checkpoint, he stopped in front of a full-length sliding mirror. It separated the space nearest to his front door from a closet containing outerwear. He looked up and down at his own impressive physique. Even without the vascularity of a recent workout, he looked better than most. He turned sideways to admire the slimness of his waist and the way it contrasted his powerful thighs and chest. He then rotated into a Hercules pose, extending one arm to the sky, and curling his other to accentuate his bicep. Shallow but defined lines separated his pectoralis, deltoid, and abdominal muscles. He refused to look into his own eyes. The way he felt would be displayed and seeing it reflected would make it too real. He returned his eyes to their comfortable closed position, feeling the moisture squeezing from behind his lids, and let his body resume its odyssey.

Finally, in the centre of his living room, he stopped. He pressed his feet, shoulder width apart into the floor and reached skyward, allowing his head to rest backward. Had his eyes been open, he would have seen the tips of his fingers nearly grazing his ceiling. He brought his hands down slowly and rested them, fingers laced behind his head. After letting it ricochet aimlessly for too long, Roman forced his mind to focus on that which disturbed him. His knees weakened and he let his weight drop. He opened his eyes in time to catch his weight and from behind the couch, he stared at the bottle which had been left since the morning. Playfully, he rolled over the leather into a sitting position, legs spread eagle.

He lifted the glass to eye level and inspected the remaining liquid before flicking it out onto the floor. The tonic in the already opened can would have lost its carbonation. His hands shook as he poured. For the expensive gin, he opted to put the glass on the table before mixing his drink. Despite his focus, it splashed over the sides. He gagged on the strength of the drink and flatness of the tonic. It spilled from the corners of his mouth. He finished the drink on his second swallow and placed the glass down to prepare a another. He retrieved a fresh can from the fridge beside his TV and savoured the crisp, bitter cocktail. Between sips he rested the cold glass in his crotch, barely holding it with one hand and resting his head backward. After finishing the drink and preparing a third, he could feel the warmth seeping into his blood. He sank deeper into the leather and closed his eyes, trying to force himself to sleep.

His peace was disturbed first by the ping of a text message and by the phone call that followed. He turned his head and peered with deep contempt at the source of the noise. His rage focused on the bloody laundry at the top of his stairs. In a quick and aggressive motion, he turned and threw the glass across the room. It shattered against the wall. Shards landed in the careless lumps and folds of his laundry. He sneered at the stain it had left on his blue accent wall, the colour of which he had spent so much time deliberating.

The pile of clothes, sprinkled with broken glass, reminded him of what would normally have been the most significant event of the day. He stood up quickly like a startled deer. For a moment he was motionless and then broke into a full sprint. He slid on his socks and then his hands and knees before stopping in the broken glass. He dug wildly at the pockets of his pants until he found the small envelope that Moussa had given him. The shards cut shallow into his skin, and he sat, legs bent in front, as he tore it open. Inside he found a USB stick. He stood. Blood flowed easily but not dangerously from the fresh lacerations. It soaked into the rear of his boxer briefs and stuck in his leg hair.

He threw the USB stick onto the couch and ran up his stairs, returning a moment later with a laptop computer in one hand. In his haste, he lost his footing and descended the last few stairs on his backside. The glass pressed deeper, but he easily ignored the pain. He opened the computer, typed his password, and inserted the USB stick. It would take a minute to fully start, so he made a quick trip to his mini fridge and opened a can of AGD. He finished the entire beer in anticipation and opened another. When the computer was fully booted, he opened the USB drive. There was one folder and inside that folder just a single audio file. It had not been renamed since its creation. Anxious to see what important information had sent his partner into a frenzy, he opened it and turned his volume up. He leaned close. At first it was just sounds, similar to what one would expect from a pocket dial. Then a voice. It was heavily muffled, but he was sure it was a conversation. He turned the volume to the max and restarted the recording. Through what sounded like background noise, he was able to make out the familiar voice. His own voice. His living room shrank. The walls leaned over him, and his vision tunneled until he had no awareness other than the computer screen and the sounds that accompanied it. He dropped his nearly full beer and covered his face in his hands. For the next several minutes, he listened to himself carefully outlining to Sacha the information that Higgins had provided to him about Igor Kovac and his associates.

He took the USB from the computer and bent it in half. The feat proved to be harder than anticipated. He closed the computer and took two attempts to break it over his knee. After failing he screamed in frustration and frisbee tossed it into his seventy-inch 4k television. This was the first time that Roman noticed he had not turned it off since last night. The image of a hockey player taking a penalty shot was now disrupted by a purple and black vertical line that extended across the full height of the screen.

"God Fucking Damn it!" he screamed with no holdback on volume. The detective on administrative leave lifted his knee to his chest, and then stomped his foot through the glass surface of his coffee table. A thin gash opened from his ankle to mid-calf. He looked down at the wound and watched nothing happen for the first second, and then blood started pouring out. He immediately recognised that the flow was even and not pumping. An arterial bleed would have been much worse. He stomped over to his discarded shirt. Unlike a misinformed movie character, he did not attempt to make a tourniquet that would have caused more damage than the cut itself. Instead, he folded it and pressed it into the wound to absorb blood. He tied his jeans over top to apply pressure and laid down in the mess of blood and broken glass.

"Doing some redecorating or what?" The voice blindsided Roman, who believed he was alone, and forced his heart to slam painfully against the inside of his chest. Every muscle in his body contracted and a tingly rush flowed to his extremities. He rolled to a lunge position and instinctively grabbed for a sidearm that was not there. He turned to face the intruder, and like an impossibly

319

charismatic asshole, Anthony stood beside the couch with a case of beer and an amused smile.

"If I had my gun, I would have shot you. You scared the fucking shit out of me."

"And then I would become a stat. Another unarmed civilian gunned down by police." His sarcasm ripped through the tension.

"Not funny. What the fuck are you doing here?" Roman shrank as he stood, lowered his shoulders, and relaxed his core.

"Well." Anthony made his way into the kitchen and started loading the beer bottles into Roman's fridge. "I heard the news. Saw your truck outside and thought you could use a friend." His voice was level, almost playful. Roman appreciated it. In his current state, he would have loathed any unauthentic sympathy in his friend's voice. He knew Anthony felt it but didn't need to see it on display. Anthony twisted the top off two beers and handed one to Roman. "How you holding up?"

Roman responded with a smirk and a shrug and then took a long sip of the cheap local beer.

"I mean like, aside from being covered in blood and broken glass, in your underwear?"

"I've had better days," he answered. It was hard to be upset in Anthony's presence. The way he spoke, always happy, even in the worst moments. It wasn't a wide smile, that would have made light of the situation, but just better than a poker face. It put Roman at ease. He drank again.

"I bet. How bad is that cut on your leg?"

"It's fine."

"Mm-hmm. Looks fine. Nice dressing too. Is that a dirty shirt?" Just the right amount of attitude.

"Fucking right."

"It'll get infected."

"Least of my concern." Roman took another long sip and then raised the bottle to observe that he had likely one more before he would need another bottle.

"If all that blood came from your leg, you should probably go to the hospital. Get it stitched up." He drew out the first syllable of 'probably'.

"You should probably suck my balls." Roman dragged out 'probably' in the same way.

"Don't threaten me with a good time." Anthony finished his beer and set the empty bottle on the kitchen counter. He had been drinking faster than Roman. He burped heavily without class and opened another. "But seriously, you have a first aid kit?"

"Upstairs. I'll go get it."

"Make you a deal. Go take a shower. Maybe throw on some pants. We'll bandage that up properly."

XII

Kind of like how your brother died.

Moussa stopped the recording. He stared at his laptop, which was squeezed uncomfortably between his abdomen and the steering wheel of his issued Elantra. Since he first heard the conversation less than a day earlier, he had replayed it incessantly. At first, he had listened in disbelief to the words that were spoken. It was in his analysis, a task which he would normally delegate, that he found himself disturbed by the familiarity of the conversation. The men speaking, Roman and someone who was not formally identified, although Moussa did have some suspicions, carried on casually. They were friends.

The tone of the conversation had started his obsession. The subtext of the words spoken drew him deeper. Separated from their predetermined transaction, which was clearly some favour in exchange for information, was a disturbingly misplaced comment. Once, during the consumption of some sacrilegious pints, Roman had briefly described the violent murder of his only brother. Three years as partners, nearly all as good friends, and it came up only once. Whoever that other person was, they were close enough to bring it up, unprompted, somewhat offhand.

The case you told me about. It's kind of like how your brother died.

"Moussa?" Her voice startled him.

"Captain." He closed his laptop, harder that his had intended, and rolled down his window.

"Ma'am. What's up?" he asked as nonchalantly as he could. He had not turned in the recording as evidence for his internal investigation, and did not want to draw her attention to it.

"Working from your car? Twenty steps from the office?" Her tone was casual. Like many in their profession, Captain Massey ceased to exist at the doors to the building, and as much as possible, she became Julie.

"Yeah, I just. Uhm. I'm hung up on this Paul Derocher," he lied, which was becoming too common for his own taste.

"Because he set your mosque on fire?"

He frowned, ignoring the presumptuous question. "Can I ask you something?"

"If I say no, you will probably ask me tomorrow anyway."

"Hypothetically. You are given an option. Kill someone you care about, and by doing so, save another. Or do nothing, and by choosing not to act, they both die. Do you think you could do it?"

"I suppose I would need to know the circumstances."

"Those are them. No way around it."

"How close are they? To me, I mean?" She seemed to be enjoying the game.

"Very. You two closest friends."

"I don't know. I guess the theory is straight forward. It is an obvious decision, but then you look down the barrel." She exhaled hard through her nose. "That's a hard trigger to pull."

"Which option represents a stronger character? Does your

moral fiber disallow the action of killing an innocent person, no matter what the consequences? Or can you control your own mind, and make a cold, calculated decision that yields the best result?"

"I wouldn't wish it upon my worst enemy. It's just not fair. Are you getting at something?"

"Imagine you peaked through a window, metaphorically I guess, that you weren't supposed to see through. And you saw something. Or you think you saw something. And you have not yet unravelled what you think you saw; what you think you may know, but you do know that it's important. And if you were to pursue it, questions might arise about why you were looking through that window, and that could be damaging to someone you care about."

"So, what's the question?"

"I don't know."

She didn't respond. Instead, she gave a head nod and friendly smile before leaving towards her car.

"I don't know," he repeated to himself.

The case you told me about. It's kind of like how your brother died. Isn't that bothering you?

XIII

Roman had to shower quickly, as the bleeding started immediately after he removed the half assed shirt bandage. To avoid seeming pathetic, he rebandaged it properly before 'throwing on a pair of pants' and a T-shirt. When he returned to the living room, he was impressed to see that Anthony had done a fairly good job of cleaning the mess. Most of the blood was scrubbed from the carpet, and the glass had been vacuumed.

"Thanks buddy."

"For what?"

"Cleaning this shit up."

"That wasn't me." Anthony lied comically.

"Whatever. Beer?" Roman asked as he retrieved one for himself.

"Got one going. So, do you like your TV better like this or what?"

"Thing's a piece of shit. Can't even throw a laptop at it without it breaking. I'm going to get my money back."

"Fucking garbage." Anthony grabbed the remote. "What do you want to watch ninety percent of?"

"Don't care. Few more weeks until hockey." He collapsed comfortably into the love seat that matched his couch.

"Probably preseason."

"Preseason is stupid. What do they play now? Like eight

exhibition games?"

"Yeah, but it is something to watch." Anthony had his feet up on the broken piece of furniture that used to be a coffee table. He leaned his head back and drank all but the last sip. "You mind if I steal and AGD from that mini fridge?"

"I was just up, and you said you didn't want anything."

"That was then. This is now. You want to shotgun a few?"

"Let me get a little more buzzed first. Help yourself."

"Lil bitch." Anthony crawled like an excited child to the fridge. He popped his head up and tossed Roman a corked bottle before returning to his seat with a can of AGD. "I managed to save some of your Hendrick's. The rest is soaked into your carpet."

Roman pulled off the plastic and corked top. It opened with a satisfying squeak and pop. He waterfalled an approximate ounce into his mouth and then offered the bottle to Anthony.

"No thanks. Shit's gross."

"Drink it."

"Fine." Anthony took the bottle and finished what remained. He gagged and placed the empty bottle on the floor. "You hear what happened to Sacha?"

"No. Haven't spoken to him in a while."

"He got jumped at a BP. Fucked up really bad."

"That guy is an asshole."

"Blind asshole now."

"For real?" Roman had to fake his surprise and did it convincingly.

"In one eye at least. Still early but he'll be full pirate from now on."

"Never go full Pirate!" Roman announced in a deep, throaty voice. Anthony laughed, choking on his beer, and covered his mouth as it spilled onto the floor. "Easy, buddy. You'll ruin my carpet."

Anthony laughed even harder. "That ship has sailed my friend."

"In all seriousness. He probably deserved it."

"To be blind? That's cold, man. He's like, one of our oldest friends."

"Still. Fuck that guy." Roman crawled over, which seemed easier, and grabbed an AGD from the fridge.

"Listen, bro. I don't know what you guys have going on, but you should probably go even things out."

"Nope. That guy can fuck his couch."

"I don't think he is as pissed at you as you are at him. Plus, he's blind now."

"Half blind. And he has no reason to be pissed off at me."

"Whatever. You do you."

"How's Sam?" Roman changed the subject.

"Huh?"

"You know. Like she obviously knows by now."

"Upset. Obviously. Been on the phone with family and friends. Probably doing some version of what we are doing."

"What are we doing?" Roman made his voice serious. The dry humour would not be lost on Anthony.

"Drinking beer and watching ninety percent of SportsCentre," Anthony replied in a similar tone. They shared another laugh. Roman appreciated how casually his friend could ease the tension. "I have a weird question. And if you don't want to say, it's fine."

"Fire away, little buddy." He took a refreshing sip from the wide opening.

"Just wondering about Kim's death. Like, what happened? She slipped, right?" Roman saw from the distortion in his face that it made Anthony uneasy.

"Oh, man. That's a whole fucking thing." He shook his head slowly, looking down at his hands.

"Yeah?"

"I don't think so. I went there. Doesn't add up to me."

"What are you talking about?"

"They won't let me investigate it. Conflict of interest." He was only half-lying. Had he not been on administrative leave, they still may not have let him take part in the investigation.

"What do you think happened?"

"One sec." Roman crawled to the fridge and grabbed two more cans. He drank the first in two breaths before opening the second. "I think she was killed. Honestly." He burped in his mouth and exhaled it through his nose.

Anthony looked even more disturbed. "Killed?" He cleared his throat. "Why?"

"I just have this feeling. It's this weirdo. His name is Paul. I thought he did it. And then today . . ." He stopped himself. "You know what? I don't have it put together yet."

"You brought me in this far. Now you're just going to cut me off? The fuck?"

"Fine. Fine. You know what? Here's the thing. So, I randomly bump into this guy, Paul, at the church."

"Which church?"

"St. Joseph's. Doesn't matter. We shoot the shit while we are waiting for the confession booth."

"Hold up. You were giving a confession. You?"

"You want me to tell you or what?"

"Proceed." He made an over-the-top rotating gesture with his hand.

"The next day I'm heading back to the church. I run into this guy again. We have another talk about God and what not. He seems really interested in me. And we go our separate ways. Oh, I forgot to say, I'm going back to the church because the priest called and said someone gave a concerning confession."

"They call you guys for that shit?" Anthony stirred, somehow uncomfortable on the expensive leather couch.

"Only if someone confesses to a crime or something. Anyway," Roman continued firmly, annoyed by the constant interruptions, "it's the same guy. We check him out. He has a history of violence. And a connection to Max."

"Max?" Anthony tucked his phone in his pocket.

Are you not even listening to me?

"Cardinal. He is an old army friend of mine. The third victim I told you about."

"The one that you identified?"

"Yes! Fuck." He felt his voice slip and get louder.

Derek Lukachko

"Look, you're getting agitated and that's not why I'm here. I don't understand what this has to do with Kim. She slipped, man."

"Maybe." Roman paused. "I don't know. No." He exhaled thoughtfully. "I don't think she slipped."

"I know the way you work. Bottom of your heart. Do you think Kim was murdered? Do you think that you have the right guy?" Anthony raised the beer to his mouth, didn't sip, and then placed it on the floor.

"The first three. There is a connection and motive." Roman trailed off, hung up on his own word. *Motive*.

At first, Anthony didn't respond. Roman guessed that he was waiting for him to continue. He let Anthony speak. "If Kim was murdered, what evidence would you have? Was there some kind of, like, DNA at the pool? Blood or something? How well do they search for that kind of stuff?"

Roman cocked his head to the side, trying to see what, under Anthony's messy bangs, looked like a small laceration on his hairline. "No," he answered, straightening out, "There wouldn't be. In a pool area like that, the cleaning chemicals destroy any DNA evidence."

"Listen to me." Anthony's voice raised and lowered a half note. "You have a lot going on. I think you need to take some down time. Relax. Let Moussa deal with Paul or whatever."

"I'm off the case anyway." Roman settled his tone and eased deeper into his seat. "Administrative leave. So, I can have some time for the funeral and all."

"Probably for the best." Anthony's phone rang in his pocket. He took a quick look to see who was calling. "Do you mind if I take this?"

"Go for it." Anthony left through the front door. After a few seconds of silence, Roman retrieved his own phone from his pocket. He had missed calls and text messages from most of his friends and family. His Facebook feed was riddled with half-hearted condolences. He switched to Instagram and, after seeing nothing of interest, returned to Facebook. He scrolled, looking for anything that could distract him. A particular post caught his attention: "What a day. I'm exhausted."

Roman stared for a few seconds, blinking in disbelief. He checked twice the time that it was posted, then closed the app and reopened it. The post was still there, mocking him with its similarity to his own post from just a few days before. "Who was that?" he asked Anthony, who was returning from his brief call.

"Work."

He wasn't sure. It may have been from the sound of his voice. It may have been from his posture or the way he held his eyes. It was most likely the short, pregnant pause that proceeded the one word that Roman decided was a lie. It was a truthful, sincere lie, but in the context of the conversation, he had no doubt. With feigned composure, he spoke easily, calculating each inflection and break, punctuating each word deliberately and reading the subtle cues in his friend's eyes. Roman said, "Hey. I was thinking. We should go fishing."

"Sure. You know I'm down. Maybe after the funeral?"

"How about tomorrow? We can drive up to Cold Lake, camp for a night, and come back on Thursday."

"You don't think that maybe you should be dealing with Kim

and stuff?"

"No. I really fucking do not. It has been a bad week. And you don't even know half of it."

Anthony sat back down beside Roman and leaned forward. "I think that maybe your girlfriend's death is more than half of it. I'll go, if that is what you really need. But are you positive that's the right thing right now?"

"Yes, I really am. I don't know how to explain it."

Anthony didn't answer. He sat quietly while Roman spoke.

"Five days ago, I went to sleep. In the morning I should have woken up to go fishing. You, me, Kim, and Sam driving to Cold Lake to catch monster trout on an unnaturally hot weekend in September. It's like, it's almost as if the universe *knew* that I would be on call that morning. A body was left to be discovered, placed in such a way that it would not be found until morning, but that it would be found before my shift ended. From the moment I received that call, it has only been down. One event after another, piling up and driving me into this spiral. No matter what I do, I just cannot climb out. It couldn't have been anyone else. It had to be me. In my jurisdiction. It had to be a murder for which I would take personal responsibility. And from that, my own eagerness would overwhelm me. I can't wrap my head around it."

"Because it needed to be you," Anthony finally answered. "*You* found the guy. From what you told me, *you* followed a feeling. Something in your gut that drove you. I know you. I know the way you work. I know that it works because you nail criminal after fucking criminal. You absolutely slam these kinds of cases. The events that followed are unfortunate and uncontrollable, but a dangerous man is in custody because you fucking got him. I agree. The universe chose you. *God* chose you." He paused, scratching behind his head. "Fuck it. Let's go. Tomorrow. You and I to Cold Lake. Bring Sam?"

"Nah. Sam can stay and start planning a funeral. If the universe really did choose me, if *God* really did choose me, then it should let me pick up where I left off. If what I have lost was part of some greater plan, then let me take what is owed to me. Whether or not it is *God* that owes me or fate or chance. I need to have that back, and maybe in the end I can break even."

Wednesday

"We brought nothing with us when we came into the world, and we can't take anything with us when we leave it"

-Timothy 6:7

I

Roman Owen walks out of St. Joseph's Basilica and marvels at the day. The sky is a rich dark blue that fades into the horizon. The heat from the weekend has returned and what remains of the storm is drying in the gutters and muddy edge of the sidewalk. The leaves still hold their colour, crunching against each other in the gentle wind. He can smell the fall.

His body feels light as he descends the cold, hard staircase. On the last step, he sits, leaning against a concrete barrier with his back to the street. He has a fresh pack of cigarettes in his pocket. He retrieves it and pops one out by tapping it against his palm. He stuffs the plastic wrapping in his jeans. In the shadow of the magnificent structure, whose beauty he had not previously appreciated, he enjoys the cigarette that would be his last. The final drag lingers in his lungs and on his breath. He rolls the filter between his fingers, pinching out the embers and marveling at its subtle lethality. It goes in his pocket, so that it may never decompose in some other place.

With a calm satisfaction that had previously eluded him, Roman drives home. He is not pressed for time, and so he maintains an easy speed. It is relaxing to him that his sense of purpose is no longer expressed in his hurried movement. He passes under a familiar bridge, one that often hides photo radar, and enjoys not braking to avoid penalization. Drivers pass aggressively around him, as if their quick motions and ugly stares might persuade him to adopt a more hurried driving style.

At home, he backs into his driveway, lining up his hitch to the boat trailer. The camera in his truck eases the manoeuvre and he completes it on his first attempt. The boat is prepared. The truck is prepared. His bag, packed with clean clothes and toiletries, is in the back seat. His friend arrives shortly after with his own equipment. Roman smiles. Anthony, Roman's best friend of many years, asks if they need to refuel before departure. Roman assures him that they have enough gas. Anthony is satisfied with the response.

With the higher axle ratio, the fibreglass boat, which can be easily used for fishing, does not stress the truck. Roman can hardly feel the extra weight. He is pleased with his decision to buy a Ram. The passenger, Anthony, suggests that they get coffee and breakfast. The driver, Roman, agrees. They park the truck, knowing that with the trailer a drive-thru is not possible. The driver exits the vehicle to retrieve food and drink. The passenger waits in the truck, feeling empty about the abandonment of family for fishing. The driver returns and divides the food between them. The cheap breakfast has never tasted so satisfying.

With their last task completed, they embark on the journey. Shortly into the drive, the passenger suggests to the driver that he should increase his speed if they are to arrive with ample time for fishing. The driver obliges and accelerates to accommodate the passenger's wishes. Displeased with what he determines to still be a slow pace, the passenger grumbles about the crepuscular period. The driver ignores him.

After finding their way out of the city, they drive quietly. The driver has recently lost his spouse and the passenger does not pry for conversation. He believes the driver is stressed. They briefly discuss the best possible route and end with an agreement that the navigation system, having live traffic updates, will guide them best. The driver gives the passenger permission to discard his food containers on the floor.

After an agonizing period, in which few words are spoken, the passenger forces a conversation. He tells the driver, whose cousin he plans to marry, that he wishes to drive a Volvo. He prattles on about the safety features that are important and that he wants to have a family. The driver responds dutifully to the conversation. The passenger tells the driver about the diagonal slash across the front of most Volvos. He speaks with a pride one would expect from an engineer or employee. He has not shopped for the car and has already taken mental ownership. He would be the best customer to a seasoned salesman. He tells the driver about how it represents their invention of the three-point seatbelt. The driver does not care.

The driver normally stores his sunglasses between the visor and headliner. Driving east, the morning light reflects off the polished hood of the truck and compromises the driver's vision. He squints and dons the protective eyewear. The darkened lenses protect his eyes from the sun, and restrict the reflected light, so that the passenger cannot see his tears. He drinks his coffee to hide the quiver in his lips. The passenger notices the poorly hidden emotions, and offers his support, misjudging the situation. The driver ignores him.

When they pass halfway to what the passenger believes to be their destination, the passenger directs their attention to the diagonal slash across the front of a semi-tractor-trailer. The driver has an amusing thought. He considers the irony of a front-end collision with such a vehicle moving in the opposite direction. That diagonal slash, a symbol of vehicular safety, across the front of the truck would be an ironic place to end their lives. He listens to the sound change as he passes the truck at the bottom of the valley and gently increases his pressure on the gas pedal until it meets the floor. The driver whispers a prayer, his first since childhood, and in those final moments he ignores the rumbling of intentionally uneven pavement, the flashing red lights that encircle an oversized stop sign, and the desperate, pleading cries of the passenger.

Epilogue

The concrete is old and worn, but immaculately clean. With every step against the cold and soulless floor, his soft sole shoes touch almost inaudibly. He does not allow his vision to rise from the path immediately before him and presses apathetically forward, guided against his will by those beyond his peripheral. His mind wanders as he pushes back without contact against those that drive him forward. When audible instructions force him to continue, he obliges for fear of physical correction. If the good grace of some unknown being frees him of this hardship, he will vow to refrain from any activity that would return him to his present circumstance. It is a delusion, he knows, that will not come to fruition. Despite that realisation, this will be his final procession through the corridor or any that bears a resemblance.

Lost on him are the taunts and threats that echo metallically.

Attenuated will be the punishment if in this chapter he is able to find one lost soul and correct its path. Permitted he will be to attend services and, in time, to vocalize his reflections.

When the formerly unnamed man, known to the system by some not yet memorized number and a name with which he chooses not to associate, arrives at the threshold, he draws a final breath. That breath symbolizes to him the freedom that in this human form he has exchanged for future grace. This extended confinement will do nothing to diminish his passion, his zeal, his devotion. Deeds of this reality will be rewarded greatly in an existence beyond the reach of man.

Another, to whom he has not yet been introduced, will occupy the same space. The soul belonging to the other, who has also committed crimes against the perceived greater good of humanity, could be the first that he saves during his incarceration.

The belongings on the lower level imply that his place would be elevated, physically anyway, in the enclosed concrete room. He scales the metal frame and stretches out above the woolen blanket. Immediately above him is an unmarked grey surface, centred by a light fixture that is installed flush with the ceiling. That flush and even construction, he figures, are due to the likelihood that one might choose to accelerate their transition from this dull, hopeless place. Time will pass slowly and painfully for those who are less enlightened.

He wonders, should his own transcension into the judgement of greater powers occur during his imprisonment, will that cold, hard barrier above his bed contain his being? If God's grace allows it, and if not for the structure in which he is now forced to live, he wonders, would he ascend? If the axis of existence were to be inverted, and if his deeds of sin were not cleansed in human form, might he fall through the ceiling, descending for an eternity into the abyss?

Until then, stiff mattresses and, in his dreams, the echoing cries of burning children.

Derek Lukachko

Cold Lake Fishing

Acknowledgements

Thanks to Kasandra, George, Shirley, Lorraine, Russel, and Christine

You all know what you did.

Derek Lukachko

Photo taken at Lac Sante, AB by Kasandra Price

Derek Lukachko is a Canadian Forces veteran and outdoor enthusiast. He is originally from the Toronto area, and now lives in Edmonton with his girlfriend, Kasandra. He carefully observes the personalities of the people he meets and uses their tendencies to inspire his character-based writing.

You can get to know him better at www.dereklukachko.ca or follow him on Instagram @all.is.lost.moment

Derek Lukachko

Manufactured by Amazon.ca
Bolton, ON